UPPER HAMPTON

John E. Poulson

UPPER HAMPTON

FICTION4ALL

Chapter 1 - Upper Hampton

Upper Hampton was a small town in the area where Chief Inspector Julie Ashton was stationed.

After she had successfully captured an international assassin whilst stationed as an inspector in North London, she was promoted to Chief Inspector, but her volatile nature and bullish ways needed to be contained, so the powers that be moved her away to the country. It was a large rural area with small towns and villages dotted about. It wasn't that she did not respect their authority, just that she was not afraid to speak her mind and, if asked to ignore a situation, she would tell them why she was not going to do that and invariably proved them wrong. This did not go down well with the powers that be.

Banished to the countryside, which was better than to the Outer Hebrides, she began to settle in, but even that was not to last. On her first day she was handed a murder case. A prominent businessman's wife had been poisoned and more were to follow. It was a complicated case and took time to solve, but with her tenacity and knowledge; she managed to solve the case. It took until four more deaths had occurred in the town where the main station was situated. She could not work out how the murderer managed to poison the wine, because no-one had been in the cellar and the victim's husband had personally selected the wine for the dinner, which made him the prime suspect, that was, until he became a victim himself.

Julie had left school and joined the army for adventure and then, because it did not provide the adventure she craved, she joined the elite special services. She was a sniper, trained for bomb disposal and became a martial arts expert. However, a roadside bomb put paid to her elite service and the injury she sustained made her no longer combat ready. She was offered a promotion in the regular army, but that wasn't for her, so she left under the premise of unfit for duty.

At mid-twenties, she decided to begin a solid period of training to ensure she was fit enough to follow in her father's footsteps. She joined the police force.

Her guile, quick wit and intelligence meant that she gained promotions quickly, but her blunt approach also brought resentment from her colleagues and, mainly, her superiors.

At mid-thirties, banished to the countryside where the cases usually amounted to the odd stolen tractor, there was a bout of sheep rustling and bar room brawls at the local pub, not the most challenging of jobs, but it wasn't all bad.

Solving the case gained her a lot of respect in the town; her blunt approach to a pub brawl did not go un-noticed, either.

"Gentlemen, take this outside, please," she would say and if they didn't then she would throw them outside herself. "Yes, it is pouring down and you are getting wet, go home, or stay there and cool off, but do not try to enter this pub until I say you can," she told one pair of fighters, who looked at her stood just inside the doorway, then at each other, got up and went home. They knew better than to argue with her.

This incident was preceded by one in the pub she used, a country pub with rooms and she regularly ate lunch there. An argument became heated at the bar; Julie turned around and looked at the two men. The barman pointed to Julie. They turned to see her looking at them and walked away from each other, leaving the argument alone. No need to speak, the look was enough, they had disturbed her lunch and that was not allowed.

Julie was not what you might call a hard person to look at, by any means; her steely blue eyes could melt your heart. She had compassion for the injured and empathy for the bereaved, but this could never be confused with being soft. She could break your arm in an instant. She has, as an operative in the Special Forces, slit Taliban throats and broken their necks with her bare hands. It was not to be bragged about, just part of her job as a lieutenant.

Now those steely blue eyes told the men that they were disturbing her lunch, as they bore into the men's souls.

"Gentlemen, please," the barman said, with a nod of his head in Julie's direction.

They turned, gave her a smile, doffed their hats and. with a nod, they left the bar.

The barman offered Julie a free coffee, which she accepted with good grace, but she always paid for any meal she had in the pub, even when offered for free, she paid. She felt it would constitute a bribe to accept the free meal, but accepted the coffee in good grace.

After lunch, it was back to the office to file more papers, or to take a trip to a farm where sheep had been rustled, or a piece of machinery had been stolen and then to the office to file the report.

"If I were prone to swearing, the air would be blue in here, Sergeant. What is this?" Julie demanded of Sergeant Collins, newly promoted.

"The head office …erm, the super and her cronies now want a list of crimes day by day, separated into each element and cross referenced by crime number," he told her.

"Sorry, they want me to spend my time listing each separate crime by what the crime was, when it happened and then list it again by the crime number? Do they not realise that it's creating double work for my overstretched officer? We are rural and do not have an army of officers to sit at desks writing all ***** day. They are expected to solve crimes, not write about them," Julie said, leaving a blank where she felt like swearing.

"It is to do with the computers, apparently they work better with the numbers, correlating the crimes, a tractor stolen from around here can then be linked to one stolen from Berkshire say, but the computer can't do that with the old method of listings, which they like and want to keep, so we now make a double report," he said.

"Like hell we will. Look here at the map. Four farms hit and they are beginning to make sense. Each one is an hour out of London. That leaves these two farms before the thieves have to travel further afield. Put surveillance on these two farms and increase patrols. I want my coppers where they can catch the criminals, not sat at desks," Julie said.

"Ma'am, I have to say it. You do realise that this came from the Super and it is not a suggestion, but a dictate," Collins said.

"I also realise she has nothing better to do than create work, when she gives me the staff to do the un-necessary work she is creating, then I will ensure it is done. Until then, I will follow Denis the Menace's idea and put a Beano down my knickers," Julie said, joking.

"Have you heard from Everet, Ma'am? She is sitting her Sergeants' exam today," Collins said.

"It's too early yet; you did know she was to sit it this afternoon and not this morning?" Julie asked.

"No, sorry, I didn't, I thought it was this morning. What if she passes? We won't not be allowed to have two sergeants in this station, will we?"

"No, I don't suppose we will, so one of you will have to transfer out, where do you fancy going?" Julie asked, with a wry smile on her face.

"Erm, isn't it last in, first out, Ma'am?" Collins asked.

"That is for me, to decide," Julie said.

"Are you being sexist, Ma'am?" Collins asked with a smile.

"First of all, she needs to pass the exam. Then there needs to be a position for her, or you, so I would not get too excited at this moment in time. I have known qualified Sergeants wait for months for a position to open up, so let's not get too far ahead of ourselves, OK?" Julie asked him, smiling.

"OK, Ma'am," he replied, "I have a gut feeling this farm will be targeted next, if they follow the sequence. Can I suggest I keep watch on the place tonight, Ma'am?" Collins asked.

"Yes, you may suggest it, well?" Julie asked.

"Sorry, Ma'am, I suggest that I set up surveillance on this farm because I believe it will be the next target," Collins said.

"Why didn't you just say that then? Do not ask if you can ask and then ask anyway. I want you at Low Valley Farm at twenty-two hundred hours, so go home and get some sleep.

"I agree with your suggestion that Hill Top Farm is more likely to be the next target so I will be there as well. Do not notify the farmer, this sort of thing can leave it open to a con. I do not want to be notified of a lost piece of machinery; I want us to see it go. Take an infra-red camera with you and snap to your heart's content, but do not interfere. Contact me by phone and then I will tell you what to do," Julie told him.

They both left the office and went home. Julie did manage to get some rest, as did Collins before they left for their respective farms for surveillance.

Julie managed to find a side lane in which to hide her car and then walked to a position to watch the access to the farm. It was late summer and she saw them bringing in the harvest as she hid carefully, settling in for the night.

If the criminals followed their usual pattern; then tonight was the night they would appear and this was the farm they would probably target, but they might not show, a chance Julie and Collins had to take.

Organised thieves would have a radio that listened in to the police radio, which was why Julie had told Collins to ring her mobile and why she left a message at the station desk to use her mobile if she was needed during the night.

Settled, Julie and Collins began the long hours of waiting, positioned early enough to avoid detection, yet not too early with un-necessary hours of waiting.

Julie smiled as she watched the last load of the day's harvest being brought in, followed by the stream of farm vehicles, tired and weary after a long day trying to get the harvest in and beat the forecast rain. No-one saw Julie or Collins, as they had both selected a good viewpoint. Hidden from the casual person by bushes and hedgerows, they began the long wait. Julie expected the criminals to arrive between one o'clock and two o'clock in the morning, when the farmer was sound asleep, worn out from his toils of the day.

Julie expected him to be in the deepest part of his sleep around one o'clock in the morning, which was she felt the best time for the thieves to do their dirty work.

She was disappointed, but not totally surprised that her farm was not the one to be robbed, but they did arrive as she expected at one fifteen in the morning and at the farm guarded by Collins.

Julie answered her phone to the news that Collins was watching them arrive and entering the barn, where the combine harvester was located. She knew a machine of that size would not fit in a covered wagon and they would need one to avoid detection. They waited an anxious three quarters of an hour while the thieves dismantled sections of the machine to make it fit inside and to load it. This gave Julie time to join Collins before the thieves left.

"Ma'am, they are loading a tractor as well and to avoid noise they have serious electric winches and are hauling the items into the trailer," Collins told her as she helped a farmer herd his cows into a different field after they had gone through his barbed wire fence and were blocking the road.

"Stirks, randy sods and no pun intended, bullish. Right through a new barbed wire fence, they ran," he said, as an apology.

"Can't stay, must hurry," Julie said and jumped into her car. The delay was not welcomed at all, it delayed her arriving at the farm, Collins was watching.

"Do not move, I am on my way, I am about two minutes away," Julie told him as she sped down the deserted country lanes to Collins.

Chapter 2 - The Price of Success

"Ma'am they are closing the wagon doors, but they are not taking the whole harvester, just the parts. This is robbery to order. I am going in," Collins said.

"And I am ordering you to wait," Julie said.

"I will just move and park my car across the gate, blocking them in, that delay should be enough for you to arrive," Collins said.

"Collins, wait, I am in the lane, wait!" Julie almost shouted down the phone.

"I am," he said as a loud bang rang out, followed by silence.

"Collins, Collins, Collins!" Julie shouted down the phone as she saw the thieves moving off in the direction she was travelling and away from her. They were in large vehicles and moving slowly, whereas she was in a car which made her faster, much faster.

She closed the gap rapidly and then became stuck behind them, unable to pass in the narrow country lanes.

Her time here had taught her the places certain things were possible and on this particular road there was a bridge. Not strong enough or wide enough for a heavy vehicle, they needed to ford the stream as the farmers did. As the wagon entered the stream, Julie hit the accelerator and flew onto the bridge. The car left the ground and landed on the far side, just ahead of the wagon, far enough for her to slam the brake on into a hand brake turn and jump out. She stood, gun in hand, on the far side of her car and pointed it at them.

She knew her steely blue eyes could not be seen showing the depth of hatred she felt towards them, or her commitment to stop them no matter the cost. The first shot rang out, killing the driver. She moved a fraction and took aim at the passenger. The wagon, now driverless, slowed, rolled into her car and stopped.

"I have no intention of being kind, you do as I say, or I will shoot," Julie said in a blunt, authoritative voice.

She watched as they began to scramble and then a gun appeared. She did not hesitate in shooting the man holding the gun. No second warning, that was not Julie's style; you did as told or accepted the consequences. The assailant's gun clattered to the floor and the men still inside began to leave the cab, their hands held high in surrender.

"Go around the back and open the door," Julie ordered them.

They began to move and she followed, holding the gun on them.

They opened the back doors and she told them to get inside, they did and she closed and locked the back door. She reversed the wagon, backing it up the stream, then got out of the cab and unhitched the trailer, leaving it in the stream, while she went back to the farm after calling the incident in.

One of the extra patrols she had ordered was on its way to the farm when she rang it in and they arrived within five minutes of her call.

14

They found her stood by the side of Collins' car.

"Ma'am, we were on our way here when the call came in," Officer Harris said.

"Down the road half a mile there's a wagon parked in the stream. Listen to me, do not, I repeat, do not open the back door for any reason. They can suffocate for all I care. Do not open the back door; just stay there until help arrives. They shot Collins and I want them charged with murder, so they stay exactly where I left them," Julie told them. There was sympathy in her voice for Collins, but they understood her meaning and order.

"Ma'am, how is Collins? Is it serious?" Harris asked.

"The black dot between his eyes is a sure sign that it is terminal. Keen to help arrest them, Collins did not follow orders. Do not make the same mistake. He was a good officer and I thought of him as a friend. He will be missed, now do as I said," Julie told them.

The officers left Julie and she went to the farmhouse to wake the farmer. He answered the door and Julie informed him of what had happened and apologised for the inconvenience he would now face.

The farmer's wife arrived at the door and offered Julie a cup of tea.

"That would be nice, thank you, it is going to be a long night," Julie said.

Slowly officers arrived at the farm and secured the scene, forensics began their work and when they were happy with what they needed, the bodies were removed.

Mid-morning the Super arrived on the scene. "Well, Chief Inspector, quite a mess, isn't it? Three dead, what happed did you run out of bullets?" she asked, shocked at the death toll.

"Ma'am, they shot Collins and then drove a wagon at me, using it as a weapon, so I shot the driver in self-defence. I wasn't happy they pointed a gun at me, so again, in self-defence, I shot the gunman. They knew I was an armed officer of the law, having told them earlier, apart from the fact that I was using the siren whilst following them. I did not stop with Collins, because I saw the black dot on his forehead.

"Now you may not know what that means, but I have seen it far too often not to know; he was dead and there's no coming back from that shot." Julie said in temper.

"I agree with what you are saying, not how you said it! Be careful, I will not be spoken to like that; you are on very thin ice, Chief Inspector. There will have to be an investigation and I will need your gun," the Super said, holding out her hand.

"Ma'am, with respect, you are an officer who has not been firearms trained, therefore I will hand my weapon in to a qualified officer, if you don't mind. It is not police issue, it is my own weapon.

"I am a licensed firearms officer and registered firearms collector, I am allowed to carry this weapon approved by MI 5. Brown. Put this into evidence, will you?" Julie said to an armed officer, handing over her gun. "I also respectfully request that Collins be put up for an award, because of his commitment to his job and his sacrifice," Julie added.

"Oh, interesting, is this the first time you have lost a colleague?" the Super asked.

"Of course not, I lost half of my platoon in Afghanistan, including two very close friends. Had Collins not acted as he did, then they would have got away, he delayed them just enough for me to be right on their tails and made it possible for me to arrest them, just to make sure it is clear as to what happened, Ma'am," Julie said forcefully.

"It is very clear Chief Inspector, and I suggest you go home and calm down before you exhaust my patience, and tolerance," the Super said.

"After I have spoken to Collins' wife, Ma'am, something I do not like to delay, bad news is better dealt with as soon as possible, so that healing can begin," Julie said.

"And do you think that in your current state of mind, you are the best person to deliver the news?" the Super asked.

"My state of mind has nothing to do with it. I am a professional and can answer questions other people are not able to. I will not suffer it; I will relieve my anger and frustrations later at home, not in front of anyone, because I am professional. I considered him not only my work colleague, but a friend. I can empathise, because I feel her pain, too. I am not the best person, I am the only person," Julie said and made to leave.

"My office tomorrow morning, ten o'clock, Chief Inspector," the Super said, as Julie left the scene.

The officers returned the trailer to the farmyard and unloaded it with the help of the farmer who set about rebuilding his machinery. He had lost the morning and early afternoon, but not the whole of the day.

Julie went to Collins' house and sat in the police car for a few minutes, bolstering her courage. She was afraid she might break down when she told Mrs Collins the devastating news.

She got out of the squad car and sent the driver away, deciding to walk home afterwards, and went to the front door. It was a long walk, weighed down by the message she had to convey. It was inevitable what was about to happen when she told Mrs Collins her husband was dead, killed in the line of duty. It was something she had done a few times before, unlike a death caused by an accident to someone unknown to her, where it was a message of sympathy, this type struck home. The loss of a colleague and a friend was the hardest to convey, yet because the feelings were shared, a mutual feeling of empathy was the result.

Julie stayed for an hour with Mrs Collins and then left for home.

She now had to bury her feelings and be subjective; she needed to prepare for the interview the following morning and she needed not an excuse, but reasons for what happened.

It would be easy to put the blame on Collins for not obeying an order, but Julie was sure there was more to it than that. For one thing guns had not been mentioned before and the robbers had been seen leaving the crime scene. Several farmers had fired at them. Perhaps that was why they were armed; it was common for a farmer to have a shot gun on the premises. This crime had been elevated by the use of guns; they were prepared to kill the farmer to get the machinery.

So, it was now armed robbery and murder, which the police had not been made aware of. Julie being a qualified firearms instructor and licensed to carry one as an armed officer usually had one with her. Collins was due to go on the course, but was not as yet registered and he did not have one.

If a situation required firearms support, then officers were drafted in from the nearest large town. Julie's force was not large enough to have its own tactical support section and considered too quiet, being rural, but it was something Julie wanted to address, after the case involving Sir Andrew Mac Adams. Julie felt that guns were far more prevalent in the country than the city, although a crime may not be by an armed thief. They were more likely to come in contact with a firearm than in a household in the city, hence the need for firearms trained officers.

Julie went into a solemn office the next morning; everyone down in the mouth about the death of Collins.

"Look, it has happened, we will miss Collins, but thieves do not take a day off and we have a job to do. As they say, 'get over it and get back to work.' I want an honour guard for the funeral to show them he was well respected and that we will miss him, but this will not stop us from doing our jobs.

"Sergeant, select six officers to walk beside the funeral car and they will also carry the coffin into the church. Apart from that it is business as usual, this is not a free pass for criminals," Julie said as the officers paraded.

Julie entered her office to see Everet, her eyes blood shot.

"I am promoting you temporarily as Sergeant until the appointment is confirmed. I want them interviewed, formally charged and every 'I' dotted and every 'T' crossed. If they get off on a technicality, your life will not be worth living," Julie told Everet, "This is just between us and never to be repeated. I told Collins to stay where he was and he disobeyed the order, trying and succeeding to delay them, but it cost him his life. If you ever disobey an order, you will think being a traffic warden is a promotion," Julie told her.

"I didn't know he disobeyed an order, Ma'am, does anyone?" Everet asked.

"I am betting not. We used our mobiles to communicate and no-one must know. I have put him up for a commendation, disobeying an order will go against him, so as I said, it is between us and must not leave this office," Julie said.

"But Ma'am, won't that go in your favour when they investigate what happened, the fact that he disobeyed a direct order?" Everet asked.

"Yes, it will, but then again; I did not order him to act, he did it courageously in the line of duty, without forethought for his own safety. That way we can honour him," Julie said.

"Yes, Ma'am, he was that type of guy, Ma'am, to act when required to do so in the line of duty; Ma'am," Everet said.

"Indeed, he was, thank you," Julie said and put her coat on ready to leave for headquarters.

At headquarters, after a short wait, Julie was told to enter and then she began to tell the Super the details of what had happened and their plan.

"So, Collins was not supposed to engage with the thieves, just watch and make notes, like the registration number of their wagon?" the Super asked.

"It was meant to be surveillance, but as I am sure you know that is not what happens in a lot of cases, as things change. I rely on my officer's intelligence to make decisions as things develop. Collins knew I was on my way, after having informed me of their arrival. They were about to make a move and he knew we wanted to apprehend them, so he used a delaying tactic, unaware that they were armed and that I had been delayed, by the herd of bulls, stirks, ma'am. The information that they may be armed had not filtered down to our station. Were you aware that the thieves were now armed?" Julie asked her.

"Be careful. Chief Inspector, that ice is very thin. As an ex-Met officer, you are used to thieves being armed, wouldn't it have been a good idea to have armed officers, on stand-by?" the Super asked.

"I was armed and Collins was supposed to have been on the course two weeks ago, but it was postponed until next week, which was why I raced from my surveillance position to be by his side, but it took too long, yet I was a lot quicker than having armed officers on stand-by. Had he attended the course as agreed, then he would have been armed. Do not blame me for head office incompetence," Julie said, allowing her temper to surface.

"It was a decision we took with good reason; we knew you were annoyed about it, you said so, but the officer from the other station took precedence," she told Julie.

"Water under the bridge as it were, Ma'am, had Collins been armed he would not have been able to get his gun out before they shot him. The way I see it is that they decided to leave. When Collins heard the engine start, he started his engine and they heard him as he moved to block the entrance. The gunman shot him, being aware he was there, he was ready, but the gunman was not aware that he was a police officer. Instead he assumed he was a farmer, say, guarding his property, because of the thefts. They may also have assumed that he would have his shotgun with him.

"As for me, there is no way they did not know I was an officer of the law in pursuit, blue lights flashing and my siren blaring away. They knew damn well who I was and still tried to run me over, justified at the very least. I would expect self-defence, a forty-ton wagon is one hell of a weapon, Ma'am.

"I am waiting for confirmation that the weapon found at the scene is the same one used to kill Collins, if not, then, someone else in the wagon had a gun, Ma'am," Julie said.

"Were your instructions to Detective Sergeant Collins sufficient? What were your instructions, or orders?" the Super asked Julie.

"I told him to observe and report, but I allowed him the tolerance to make decisions. He was astute enough to make decisions on his own behalf. He was there, I was not, so I could not make the decision for him, nor would I. I do not want puppets that react to their strings being pulled, I want proper police officers and I am lucky enough to have them. Collins was a very good police officer," Julie said forcefully.

"So, he was told to observe and report, yet we have no record of him reporting?" the Super asked.

"Thieves have equipment which is considered illegal, but being thieves, they do not take notice of the legalities and listen in to our radios. To avoid alerting them to our presence, we decided to use mobile phones for reporting. Collins rang me and said, "They are on the move; I am going too," and then I heard the bang. I had already left my position and was about one hundred yards from Collins' position when I heard the bang. I thanked God for the advanced training I had received by the army for protection duty.

"As soon as the wagon began to move to the right, I hit the accelerator and hit the hedge as I squeezed past it. I headed over the bridge, the car flew up over the brow and slammed down; I think it may need new suspension it did bottom out when I landed. I skidded to a halt, side on to the wagon, blocking the road.

"I had checked on Collins. You may not think it, but when you have seen it as often as I have, execution style, eyes closed, a pallid complexion, a black hole and a trickle of blood between the eyes, there is no doubt what I saw as I passed him. There was no need to stop, he was dead and the killer was getting away, so I didn't stop. I pursued them and caught them; that is my job, isn't it?" Julie asked, once again allowing her temper to surface.

"At what point did you tell them you were an armed officer of the law?" the Super asked.

"The flashing blue lights and siren informed them that I was an officer of the law. Before they ran me over, I shouted that I was armed and then fired; did I wait to be run over before I fired, giving them time to give up? No, I decided that my life was important, as was Collins' life and they knew that I was after them. They were lucky I had time to warn them that I was armed," Julie said bluntly.

"I do not believe you; I think that in the heat of the moment you killed the driver, fearing for your life, perhaps? Then again you are agile enough to have jumped clear, but they had killed Collins and that was why you fired. Rather than fearing for your life, you are far too experienced to act without knowing what you are doing.

"This is off the record, when the internal affairs interview you that will be on record. My report will show you as acting in accordance with guidelines.

"I am sorry for the loss of Detective Sergeant Collins and support your actions; unofficially, I applaud them. How on earth you could stand there with a forty-ton articulated wagon bearing down on you and calmly shoot the driver between the eyes before jumping to the side to avoid being run over amazes me and then to recover enough to shoot the gunman. Did he manage to get a shot off?" the Super asked Julie.

"No, Ma'am, it only takes one bullet to kill, I didn't allow him the time. Between us, Ma'am, as soon as I saw the gun, I fired. He knew I was armed, having shot the driver, there was no need to warn him and he knew I would fire," Julie said, relaxing a bit.

"I have no option but to suspend you pending the internal investigation into the shooting. I suggest you have your solicitor present; most of this has been off record, as I said. The interview with the officers investigating the shooting will not be easy, do not let your guard down," the Super told her.

Dismissed, Julie went home. She slammed her car keys down on the hall table and went into the kitchen where a slab of steak felt her anger as she diced it up. She sliced an onion and chopped carrots into a casserole dish; she added wine and seasoning and slapped it in the oven, then slamming the oven door shut.

Julie picked up the phone and rang without thinking about it.

"Julie, all well?" Dan asked.

"Like hell it is, I.ve been suspended, the b-b-b shot and killed Collins, so what was I supposed to do? Let him walk away, ask nicely for him to put his gun down; the one he was pointing at me? Like hell; I shot the b-b-b," Julie said.

"I see. It sounds as if you need some support. I am due a week's leave starting next week; would you like Alex and me to come down? You can take her shopping in that new centre they're advertising." Dan said.

"I appreciate your offer but no. By the way how do you know about the new centre? Manchester's a long way for the adverts to have reached you," said Julie.

"I placed an order with the local rag and get the weekly news. I suppose your exploits will be in this week's paper. You know how much Alex likes shopping and a new centre would interest her. I could well rest and pay, as usual," Dan said, as if disgruntled.

"Dan, if memory serves me correctly, Alex earns twice what you earn and she pays, not you. Interior design is very lucrative, so I understand," Julie said.

"Actually, far more here than in London, believe it or not. We will see you on Sunday," Dan said.

"I would love to see you both, but this I need to fight alone. It will be character building for me to use politics rather than my fists, it may help me to conform more," Julie said, laughing.

"Ha, you conform? Never! Keep me informed; I will expect a daily call from you," Dan said and they hung up.

Julie went into the garden and pulled some weeds and then had a shower. She took her now over cooked casserole out of the oven and sighed. 'It's never a good idea to cook when in a bad temper,' she thought.

She had prepared it too early and now it was over cooked, but she needed to take her anger out on someone or something. If she took it out on someone, she would in all probability kill them; the casserole was her best option.

She left for the pub and ordered a glass of white wine, Chardonnay, and sat in a corner watching the people as they lived their lives, enjoying a night out. It was a hobby she really liked, watching life pass by. Drunks, socialites, housewives, businessmen and women all gathered for a drink, chatting, laughing and arguing, rather debating, the colourful mix of society.

Julie liked to guess who or what they were, here it was not as good as London, there she seemed to know no-one and here she knew fifty to sixty percent of the people in the bar.

A man entered, dressed in a tweed jacket and slacks. His shirt was pink and he wore a cravat along with highly polished shoes and tartan socks. Julie looked again. His attire was abstract to say the least, some sort of artisan, perhaps? He did have the long hair associated with an arty farty or beatnik types. A traveller perhaps, but they did not usually have such highly polished shoes. He gave the impression of being well to do, but had an air of being impoverished, as if his clothes had been stolen from a washing line and did not match.

Julie got up and moved towards the bar, she needed to understand the man and to do that she needed to hear him speak, perhaps engage in conversation with him.

He was an anomaly, he did not fit in the pub, or society somehow.

"A pint of your finest amber nectar, my good man," he said in an aristocratic voice.

"Allow me. You are not from around here, are you?" Julie asked, offering to buy his beer.

"My good lady, indeed not, t'would be impolite of me to allow such a delightful young lady to purchase my beverage. May I have the honour to purchase another libation for your good self?" he asked.

A throwback from Victorian times, perhaps, he became more and more of a contradiction which intrigued Julie, so she allowed him to purchase a drink for her.

"Allow me to introduce myself. I am Julie and I am sat over there. Would you care to join me?" Julie asked him.

"It would be my honour to join such a delightful lady as your good self. I am Professor Eugene Algernon Blackthorn, at your service, my card, Madam," he said with a slight bow, handing her his card, another throwback from Victorian or Edwardian times.

Julie couldn't decide if he was a time traveller, or just nuts, but she was intrigued and took his card, smiling at him.

"I live in the town and know, by sight, most of the town's inhabitants and I am sure I have never seen you around here.

"Where have you come from? Are you here on holiday?" Julie asked.

"I do not hail from these parts; that is correct. I have travelled far this day and require libation to ease my tired and weary body. I must admit that being in the company of such a delightful creature as your good self makes the libation far more pleasant," he said, added a slight bow, and took a drink.

"You are very interesting, a Professor, you say, what brings you to these parts? Being an inspector, makes me nosy, DCI Ashton," Julie introduced herself to him.

"Music my dear, the noble art of intricate melodies, soothing but complex by nature," he said.

"I see, so you are a musician then, where is the gig?" Julie asked.

"My dear lady Inspector, do not be so crass and defamatory, I am surprised that an articulate person such as your good self decries the noble art with such crude terms as gig, it is a feast of melodious concoctions, delivered via an ensemble of virtuosos, such as myself," he said, as if aggrieved.

"My apologies, obviously it is not just a group doing a gig, but more of an orchestral rendition by superior musicians," Julie said, trying to appease the man.

"Indeed, it is, you are very astute, my dear," he said.

"Then I hate to burst your bubble, but my dad told me about a group in the nineteen sixties called "The Temperance Seven," led by a Professor, not a real professor, just an acting title, for entertainment. He liked their music and enjoyed their antics, so where and when?" Julie asked, smiling broadly.

"And there I was, thinking I was imbibing with a lady of distinction," he said, as if hurt.

"I can be, but after my day, I am very much down to earth," Julie said.

"A tiresome day, mayhap?" he asked.

"You could say that, so some light relief would definitely not go amiss, my dear, dear, Professor?" Julie said as a question, adding a smile for him.

"Then the morrow, at nineteen hundred hours, on the green at Upper Hampton and I will be delighted if you would deign to be my guest at our rendition," he said.

"Yes, the stage they were erecting, I wondered why. I will feast upon the libation of lyrical notes and phrases, thank you, Professor," Julie said and left before she burst out laughing.

It had been a very formal conversation, yet lighthearted, she had enjoyed the formality of the conversations of days gone by; it had been a relief for her from the hard facts of the last twenty-four hours.

She got into bed still smiling, being correct had made her think, filling her mind with what or how to say anything and pushing her suspension to the back of her mind.

The shrill tone of her phone woke her. "Sorry to disturb you, Ma'am, but there is a weird guy here who insists he spoke to you last night at the pub and will not speak to anyone but you. Apparently, a, I use his terminology, 'a crime of horrendous proportions has been perpetrated upon a dear, dear friend of my acquaintance.' That is what he said. Is he for real, Ma'am?" the desk Sergeant asked.

"I presume he is wearing a tweed Jacket, tartan socks, pink shirt and a cravat?" Julie asked.

"Yes, Ma'am," he replied.

"Ask Professor Eugene if he would do me the honour of partaking of a herbal libation in our rather sullied, refreshment area whilst I prepare myself to greet him more formally. Can you remember all that, or shall I repeat it whilst you write it down?" Julie asked him.

"Ma'am, what, can you repeat it? Why can't I just tell him to get a cup of tea and wait in the canteen?" he asked.

"Because I asked you to say it that way," Julie said and repeated it whilst he wrote it down.

She got dressed, made her way to the station and entered to comical and confused looks.

Chapter 3 - Professor Eugene

"Professor, may I say what a delight it is to see you again, although the circumstances are not as conducive to good conversation.

"Let me begin by making the introduction complete, I am Detective Chief Inspector Julie Ashton, as you may have guessed, or been told, and currently not able to assist you as much as I would be honoured to do so. I have asked Detective Sergeant Everet to join us. I hope the libation was to your liking and the accommodation was acceptable?" Julie asked.

"I am distressed that you feel unable to assist me in what is an already very distressing situation," he said.

"I cannot go into details because of our connection last night. I came, but officially I am not allowed, to act. This does not mean that I will not be involved, but it will be just on the side lines, as it were, Professor," Julie said.

"Then pray tell me if your companion will be able to converse as amiably and convivially as we conversed, last evening?" he asked.

"Alas and with much regret, my colleague may not be as conversant with etiquette as am I. With regard to your distressing situation, then I am sure you will have nothing to worry about, talking to my colleague, plus I will be on hand to advise where necessary," Julie said.

"Then it is with much regret that I must inform you of a tragedy, our syncopated performance of musical renditions must be cancelled," he said. Julie wondered if he was about to cry and Everet looked at Julie, confused.

"Ma'am, why are we in here with, well, a nutter?" Everet asked, taking her out of the room.

"Know the man, know the reason, music is his life. There is nothing more important than his music, give him time and he will explain why, that is why he is here, not the fact the concert is cancelled," Julie told her and then re-entered the room. "I apologise for mine and my colleagues' abrupt and rude disappearance. Pray continue, I presume there is a very good reason for the cancellation." Julie mused. "Indeed, very distressing, our dear Bones, a syncopated percussionist, capable and highly skilled with skulls and pig skin, is no longer with us, having passed away. His demise was not expected and came as a shock, foaming and writhing in a convulsive manner," he said.

"I am sorry to hear of his demise and the manner of his demise, but we need more information. Where is he now?" Julie asked.

"The syncopators and I did not touch him for fear of it being contagious, he lies where he fell, across his beloved percussion," he said.

"I see. Where may we find his percussion? An address would be nice," Julie said, tiring of this now.

"On the stage, where else?" he said.

"So, you left him on the stage in full view for everyone to see. Did you cover the body at all? Why didn't you call an ambulance when he started to convulse?" Julie asked, shocked.

"It was not a long time, he just shook for a few seconds and then fell face down on his percussions with a cymbal crash," he said, falling face down on the table with his hand outstretched as if hitting a cymbal.

"Everet, get a car and call for an ambulance to join us there. Professor, what are you saying? He was murdered, or he took a drug overdose, or he was ill, which is it?" Julie asked, now with some force.

"I am a syncopator, a professor of music, unfortunately not of the medical profession, so the answer eludes me as much as it eludes you, until we arrive and survey the situation. Although some of my persuasion may partake of innocuous substances. I, and my fellow syncopators, do not," he said.

"In the pub it was fun and earlier I allowed it, but from now on we talk normally. You will be dealing with normal people who will not understand your words and therefore decry your validity as a witness and we cannot afford that.

"Once this is over, perhaps we could have a chat. I have enjoyed the experience, but not now. Was there a gunshot, or did you see anyone else?" Julie asked.

"Nay, we were alone, just the syncopators tidying up," he said.

"So, drugs do not usually have an epileptic effect, but can do. He did not suffer from epilepsy, did he?" Julie asked.

"Nay, he was fit and of good health," he said.

"I will need you to show us where he is, will you do that for us?" Julie asked him.

"I am at your service," he said, with a slight bow towards her.

Julie led him out of the police station and into the waiting car. He joined Everet in the back and Julie sat in the front as she now ordered the driver to put his foot down.

"Blues and twos, but don't use them unless you need to. Well, have you forgotten where the accelerator is?" Julie asked as he stuck to the speed limit.

"Sorry, Ma'am, you meant for me to rush?" he asked.

"Officer, there is a dead person, obviously we need to hurry, we need to secure the scene before all the evidence, forensic and visual, is lost," Julie said.

"Jonas, please hurry, do not let the chief drive. The last time she drove is the only time I have been in a car taking a corner on two wheels. During the chase after Collins had been shot, she took Bridgeford Bridge so fast the car landed six feet further down the road, it flew and I have not had my breakfast yet, so there is nothing to come up," Everet said.

"Ma'am, can you teach me how to do a handbrake turn," Jonas asked.

"Yes, I can teach, but can you learn? Brake hard, now turn and now accelerate hard, no, no, no,

35

you brake going into a corner and then hold as you turn and then accelerate. Do not brake when trying to turn or you will lose it," Julie said, sitting back comfortably whilst Everet's knuckles were turning white as she gripped the handle over the back door.

They arrived safely with Julie's tuition and she went to the stage where the body was waiting, accompanied by the rest of bandr.

"Professor, please wait on the grass, this is a crime scene. Jonas what are you doing?" Julie asked him.

"Erm, checking for a pulse, Ma'am," he replied.

"Come here, right, now find the carotid pulse in your own neck. Found it yet, no, just as I thought, you are dead, well from the neck up, at least. Never use the carotid pulse, it is not only hard to find, it is deep so you need to press hard, use the wrist and not with the thumb. why?" Julie asked him, lifting a wrist to feel for a pulse.

"I, erm, sorry Ma'am, I don't know."

"Very simple, there is a pulse in your thumb, but not in your fingers, so you never use your thumb. And there is no pulse, but I am a police officer, satisfied he is dead, but not officially, we will have to wait for a doctor to confirm his death.

"Everet, what have you concluded?" Julie asked.

"That he is dead, there is foam around the mouth consistent with drugs and poison, so he died from an overdose, or poison. There are no bullet holes or stab wounds to make me think differently," Everet said.

"Not everyone can detect it, but there is a smell of bitter almonds, which is a sign of cyanide poisoning, but we will have to wait for toxicology."

"Professor, when did he last eat, or have a drink? What did he eat and where was he when he had it, so what, where and when?" Julie asked him.

"I can't remember. Are you proposing my dear percussionist friend was robbed of the very life he was enjoying?" he asked.

"I am suggesting he was murdered, but until we have toxicology, I cannot be decisive, or confirm the means of his demise. At last, the ambulance has arrived, along with Wilson."

"Right Jonas, secure the area with Wilson. Everet, have you called for forensics?" Julie asked.

"Yes Ma'am, at the station before we left, they will be here in about an hour, once the on-duty people have been called. I have asked that a doctor attend in the ambulance, Ma'am," Everet said.

"Then I can go home, seeing as I am suspended," Julie said laconically.

"Ma'am, may I call on you in the morning?" Everet asked.

"Everet, it is morning and yes call me later; I am going back to bed, the joys of being suspended. Everet, you have been involved before in this sort of thing and I have every faith in your abilities, but if in doubt call me at home, but not for a few hours," Julie said.

Julie got in the patrol car they came in and left Everet to do her job as she drove to the station. Once home, she went back to bed.

Julie was up and in her garden when the phone rang, asking her to attend the interview at eleven o'clock that morning. She knew they did not mess about, they usually acted quickly. A senior officer suspended was not a good thing, leaving a station without its leader.

Julie drove to the main station, registered at the desk and waited to be called.

Two officers came to escort her to the interview room and sat facing her.

After setting the tape recorder going, and giving their introductions the Super, from a different area, opened the interview.

"Chief Inspector, tell us what happened?" he asked.

"There had been several large machinery thefts, we noted that they were targetting farms approximately one hour's drive from London' We found two farms which met the criteria. Detective Constable Everet was on leave and that left Detective Sergeant Collins and me, so we took a farm each," Julie said.

"What were your instructions to Detective Sergeant Collins?" he asked.

"To hide, observe and report," Julie said.

"Not to try to arrest them?" he asked.

"No, just observe, and report," Julie said.

"So, he took it upon himself to disobey your orders?" he asked.

"I do not order my team members, they are intelligent and astute, they also have a brain and can assess, a situation," Julie said.

"You ordered him to observe only; that was what you said, wasn't it?" he asked.

"I have been told that I have little respect for authority. When authority puts words into my mouth, or being in such rarefied air their brains do not function as they should do. Then, I do have little respect, for them.

"I said that I do not order my team; I give them an instruction and then allow them to use the brains they were given to amend my instruction as the situation changes. What changed the situation I do not know and never will know, but for whatever reason, Detective Sergeant Collins decided to move. I know it was the right decision, although it led to his death. We were not aware that they were armed," Julie said forcefully.

"Where were you, armed as we know, while all this was going on?" he asked.

"Having checked his mobile phone records, you know he rang me later, after the first call. I left the farm I was watching and went as fast as I could to his location. Some stirks had managed to escape their field and clearing the road delayed me. They move fairly quickly, but not fast enough for me to arrive before he was shot. I was driving into the lane, approximately one hundred yards away, when I heard the shot.

He said, 'I am going to-' and then I heard the bang, then silence, so as I said, what and why he did what he did I do not know, but I know it was the right thing, apart from the fact that we did not know they were armed," Julie said.

39

"That brings me to the fact that you were armed. Why was that, if you were not aware, they were armed?" he asked.

Julie felt behind her and slapped her Colt 45 Magnum on the table.

"The security here is crap; I usually have my weapon before I even put my knickers on, army trained. I never leave home without it and as an expert for the police force on firearms and security. I am surprised you did not check if I was armed today," Julie said.

"There are two dead, why did you not arrest them? It seems like excessive use of violence which you are also renowned for.".

"You tell me what to do then when a forty-ton articulated lorry is driving straight at you and gaining speed? Your colleague lies dead, so they are obviously not afraid of killing a police officer, now what was I supposed to do?" Julie asked them.

"We ask the questions, Chief Inspector," he said.

"Then I had two options, allow the bastards that had shot and killed my sergeant to drive off into the sunset, or shoot and, seeing as my life was in danger, I chose the latter and shot the driver. When the barrel of a gun appeared at the window of the cab, I knew my life was once again in danger and acted in a manner commensurate with the danger posed. I shot, the bastard," Julie said, with feeling.

"Did you alert them to the fact that you were an armed officer?" he asked.

"Yes. I had the siren blaring away and the blue lights flashing as I chased after them. I stopped my car in their path, with the siren and lights still switched on, which was enough to alert them to the fact that I was an officer of the law. I do have a strong voice, but over the noise of the engine, and in a closed cab. I very much doubt that they would hear me tell them that I was armed. I fired a warning shot, now at one hundred and sixty decibels, that would be heard over the engine noise.

"If you want to try searching for the bullet, well now, let me see... A bullet travels at over twelve hundred miles an hour and fired upwards at a forty-five-degree angle, that makes the landing point approximately half a mile from the point of discharge. When you take into account the three-quarter charge I use, well, good hunting," Julie said.

"Why not take down the registration number and let them pass, then put out an all points for the wagon to be tracked?" he asked.

"Because they threatened my life. Point a gun at me and I will shoot you and I do not miss. I always use sufficient force to stop the offender. Point a gun at me and I will fire, especially if I'm not in a position to disarm you. Being in the cab of a wagon I was not able to disarm the gunperson, so I shot them, simple," Julie said.

"We have asked the farmer who was awake after the first shot and he only heard two more shots, yet you say you fired three bullets. One into the air as a warning shot and then two at the driver and the gunman, making three," he said, making the point.

"You have not seen me shooting, so I accept you do not know just how good I am. I shot the driver and took the dive, firing as I flew through the air. It could have sounded like an echo and been missed coming so soon after the first shot," Julie said.

"You cannot aim and fire a gun as you fly through the air. I also am a trained firearms officer," he told her.

"Do not confuse army and police training, do not think what they both teach is the only way. When in a tight situation, an ambush say, you learn very quickly just how good you are. I am here because I am good and didn't die in Afghanistan. I lost half my troop when we were ambushed, but that means that I got half of them back safely. You can't fire from the hip, I did, you can't fire when flying through the air, I did. When the adrenaline is flowing you can move mountains and do things you can't do normally. Now sack me, or end this witch hunt.

"A colleague and friend lay dead and I saw red so yes, perhaps I could have wimped out, but I do not let my friends down. They were there and I did my job, killing where necessary and arresting the others. They had two options, give up and be arrested, or shoot their way out and they chose the wrong one and ended up dead. I fired in self-defence and it is up to you to prove otherwise," Julie said, throwing down the gauntlet.

"I have an appointment on the firing range this afternoon, but I am going to give it to you, so I can watch you firing whilst flying through the air, because I do not believe it is possible," he told her.

"What time?" Julie asked.

"Three o'clock," he said.

"I will see you at three and watch you eat your words," Julie said, regretting her promise as soon as she had said it.

He was right about it being almost impossible, but he had called her bluff and she was too proud to accept defeat.

She knew to hold the gun when it is fired takes strength; to avoid missing when it recoils, but as she had said when the adrenaline is flowing; you suddenly acquire strength, as had happened many times in Afghanistan.

Her main advantage was that she knew how to use the recoil to her advantage.

At three o'clock prompt, she arrived at the range and was met by the trainer who smiled at her.

"This is very unorthodox; you do know that, don't you? I believe he wants to see you take a dive whilst firing a Colt 45 Magnum. I would be asking you if it was possible?" the Trainer asked.

"No, it isn't normally, but here I do not need long range power, so I use a three-quarter charge, even so the kick is powerful, but I can control it and I will not be firing from behind the guard. For it to be just, I need to be twenty feet from the target, as I was when I shot at the wagon," Julie said.

"Well, Chief Inspector there we are, the two targets are set for you, now show me exactly how you did it."

"First of all, Sir; that is not how it was, do you want to recreate the actual situation, or do you want to engineer a result to suit you? To be correct, I need to be a lot closer. The range will have to be closed and the wagon was about twenty feet away when I took the first shot. This means that I need to move down the range and I use my gun, not the one you have selected. As I said, three quarter charge, less recoil, but just as effective in close range situations," Julie said, making sure it was at least fair.

He accepted her demands, because the firearms trainer was present and he agreed with Julie to ensure it was fair.

Julie walked down the range to about the right position and looked back. The trainer nodded to her and spoke to the Super investigating her and he nodded to Julie, a reluctant nod.

Julie stood erect and then snatched her gun from the waist band of her trousers and fired, taking a dive to her right as she had said in the interview and fired again. She came back to the Super the trainer wheeled the two targets in and looked at them.

"Sir, two direct hits, the first is a bull's eye, the second an outer bull's eye, had I not seen it with my own eyes I would not have believed it," he said.

"I have no other option but to accept your word," the Super said.

"It is not my word now, Sir, it is fact, you cannot deny your own eyes, can you? Add the power of adrenaline to my actions and you have two bull's eyes. I presume the suspension has been lifted and I am allowed to do my job now," Julie said and turned to leave.

"I have not completed my investigation yet, there is still the other bullet, the one you say you fired into the air," he said.

"Then I suppose I should apply for my pension! Have you any idea how big the search area would be and what for? You failed to get me sacked in London, but managed to have me moved. At first, I was upset but now I like it here and it grates with you that I have settled and like the posting, so you are trying to get me sacked, again.

"Ask Simon here about trajectory and power and see if he can advise you as to where to look. Simon, I fired a bullet up in the air at a forty-five-degree angle, with a three-quarter charge and in a westerly wind. Where should he look?" Julie asked.

"How strong was the wind?" he asked.

"I don't have the accurate speed, but about ten knots," Julie said.

"About one, to two square miles," he said.

Julie felt he had over exaggerated, but that was in her favour, so she said nothing.

"I will confirm the end to your suspension in the morning, you have more lives than a cat," he said, disgruntled.

Chapter 4 - Back to Work

"Morning, Ma'am, good to see you back," Everet said.

"Good morning, it's good to be back. Now, where are we?" Julie asked.

"It took some time Ma'am; they are weird to say the least. I presume you do know he is not a real professor, just as Skins Malloy is not his real name, but could I get them to tell me what his name was? I ended up threatening them with jail for withholding evidence.

"He was Alan Bunburry from Chelmsford, but currently of no fixed abode. They all lived together in a mobile home and a tent. There were seven of them and not one of them has a name I could recognise or list without a back lash from above. Windrush Adams, he plays the trombone, Butterfly Jones, he plays the flute and saxophone and need I go on?" Everet asked.

"Are their surnames real, or are they a figment of an over-active male brain, sorry dysfunctional, male brain?" Julie asked, laughing.

"How could I check, Ma'am? Have you any idea how many 'Adams' there are in the UK? Without an address or name, I can't begin to narrow it down. I know we have odd names out there, so I began by accepting the names given, but nothing came up, so I went back, to no avail, Windrush actually hit on me, I am not sure if it was drug induced or not, Ma'am," Everet said.

"Ha, apart from the fact that you are a good-looking woman, so it does not surprise me, could it have been to take the upper hand, to catch you off guard?" Julie asked her.

"I did wonder but if so, it did not work," Everet said forcefully, for effect.

"I never doubted it; do not be surprised if they were straight 'A' students with degrees and not a minor degree, in fact I suspect they are very intelligent people, somewhere on the border between genius and insanity. Balancing that very fine line," Julie said, smiling.

"I think they have crossed over, Ma'am, into insanity," Everet said.

"Perhaps, but they are harmless enough. Try tracing their gigs, someone may know more, where did they perform last?" Julie asked.

"Ma'am, can't we force the issue, I mean, surely they have some connection with society, like social security numbers, a driving licence even?" Everet asked.

"I presumed you did ask for some form of identity?" Julie asked.

"Yes, the driver lives close by, he was the only sane one. Clive Burrows from Ashton-on-Cherwell, he lives with his mother when not on tour," Everet said.

"I presume that is most of the time, they are what I would call musical gypsies, nomadic musicians. The problem we are faced with is that you can call yourself anything you want. You do not have to change it by deed poll, just by common usage, but unless you change it by deed poll, the assumed name is not legally recognised, so it cannot be used on legal documents.

"We can use this to find out their real names, or their given names, by asking them to sign their statements, now we can ask to have their signature verified.

"What about the crime, where are we on that?" Julie asked.

"I did as required and sealed off the crime scene, then began the interviews while forensic did their jobs and the coroner took the body away. I am currently waiting for the forensic and coroner's reports. I planned to have another go at the band. I do not know if they were drunk or drugged up, but I could not make head or sense of what they were saying," Everet said, frustrated.

"Then we will help them make sense of it, a night in the cells will clear their befuddled brains, I am sure, if not two nights should do the trick," Julie said, smiling.

"My thoughts exactly, Ma'am," Everet said, as they put on their coats and left the office.

"Professor, lovely to see you again, but alas, and without fortune it has come to pass that I require you to tell me about the unfortunate events of the other night. It is beholden upon me to acquire facts and for this I will need you to have a clear functional mind. If for any reason this not be apparent, then I have a nice cell awaiting you, withholding or perverting the course of the law is an offence and can cause the transgressor to spend time in incarceration.

"OK, the bull out of the way, what is your name?" Julie asked, changing her approach.

"Professor Eugene Algernon Blackthorn, at your service," he said.

"I will require proof of that," Julie said, adding a contrived smile for his benefit.

"Under English law, a name is but an identifier and can be changed at any point without application for legal acceptance as long as it is in common use and for the last seven years I have been, as I said, ergo common use and therefore my name. Check if you will, Button versus Wrightman, fifteen ninety-four or Williams versus Bryant eighteen thirty-nine," he told her.

"A degree in law, I presume?" Julie asked him.

"There was confusion back in those times with regard to Christian name and Baptismal name, the first name being referred to as Christian name, but it could be any name chosen by the parents. Whereas at baptism the name had to be one of the saint's names, Mark, Luke, John for a male, or Margaret, Mary, etcetera for a female, but you cannot have two first names, just to add to the confusion. So my Christian name, or first name under their ruling, is Eugene Algernon, not Eugene or Algernon but both and, unlike many of my counterparts, the title is genuine as a professor of law," he told her.

"Then as a professor of law, you will understand just how important it is that we find out how your friend and fellow musician died, was he murdered, or was it suicide?

"In the pub it was fun and I did enjoy our time, but now I am a police officer investigating a death

49

and I am professional and will use the law to get at the truth. I will have no qualms about putting you and your fellow musicians behind bars, if they mess with me or my officers. You have been warned," Julie said firmly.

"And I will defend the rights of my fellow musicians, now, officer of the law, how can I be of service?" he asked her.

"I am usually accused of skating on thin ice, but that is exactly where you are, as of now. I am perhaps your alibi for the most part, but where did you go after I left the bar?" Julie asked him.

"Ah the merriment of the evening was not yet complete and I continued my merry way in discourse with fellow imbibers until one in the forenoon of the morrow," he said, adding a smile.

"So, you left the bar at one in the morning, with whom did you converse?" Julie asked.

"A merry widow, with associated single females, of certain attributes and requirements, not to be discussed, or divulged by a gentleman," he replied.

"So, you chatted up single women, one of whom was a widow with the intent of having sex with them, but failed, unless you did it in the bar. I will have it checked for forensic evidence to confirm your story, unless you would like to give me the name of your partner." Julie said.

"Alas, t'was not given to, nor required by myself, the ladies chamber was more conducive to our intentions, so we retired to said chambers," he said.

"That is helpful, I can get her name from the register, even if I have to visit every resident. I will find her and, assuming she was telling the truth with regard to being widowed, when I interview each one of them in front of their husbands. There was a hen party in the hotel, so you can help me save their blushes, by telling me with whom you slept." Julie said.

"Is there no concept of decency, one's desires and the fulfilment of those desires is private and not for general discourse, or disclosure? It is a very basic requirement of our very being; 'tis the basis of life, the requirement to, procreate," he said.

"I did warn you, now I am arresting you for withholding evidence and obstructing an officer of the law in their lawful enquiries into a serious incident. Perhaps a night in the cells with time to consider a much longer period in there will help you answer my questions. The flowery nature of your answers does not faze me, but not telling me what I need to know, I consider an insult. Brown, take him away, he has been arrested for withholding evidence," Julie said.

Julie left the motor home she had used for the interview and went to Everet in the tent, where he asked to speak to her outside.

"How is it going?" Julie asked.

"Not that well, Ma'am, he has told me that as long as he uses his name regularly and it is in common use, then that is his name and I am struggling to get past that point," Everet told her.

"Then take them all down to the station, they play my game my way or they will face the law," Julie said.

They were all taken to the station and put in the cells as directed to by Julie, much to their objections, but they went in and were locked in until Julie decided differently.

Julie and Everet went to the pub and spoke to the landlord.

"Jim, sorry to have to disturb your routine, but I need some answers. Last night I was chatting to a man, I am sure you saw me and him chatting, you don't miss a thing. After I left, what did he do?" Julie asked.

"He came back to the bar and started to chat to, erm, Mrs. Erm, yes, Mrs June Bakewell, you know she is mid-forties, quite a good-looking woman for her age. She lost her husband three, no, four months ago, the big C. Mind you he never had a cig out of his mouth, chain smoker. How he could afford it I'll never know, sixty, no eighty a day. He had a friend who sent him some from abroad, even so still too expensive for most people and he wasn't rich, middle management," he told her.

"Did he leave with her?" Julie asked.

"No, she moved away. I don't think she understood his ways, they were odd, a throwback from a long distant past if you ask me. You were the only one who seemed to understand him.

"After her, he moved to the hen party. Now they were too far gone and I think laughed at him more than anything, his odd ways and speech. Round about midnight the bar emptied and he was not here, the hen party had also gone. I tidied up as usual and then went to my room. I did hear laughter coming from room seven, but the hen party had rooms five, six, seven, eight and nine. They were not disturbing anyone, so I left them to enjoy whatever they were doing," he told her.

"I will need the names and addresses of the members of the hen party," Julie said.

"I have them, are they in trouble?" Jim asked her.

"Not as far as I am aware, just routine. Did they come for breakfast, or when did you see them again?" Julie asked.

"Yes, breakfast: well a late breakfast, like five minutes to ten when we finish breakfast and then they were gone by eleven, putting Alice in a bit of a spin. She was late finishing, because she couldn't get in their rooms, but they spent a lot of money, so I didn't charge any extra," Jim told her.

Jim gave Julie the register, she took a photo of the relevant page and handed it back, she thanked him for his help, and left.

Back at the office, Everet began making a list of the guests with address and phone numbers, while Julie went to the coroner to watch the autopsy.

"I know you and I will not guess, or make assumptions, but from the amount of rigour mortise, death occurred between midnight and one o'clock am. You were in all probability correct in your assumption and I am confident when the toxicology reports are in that, Cyanide was the cause of death.

"Poison can be administered by four ways, ingestion, absorption, inhalation and injection, I can see no injection sites, so I must deduce it was not injected, apart from in liquid form, there is no powder residue in the stomach contents, so ingestion, is doubtful. Considering that he was sat on the stage in the open air, inhalation is also very doubtful, the only promising method is absorption," he said, now looking at her over the top of his glasses.

"I am looking for something he has handled, which assuming, although we never assume, he was murdered and if is not suicide. I can't think of anyone who has committed suicide by absorbing poison, can you?" Julie asked him.

"It is not the preferred method, can I say, but not impossible, not wishing to be dragged screaming into assumptions," he said and gave Julie a wicked laugh.

"Far be it from me to drag you anywhere, doctor, least of all, assumptions. From the smell I detected of burnt almonds, I am led to consider Cyanide as the means of death and, by deducting injection from the means of death, because of no injection sites. I am left with inhalation, ingestion and absorption, although being in the open air, inhalation is very dubious, see, no assumptions, Doctor," Julie said and laughed.

She was still laughing or happy about the visit when she arrived back at the office, to see Everet also smiling.

"What put you in a good mood?" Julie asked her.

"I've called four of the eight hen party guests and three say they slept with him. It is not a happy smile; it is one of incredulity. Between midnight and one o'clock in the morning he has had sex three times, my husband struggles twice in one night. How did he manage three in an hour?" Everet asked.

"Wait until you have all the accounts in, there may be more to come," Julie said and laughed. "The main point is that he was there as he said and the doctor has confirmed that death occurred whilst he was satisfying the hen party guests. He also suggested that it may have been administered by absorption. Have the drumsticks analysed for residue, make it the whole drum kit, sorry, percussion kit, and warn forensics that it might be the cause of death, so be very, careful," Julie said.

"What is the difference, I mean, you corrected yourself, Ma'am?" Everet asked.

"I was reliably informed by the Professor that a drum kit is just that, but Skins Malone also played the skulls, the odd-looking balls with slits in on the front of the percussion set, percussion to hit, he also played the xylophone, again to make the sound you hit it. I need to know if he was poisoned setting it up, (handling the parts that made up the whole), or when he played it," Julie said.

"I will also ask them to check his clothes and any deodorant or talcum power in his dressing area," Everet said.

"I doubt it being any of those things, but do it to make sure," Julie said.

55

While Everet was making the arrangements, Julie went to the interview room, after asking for Windrush Adams to be brought to her.

"Good morning, yes, it is still morning, just, how is the accommodation?" Julie asked him.

"Are you for real, it is an eight by ten enclosed space, the vibes are nasty, uncomfortable and play havoc with my temperament," he said.

"Good, I'm glad you appreciate our efforts to accommodate you. This can go on for days, weeks, months even, up to years, so I suggest you acclimatise yourself to it. The duration of your stay will be determined by your answers to my questions. Where were you between the hours of say eleven thirty and one thirty in the morning, this particular morning?" Julie asked him.

"Like high, way high, floating on clouds," he said in a dream like voice.

"I presume that you have just admitted to taking drugs?" Julie asked.

"No, no, high on the euphoria of the music, the power of the session, like wild man, just wild," he said.

"I would never have thought of syncopated music being like flower power music, it seems so much more, down to earth, Victorian in essence?" Julie asked.

"You need to be one with the notes, floating through the waves of bars, riding the crest of the highs and wallowing in the depths of the lows, man, it is a roller coaster ride," he said.

"Who else was with you during this euphoric ride?" Julie asked.

56

"I need no human companionship, the music is my companion," he said.

"Excellent, yes, I am intrigued, when did the Professor return to the van, can you tell me that?" Julie asked.

"Yeah man, t' was as the moon was at its zenith," he said as if in a trance.

"I see, that is midnight, but allowing for the hour's change one o'clock in the morning. How do you know it was that precise time?" Julie asked.

"Time is relevant to one's desires, a constraint thrown upon the oppressed by the proletariat, a means to control. I have thrown off those shackles and am free, the sun and moon bear witness to my freedom," he said, "You say one; I say halfway between the setting and rising of mother sun," he added.

"That does not answer my question, would you like time to consider your answer? How do you know what time he arrived back?" Julie asked.

"The heavens, when the moon was at its zenith, the professor arrived back in camp," he said.

"Perhaps a few more hours in our accommodation may help you be more precise," Julie said and nodded to the officer to take him back to his cell.

Julie then had Butterfly Jones brought to the interview room, whilst she was waiting, she asked an officer to find out what time the moon was at its zenith, he did as asked, but gave her a confused look.

"I accept you are to be called by the name chosen because it is in general use. I do however

57

need the name you were given at birth." Julie told him.

"A name, what is a name, but an identifier of a person, to be called by any other name than that given thee by subjugated parents, is not a crime, but a freedom, a means of expression. Like the air on the 'G' string, the melodious note floating through the air in waves of rippling sound," he said.

"I agree, but how do you know it is the 'G,' string, without it being named at birth?" Julie asked him.

"It was not named at birth; it existed long before it was given a name in the abyss of nature, that voluminous cavern of being without a name. Many things exist we know not, because they have yet to be given a name, yet they exist," he said.

"How do you know it exists if it has yet to be named?" Julie asked and regretted it as soon as she had asked.

"Did not the wind howl long before man named it, was the note not there prior to, the string called the 'G' string, being named?" he asked her. "Did not the person exist prior to it being named Butterfly, under what name was it known, then?" Julie asked.

"Nay thrice nay, the person did not exist, known as Butterfly, prior to its creation, when syncopation entered its life," he said.

"Prior to the birth of Butterfly, it was a pupa, a caterpillar, by what name was it known then?" Julie asked.

"The metamorphosis clears the residual elements of a prior existence, a new brain, with new thoughts and feelings, gone the restraints of past existences, now free to float on high, carried by the wind of a thousand rhythms, created from eight single entities," he said.

"Well, float on back to your room, consider this, the door opens and you can fly back into the wide blue yonder, or it can stay closed, denying the butterfly the freedom it cries out for. When it finds the ability to tell me by what name it was called prior to the metamorphosis and what the time was when the Professor returned, then it can spread its wings," Julie said and again told the officer to put him back in his cell.

Stretch Brown was next to be brought to Julie.

"I am having a lot of fun doing these interviews; so far everyone is languishing in the cells apart from Skins Malone, who is lying on a mortuary slab. I have three simple questions; first of all; I need to know what name you were given at birth and an address we can trace. The second question is not in two parts, what time did the Professor arrive back in camp? For that one, some form of qualifying evidence would be nice. Finally, where were you between midnight and one o'clock in the morning?" Julie asked, adding a smile to encourage him.

"I am reliably informed that past identifiers are null and void, because I am now identified by my chosen name, being in common usage, as to the time of my companion's arrival. I know not, being within my thoughts and in slumber. In the world of the oppressed, ageism is rife, but in our world of freedom, ability is the key. Having attained a lengthy existence, it is onerous upon me to rest and slumber is required, after a lengthy session in practicing our craft," he said.

"So, you were asleep when he came back and cannot verify the time and as an oppressor of the normal world, you may go back to the accommodation we offer. It may not be the most salubrious, but it does focus the mind. Twenty-four hours may not seem long, but when obstruction is added, it can be extended, indefinitely. Lunch is about to be served, enjoy it in your cell; I am going to the pub," Julie said and he was taken back to his cell.

Julie did as she had said and went to the pub for her lunch where Everet joined her.

"What a morning, from the improbable to the incredible, six out of the eight have now had sex with him," Everet said, sitting with Julie.

"Have you considered that they are covering for each other, one did the deed, but by them all saying they did it; it throws you off the scent?" Julie asked.

"I have thought of that and also that it would be possible for four to do it, by having normal sex and oral, half an hour apart, but more likely that as you said, they are covering for one of them," Everet said.

"The thing is that we know he was not the murderer, one or twenty-one of them, he was not around when the murder happened, so it probably isn't him. He could have doctored say, the drumsticks prior to leaving, so not being there, does not clear him.

"My second concern is that we do not have a motive. The front they are putting up isn't helping, what is your name, a simple question and one which we usually have the answer to immediately, unless they are using an alias, which we break in a few minutes. These are not trying to conceal their identity as such, they are within their rights to state any name they have, in common use," Julie said.

"What is the point then, in keeping them in the cells?" Everet asked.

"From what I have seen, their instruments and music are like a drug and I am hoping just like a drug, they will go into withdrawal. Then I can use their instruments to get them to talk to me in a more civilised manner, erm no, natural, erm; mainstream way, normal?" Julie asked, questioning her thoughts.

"From what I have seen they definitely are not normal," Everet said.

"I agree and without some sort of history to their relationships and past events, we will struggle to find a motive, a reason, for his death. The means is more of a female trait, yet the band is all male, so it is making me think outside the band, rather than by a member, but I am not discounting anyone at the moment," Julie said.

"Could it be jealousy, like Ringo Starr, he was not the first drummer the Beatles had?" Everet asked.

"I do not see that, I mean, only if the band makes the big time would jealousy creep in and this band is definitely on the fringe. I do not see them commanding thousands of pounds for a gig, do you?" Julie asked.

"No way, but they must be making a living," Everet said.

"I would not call living in a camper van with six others as making a living, would you?" Julie asked her, smiling.

"I suppose not, but it is the choice of life they have, or seem to be happy with, they live for their music, not accolades, or money even. Like the artist who lives in a garret and is destitute. Offer him the job as a banker and he would refuse, because it would mean he could not paint," Everet offered.

"Which leads me to be happy that it was not one of the band, they all chose this way of life, even so, I will not discount them just yet," Julie said.

Chapter 5 - Syncopation

Back at the station, Julie took a handful of papers and pens and went to the cells.

"I want you to write down your life story, head it with your name date of birth and address as usual, and then write the story of your life," Julie said as she entered each cell, handing them two pieces of paper and a pen each.

"Everet, with me," she said, entering the office. "Which one of the ladies was the one most ill at ease?" Julie asked her.

Everet told her and they went to that address.

"Good afternoon," Julie said and introduced herself on entering the house. "I am not happy about your statement, more so the others. To withhold, or try to obstruct an officer of the law while investigating a crime, especially one as serious an offence as this.

"Now, if you want to stay out of prison, you will be honest with me. A man has been murdered and you are providing an alibi for a person connected to that murder. So, you see just how serious it is, six of you claim to have had sex with the Professor in one hour, it is a physical impossibility for a male to regenerate in that time, one every ten minutes! So, who had sex with the Professor, was it you?" Julie asked her, forcefully.

"Yes, it was and the bride too, but we didn't want her fiancé to find out, so we all said we had," she admitted nervously.

"Explain?" Julie asked her.

"We were sharing rooms to save money and I walked in on her humping him, I was drunk and seeing them got to me, so I joined in and we both had him. He stayed with us, resting, and then it was my turn. Please, can you not tell my husband, keep it between us, it was a moment of weakness and it has never happened before," she pleaded with Julie.

"I need you all to re-write your statements and as long as they are the truth, it need go no further, but if one of you lie, then I will arrest you for obstruction, which means it will come out in court," Julie said bluntly, leaving her in no doubt about the outcome if they lied.

"That's cleared that up. Now those miscreants in the cells, be careful, I am on a mission and it hurts people who stand in my way," Julie said, with a lot of determination about it.

They entered the station and Julie told the sergeant to have Ivories Wilson taken to the interview room. Julie and Everet stood in the ante room looking through the two-way mirror.

"I wish I was so relaxed, they are on a different planet," Everet said.

"Soon to be grounded," Julie said and entered the room with Everet.

"Good afternoon," Julie said, introducing them both as she waited for the tape to start. "I have been given the runaround by your colleagues all morning, but now refreshed and revitalised, I am eager to end this masquerade.

"I have a short fuse and I must warn you my hands are licensed and I will not put up with being messed about," Julie said, standing up and then hitting the table with her finger. "Oops, sorry," she said, pulling her finger out of the hole. "Sometimes I don't know my own strength. So, it occurs to me that you were at one time a baby and then a child. Here I have your life's story and form this I can deduce that you are seven years old. I had a really good laugh at that.

"You see that makes it you are below the age of criminal responsibility, which we all know you are not and that in itself is a crime. Withholding evidence from the police is a crime and I am arresting you for that crime. You do not have to say anything that you later rely on in court and that may harm your defence. There now, all legal, you will spend tonight here in the cells and then tomorrow you have an appointment with the court. The judge will make you state your date of birth. Refusal will mean a trip to prison and an indefinite stay, until you do tell the court your date of birth. The other option is to begin again and write your life story accurately, not missing out your childhood or your name at birth. I will give you half an hour to begin," Julie said and got up, switched the tape recorder off and left the room. They went back to the ante room and watched him for a few minutes, then left him writing his story.

An hour later they went back and looked at his life's story.

"That wasn't too hard, was it? I am not interested if you have a past record, but I do need to know with whom I am dealing. Now shall we be straight with each other, your percussionist is dead,

65

poisoned we believe, who do you know would want him dead?" Julie asked.

"He was well liked, I have no idea," he said.

"All murdered people were well liked, that is why they were murdered. Yes, I am being glib, like the youth who was stabbed; he was such a nice boy, a string of offences to his name, but such a lovely boy who wouldn't harm a fly. I have seen it all and heard it all, we all make mistakes, or have accidents, do desperate things at times of stress and you know of no such situation?" Julie asked him.

"No, I do not, can I say that I have only known him for the last seven years, since I joined the group, I cannot speak for his life before that," he said.

"I can accept that, now, when did the Professor come back?" Julie asked.

"It was one o'clock in the morning as we all said, perhaps a bit after one, he switched the light on and it disturbed me, I looked at the cloc and it said one fifteen, but it isn't always correct," he said.

"Thank you that does help me, now all I need is for the others to wake up to the facts of life, a lone pianist is not much of a syncopator, is it?" Julie asked him.

"I will speak to them, if you like?" he asked.

"Yes, please, tell them that they will not be on stage tonight unless they help me by telling me what I need to know," Julie said.

She asked the officer to take him to the cells and allow him to speak to them and then release him.

"How, did you do that; put your finger through the tabletop, Ma'am?" Everet asked.

"Years of training and practice and knowing the surface, the table in the next room had a laminated top, much denser and not as easy. That top was pine and had a thinner top to it, a softer wood, which was why I chose that room, but varnished dark to appear to be redwood or mahogany, so I cheated," Julie said and laughed.

"Pine or redwood, you put your finger through it, did it hurt?" Everet asked.

"Actually yes, it is a long time since I last did that and my finger is weaker, I need to practice more and toughen up generally," Julie said with a sly wink.

"What about the robbers, how are we doing with that?" Julie asked.

"I have confessions from four of them; the other two believe I am doing them for murder, as an accomplice," Everet said.

"You are doing them for being an accomplice before and after the fact for murder. How many knew they were armed?" Julie asked.

"I am happy that the four who confessed were not aware, but the other two, I believe they knew," Everet said.

"What time am I due in court tomorrow with them?" Julie asked.

"Ten o'clock Ma'am, it is only the local assizes, they will then be held in custody till the actual trial," Everet said.

"Mistake, do not assume, I will go in there with a strong case, but I have seen strong cases thrown out in the past, never think it is slam dunk, there is no such thing," Julie said, "Everet, collect their stories, then go home and I will see you in the morning," Julie said, putting her coat on and leaving the office.

She had her brief case containing all her notes on the case for her to read again, making sure she was in control and knew all about the case, every last detail. It was far too important to be caught off guard by an awkward question; she needed to be perfect, for Collins.

Chapter 6 - Court

Julie arrived at the court at nine forty-five and made her way to the actual court room; she then sat in the waiting area, ready to be called.

Her case was the first one, but the judge was late arriving in the room and by the time all the preparations had been completed, like opening the room and then the case and the defendants put in the dock it was quarter to eleven before she was called to give evidence.

She began as usual with her name, title and occupation as the arresting officer and that was followed by the solicitor asking her to tell the court in her own words what had transpired that evening, which she did. Then it was the turn of the defence lawyer.

"As a serving officer, do you always carry a firearm?" he asked.

"I have been trained in firearms by the regular army and as a sniper for the special forces. I then joined the police force and again I was trained by the police force in their regulations and requirements. I passed the examination with a one hundred percent mark. I am qualified to carry a weapon and do so as I feel necessary. The circumstances of that night, I felt, necessitated that I carry a firearm, because the robbers were from London and most crimes committed in London these days are by armed thieves," Julie said.

"Detective Sergeant Collins was not armed, why, if you felt it necessary that firearms be issued?" he asked.

"Detective Sergeant Collins was not qualified to carry a firearm, he was on a course the week prior to the crime being committed, but it was cancelled. I am registered as a firearms holder and officer so I did not request a firearm, I used my own, as I am entitled to do, being a registered owner and keeper of firearms and a qualified firearms officer," Julie said, unfazed by the questions.

"Yet suspecting that the robbers would strike and at those two particular farms, on that particular night you did not request firearms support. Why, if you suspected that they would be armed?" he asked.

"I have tried in the past, but the powers that be require evidence and I had none, just a suspicion which turned out to be fact. Had I asked for firearm support, it would have been refused on the grounds that I did not have any evidence, just my gut feeling and a constructed probability. His Honour would not give a 'guilty' verdict on that premise, nor would the powers that be agree to armed support, on such weak evidence," Julie said.

"You said that you saw the gunman shoot Detective Sergeant Collins, how?" he asked.

"If I may Your Honour, can the stenographer please read that part of my statement? I did not say that I saw him being shot," Julie asked, cheekily.

"I will allow it this time, but be careful, we ask the questions in here," the judge said, making sure she knew her place.

"Thank you, Your Honour; it saves a protracted session, hopefully. I heard the shot, as I said," Julie said.

"So, if you did not see the shooter, how did you know who to shoot?" he asked.

"Is he for real? It was the person pointing the gun at me: that is the person I shot, as well as the driver of the wagon bearing down on me, intent on killing me, so I shot both times in self-defence, as agreed by the investigating officer," Julie said.

"Be careful that is the second time, Chief Inspector," the judge reminded her.

"What if I told you that the person you shot was not the one pointing the gun at you, in fact, none of them were?" he asked her.

"Then having killed a police officer whilst in the execution of a crime they are all guilty of aiding and abetting murder and by association are guilty. Apart from that, I am a qualified sniper and have never missed the target, my experience and expertise are well documented, I did not miss my target," Julie said bluntly.

"I did not ask that, I said you did not shoot the person pointing the gun in your direction, but the person in front of them, now what do you say?" he asked.

"Have you ever been in a fire fight?" Julie asked.

"As the judge has told you, we ask the questions," he said.

"Let me tell you it is a mess and very easy to lose your cool, civilians running for cover and the enemy shooting at you from several positions and I

71

have never hit a civilian. But I did kill six of the enemy which can be proven, two civilians were shot by accident, but it was proven in the enquiry that it was not the gun I held,.

"A civilian was being held with a gun to her head as the enemy tried to escape, he didn't. I shot him. I spot the enemy and shoot them, the person who said that I killed the wrong person is lying. As the bullet penetrated his skull, he dropped the gun, residue was found on him from the time he shot Collins, but it could have been because he was in the cab, then again how, when it was on his hand, his gun hand," Julie said.

"Isn't it true that you are here because of your cavalier attitude and pushed out of the way?" he asked.

"I don't see how what has happened to me is relevant to this case. However, my record speaks for itself, I am now a Chief Inspector, perhaps had I been more diplomatic; then I might have been a Chief Superintendent, but I like being an officer of the law, catching criminals, so that you can try and get the case dismissed on a technicality. How you sleep at night I will never know. I wonder just how many muggers are on the street because of people like you, who should be behind bars," Julie said.

"Chief Inspector, you will observe the court etiquette," the judge said.

"Respect is earned, Your Honour. Criminals talk about their human rights. I say I will give them the same human rights as they give their victims, none and that goes for anyone who knowingly tries to get them off, when knowing they are guilty. I was there, I was the one they drove the forty-ton wagon at and they shot Collins and they are there in the dock, trying to destroy my reputation and decry me does not make them innocent," Julie said, now angry, but in control, just.

"I think it is time to have a recess, to allow you to cool down, Chief Inspector," the judge said, but he seemed to be smiling.

"I am sorry, Your Honour, to the court, but not that, yes, I am angry, a good officer lies dead because of them and who I was trying to get them set free. The only one in contempt of the court to me is that," Julie said and stepped down from the stand; before she said too much, it was not that she hadn't already.

"My rooms, Chief Inspector," the judge said.

Julie made her way to his offices and spoke to the secretary, letting her know she was there.

She was told to enter. "You are skating on thin ice, Chief Inspector, another outburst like that and I will hold you in contempt," the judge said.

"I am beginning to wonder if there is any ice that is not thin, because that is where I always seem to end up. Being in life-threatening situations for years does not make it any easier, when a forty-ton truck is careering towards you and you know they intend to kill you and then an upstart of a lawyer starts criticising you.

"He has never faced death or looked in the eyes of a person intent on killing you and you have a fraction of a second to decide: shoot, run, or be killed. Had I taken the dive to the side, then he could quite easily have turned the wagon towards me. It was kill or be killed, I had the registration number of the wagon and I could describe their faces. They could not afford for me to live. I had two seconds to decide and work all of that out, aim and shoot and then a fraction of a second to recognise, aim and shoot the gunman. That does not come out in court, just how badly the criminals are being treated, how hard done to they are. What about Collins' wife? What about the baby she is expecting, who he will never see being born, or growing up, because they can't be arsed to get a job?" Julie asked.

"Have you now got it off your chest? We will do what is right, rest assured, stay calm and just answer the questions. The last thing I want is to have you in prison because of contempt of court," he told her.

Julie left his office and went for a coffee and to calm down, until she was recalled.

"You are a violent person, aren't you? Just yesterday you punched a hole in the middle of a table, that is correct, isn't it?" he asked.

"No that is incorrect, to be precise - to punch, you make a fist, I did not, I used my finger to great effect," she said.

"Let me get this right, you made a hole in a solid tabletop with just your finger?" he asked.

"Yes, had I used my fist, it would have destroyed the table and they cost money, which would come out of my budget. The hole is not in the way for writing, so no real damage done and the prat facing me got the message and gave me what I wanted, his birth name and date of birth," Julie said.

"How much coercion did you apply to my clients?" he almost shouted.

"None, none at all, fearing what I might do to them and knowing my abilities, I left that to my colleague Detective Sergeant Everet. She interviewed them; did they not tell you that? I didn't even watch in the ante room, afraid of being incensed by their lies and my actions, so I did not get involved in their interviews," Julie said. "Just how capable are you?" he asked.

"Objection, what has this got to do with the case before us?" the prosecution asked.

"I wondered the same, but if you have no objection I would like to know," the judge said.

"Does that mean that I can refuse to answer?" she asked the judge.

"Yes it does," he said.

"OK then, as long as it is to help understanding what I was, prior to joining the police force and has nothing whatsoever to do with this case?" Julie asked and the judge agreed. "It is with regret that under the Secrets Act, unless you have signed the National Secrets Act and have the clearances necessary, I am not allowed to divulge any covert activities engaged in by the armed forces, of which I was a member," Julie said.

"Do I take it then that you are no stranger to extreme violence?" The defence lawyer asked.

"It never gets any easier; do not think I stood there unmoved, as the wagon hurtled towards me? I was afraid; I needed to be, to react to the situation. I

75

used the adrenaline to feed my need to jump clear and focus my aim. I had to kill him first, to stop the driver from turning the wheel as I jumped clear. How clear was my view? The second from the left in the dock was egging him on and leaned over to pull the wheel, assuming I would jump to my right, but that's the usual and expected action, so I jumped to my left and he did not have time to readjust. Now you know why I am here and not on a mortuary slab. He was wearing a donkey jacket like the ones worn by old fashioned coal men and a checked shirt and I have not seen the photos of their arrest. I am good, aren't I?" Julie asked, putting him down.

"No further questions, Your Honour," he said and sat down.

"Thank you, Chief Inspector, you may stand down," the judge told her.

Julie went to the back of the court room to watch and listen.

"I submit that the crime is far too serious for bail to be considered and ask for a custodial holding until the trial," the prosecution said.

"All of my clients are of reliable and good characters and want to clear their names of this horrendous accusation. A custodial duration will mean that they lose their jobs, which at the present time are hard to come by. It would be wrong to have them put into custody. They have yet to be found guilty and as innocent men, they are entitled to a court hearing before any form of sentence being passed, which holding them in custody would be," the defence said.

"I sympathise with the defence, it is never our intention to punish someone for a crime they have not committed, but the seriousness of the crime and from what I have heard, bail is out of the question. They will be held until a trial date can be confirmed," he said and banged down the gavel, ending the session.

"That was well done, Chief Inspector, but a little conceited," the prosecution said outside as they were leaving the court.

"I have never killed anyone except in the defence of my country, as ordered to by my senior officers, or in self-defence. I am as violent as the situation necessitates, six to one and I break bones," Julie said. It was a factual statement, not a conceited one.

"You do not look like a thug, erm, a violent person, quite the opposite," the prosecution lawyer said.

"My biggest asset, shock and awe, helps me stay nimble and agile. The attackers think I am weak and will collapse when attacked, after the first broken jaw they think again, it saves a long-protracted engagement," Julie said, and smiled at him.

They split up, Julie heading for the station and him for his office.

"Morning, Ma'am, I have heard the offenders are now safely locked away," the desk Sergeant said as she entered, wearing a broad smile.

"Yes, they are safe, locked away from my anger. Have the forensic reports arrived from the band murder?" Julie asked.

"Yes, Ma'am, I have sent them to your office, along with the autopsy report," he told her.

"Thank you," Julie said and made her way to the office.

She smiled and told Everet about her morning. She opened the file lying on her desk and began to read the reports.

Cyanide was confirmed as the cause of death, it also made clear that there was no sign of it in the stomach contents and that there was no injection site leaving inhalation, but because of the lack of residue in the nasal cavities that was ruled out and that left adsorption, he was not a fit healthy male, years of drug and alcohol abuse had left its mark with a diseased liver and damaged kidneys. He was not long for this earth and he must have known that.

His fingerprints confirmed that he was one Simon Malone and came from Swindon. He had a conventional education and entered Oxford where he met the other members of the band. They realised that their instruments did not lend themselves to a rock group and decided to become syncopators. Julie wanted to understand this, it was not for the money, they were to say the least, destitute. That style had died out in the sixties when it was reinvented by The Temperance Seven and had a very short life, so why select it?

The band did not fit into the big band sound, being too small for the full effect and too big for a rock group, apart from a dysfunctional sound.

None of them played a guitar, which was the main instrument of a rock group. The other thing that confused Julie was that they were all well-educated; the Professor was a Professor and Doctor of law. The drummer or percussionist was a Doctor of Physics. Both good jobs and well paid, yet they had consciously chosen a career in an obscure musical genre and lived the life of a gypsy, or vagrant.

"Everet, I want to know what the others have in the form of educational qualifications, they all met at Oxford, according to our information; I want it confirmed," Julie told her.

"According to Blowhard's story, he has a doctorate in medicine, but he does not qualify it as to what; I will check. Butterfly Jones has a doctorate in quantum physics. Ma'am, it is just a thought, but could they have burned themselves out at university and opted out, able to qualify, but unable to cope, with the pressures?" Everet asked.

"It is a thought and a good one, the degrees you mention are intense and need a high level of intellec, and study, so it is possible," Julie said, considering the probability.

"Odd though, don't you think, burnt out at twenty-four?" Everet asked.

"Everyone is different, I know soldiers who needed help to cope with the effects of war, after two years in the fray. I did six years and never needed help. I put it down to talking, I talked to fellow soldiers and made no secret of what I had seen and done. I cried openly with others who had been through the same and joked about it. I coped,

79

do not think it was anything more than coping and only just, but I did. It was when as they say, 'all around were collapsing,' falling apart, keeping it, all locked up deep inside. What I saw and dealt with burns from the inside out, so let it out, do not keep it in. I will never know if I am right or not, but it helps me cope and that is what matters, my sanity over your sensitivity, my sanity will win, every time," Julie said.

"I agree with you, Ma'am, if that helps, I mean I have heard of roadside bombs and the devastation they cause, but they do not show it, so what it must be like. I will never know and I don't suppose I want to," Everet said.

"And I hope you never have to see it, or be involved, it is disgusting, I will say that the most graphic horror films fail and not by a little, to show the real horror," Julie said and went silent as she remembered the horrors she had faced.

"Do you collect all the body parts?" Everet asked.

"The bits we can find, a leg here, a kidney there, an eyeball blown out of its socket, six out of ten fingers and five toes. Six members of my squad in four bags, after an I. A. D, and two maimed, both legs gone. I had just reached the vehicle and that was why I was not injured, along with two other soldiers. We were protected by it, but I organised the clean-up, calling in air support and the bomb squad.

"I found a secondary device and defused it, just one week before I had been on the course, and qualified as a bomb disposal officer, but had as yet not been reassigned. We found out who was responsible and I did not hesitate when we found their camp, slitting the throats of the guards, our orders were to kill, or capture. I took it literally and we killed all six of them in the camp.

I have always justified it as war, kill or be killed, there is no doubt in my mind that had they been awake, then they would have killed us, so it was justified, apart from the incident with the I. A. D, but it was murder, in the lawful sense, they were defenceless, being woken rudely," Julie said, with remorse in her voice.

"I will only say that I was not there and cannot judge," Everet said.

"Perhaps not, but I was and can judge, it needed to be done. So, we have a Doctor of Law, a Doctor of Medicine, but in what, we have to find out and a Doctor of Physics and that leaves four others," Julie said.

"I have made contact with Oxford and they are looking into their records for us. I thought it easier than asking the members of the group, Ma'am," Everet said.

"Good thinking, what could have made them opt out of modern society? They have a phone, just one, so that their agent can let them know about bookings, let's get that record as well," Julie suggested.

"Ma'am, do you think it is a member of the group we seem to be concentrating on?" Everet said.

"Know the victim, know the killer springs to mind, we do not have a motive, knowing why he

81

was killed will help identify who did it. His life story will help us work out who he aggravated so much that they wanted him dead. Lying in his history is the motive and we need to find it," Julie said.

"Like the case involving Sir Andrew's murder, when the motive was six years old, having lain festering in her heart for so long before, she acted," Everet suggested.

"Yes, like that, but in that one it lay dormant until the re-opening of the quarry brought it back to the forefront and a sudden injection of money made it possible. A robbery gone wrong is still history, the history of wealth and jealousy, but the incident is modern history, in that case, it was old history. A feud can be ancient history and so old the combatants don't know why they are involved. Ask an Irish person why they are embattled and they will say usually that it is Catholic versus Protestant, which it is, but very few know why.

"In 1609, emigrants from Scotland and England known as planters moved onto land without an heir. The owners had died and there was no-one to inherit it, so the state took it and gave it to the immigrants. The problem was that the immigrants were Protestant and the indigenous Irish were Catholic. The Protestants by descent were English and wanted to align themselves with the English crown, but the Catholics, being by descent Irish, wanted to align themselves with Ireland. So, although on the surface it is a religious war, deep down it is a territorial war brought about by King George the Third, who deposed James the Second. He was the son of James the first, who was James the sixth of Scotland and recognised as creating the union.

"One more point, King George the third was an Orangeman and from the Netherlands, Holland hence the orange order," Julie said.

"So, a foreigner gave land in an adjoined country to a bunch of settlers and four hundred years later we are still fighting, over it?" Everet asked in shock. "God, it must be the longest war ever; over four hundred years at war?" she added, aghast.

"I don't suppose it is classed as a war, more an irritation which flares up now and again," Julie said.

"Thank you," she said, accepting an envelope from an officer. "History lesson over, shall we get back to work? The report you asked for from Oxford. Now that is interesting, they have an average IQ of one hundred and fifty-four. Einstein's IQ was never measured, but these figures put them in the same category as he was. A score of one sixty IQ is as high as it gets these days. Every one of them has to have an IQ in the mid one, fifties, it is no wonder they have Doctorates and not just degrees," she added.

"I understood that there was a very fine line between genius and insanity," Everet said. "So I understand and these guys are walking it, we cannot say that they are insane, but they do not apply their intellect to good use, hence walking that line, neither side of it," Julie said.

"Or both sides, at the same time," Everet offered.

"I had not thought of that, yes, perhaps that fits even better, going in and out of insanity at will, perhaps?" Julie asked.

"What about their degrees?" Everet asked.

"As we know the Professor has a Doctorate in Law, Butterfly Jones in Medicine, an MD and a doctorate in English Literature. Blowhard Evans has one in Quantum Physics and Biology, Skins Malone has a Doctorate in Chemistry and Biomechanics, Windrush Adams only had a Doctorate in Quantum Physics, Stretch Brown had one in English Language, English Literature and Chemistry, Ivories Wilson had one in Physics, Chemistry and Music and they all got a first in at least one of their subjects. It also tells me that any one of them was more than capable of taking the raw ingredients and making, the cyanide," Julie said.

"So, are we looking at the group for our suspect, Ma'am?" Everet asked.

"Funnily enough, I very much doubt they did the deed. It was not within the group but outside, that is where my gut is taking me, but we do not write them off just yet," Julie said.

She put the report down and picked up the autopsy report.

"I was right, it was cyanide poisoning, Cyanide Toxicity Hydrocyanic Acid Poisoning, and by absorption. The forensic report states that the drumsticks were painted 'with it and he absorbed three milligrams per kilo of body weight, twice the dose needed. The deep red skin discolouration and the smell of burnt almonds was what led me to believe it was cyanide.

"You see, the cyanide stops the organs absorbing the oxygen, which means that oxygen rich blood passes into the veins, causing the ruddy colouration of the skin and at that absorption rate he was dead within seconds. So, the report tells me," Julie said.

"I was beginning to wonder if you had a Doctorate!" Everet said, laughing.

"Me? No, I went to a grammar school and then life's university in the British Army. But I did have an enquiring mind and read about things, like; when I was in Northern Ireland, why was there a conflict? So, I read up about it, it helped me understand, but to be fair I am still not sure I do understand," Julie said.

"Perhaps there isn't a reason, just a perpetuation of violence caused by parents teaching their children to fight for a cause they don't even know what it is. They, the children, then fight and teach their children to fight and so on in perpetuity, rhyme and reason lost in the annals of time," Everet said.

"Religion has a lot to answer for. Just look at the causes of wars and the torture and death of innocent humans, starting with the Romans who crucified Christians, then the Crusades, then the Inquisitions and Hitler his persecution of the Jews, all down to religion as a reason, or an annexed reason. Now we have the Taliban, again religion and that is far from over," Julie said.

"Ma'am, reading the comments from the University, did you know that Skins had a girlfriend when he was at University?" Everet asked.

"I noticed it, but I did scan the report rather than read it. I will do that tonight, it is better than any book to send you to sleep," Julie said, laughing.

"It says that he gave her drugs and she died, her elder brother was distraught and he blamed Skins. I will get the police report of the incident," Everet said.

"Do that, what else, no never mind, as I said I will read it properly tonight, along with the forensic reports and autopsy. For now, I need to visit the scene again," Julie said.

Chapter 7 - Clues

Julie and Everet left the office and made their way to the scene of his death. They mounted the stage and looked around. Julie went to the front of the stage and looked at the houses bordering the green.

"Has anyone canvassed the houses?" Julie asked Everet.

"I'm not sure, Ma'am, I don't have any reports of that, but it is standard," Everet said.

"And easily missed, accepting that someone has done it, when in fact no-one has. Get in touch with the station and organise it, please," Julie said. "While you are at it, find out who cut the grass. When I visited the site the day of the murder; I could smell freshly cut grass," Julie said, staring out at the green.

"Chief Inspector, what a pleasant surprise. I am honoured that you chose to visit us, yet alas, seeing you in this inhospitable environment saddens my heart. Skins was not a happy chappy, he dwelled in Nether Land of the euphoria of joy and the deep, deep depths of despair," the Professor said, climbing up onto the stage.

"You never said he was bipolar, were the depths of his feelings enough to consider suicide?" Julie asked.

"Who can say? Being engaged in the carnal habits of animal instincts, I was not conversant with the feelings he had that sad day. Mayhap my fellow syncopators know of his mental attributes of the day," he suggested.

"How will you cope without your percussionist?" Julie asked him.

"It is far more problematic that we seem bereft of the implements to enable a percussionist to demonstrate their prowess. Kind Chief Inspector, when would it be possible to return our instruments of percussion to enable us to pay tribute to our fallen colleague?" he asked.

"I will endeavour to get them returned as soon as possible, but I suggest very strongly that a new set of hickory sticks be obtained, in fact I insist, mayhap the old ones could be cremated with their owner," Julie suggested.

"It is a fine and noble thing you suggest, allowing my friend and colleague the honour of taking with him his implements of time and rhythm," he said.

"It does trouble me that if it was suicide, why go to all the effort of painting his drumsticks with Cyanide, why not just take the pill?" Julie asked.

"As with any thespian, musician, or member of the stage, in whatever capacity, to go out live on the stage is the greatest honour, hearing the applause and accolades, knowing you are at one with your craft," he said. Julie felt he was over acting, watching as he threw his arms up in a grand gesture.

"I do not wish to burst your bubble, but he was alone on the stage, there was no-one to hear his final drum roll, syncopated or otherwise," Julie said.

"His audience may have been unaware, but there was an audience, just look around you," he said, indicating the houses bordering the stage.

"Yes, that is very interesting on two counts, one: he died within one second of sitting down, what kind of drum roll can he have played in that time and two: how come no-one complained about the noise? It was midnight and the locals would, by and large, have been asleep," Julie said.

"He sat, picked up the sticks and died hitting the hi-hat in his death throes and the bass drum; I would have said, from the position we found him in," he said.

"You are lying to me, one for him to be as far over the kit as he was, he must have been stood up, without anything to support his arms, they would have relaxed and fallen in, not be, outstretched. You moved him, why?" Julie asked.

"I protest at the unjustified accusation, a fertile mind with artistic tendencies may have overstated the situation, to interfere with a crime scene is folly," he said.

"I agree, so can we be accurate from now on? You found him stretched and although it is poetic to add some liberal concepts, it is not conducive to finding out the truth.

"As I see it, he climbed the stage to perhaps adjust something and then picked up his sticks and collapsed, falling down flat onto the kit, rather than falling forward. That would have knocked the kit over. He just fell flat on top of the kit. This indicates murder rather than suicide, so why offer the suggestion of suicide? What are you hiding?" Julie asked him.

"Nay, thrice nay, it was not by my hand that his demise was so theatrical. Mayhap you recall, I was engaged in the pleasures of the flesh," he said.

"I do; I did not suggest that you did this foul deed, merely that you are hiding something, mayhap the perpetrator of the deed? Someone within the syncopators who held a grudge, or a past crime perpetrated by the victim, against the said perpetrator?" Julie asked, raising her eyebrows and cocking her head to one side enquiringly.

"Albeit that every associated, or association within a group, does not bode amicably all the time I can honestly say that within the syncopators, we have a very amicable and benevolent association, being of like minds and quests," he said.

"I understand your premise, but I do have reservations as to the viability of such a statement in the exclusion to any problematic situations. There surely are times when the syncopators are not synchronised?" Julie asked.

"Heaven forbid such an event, syncopators are never in a position not to be synchronised," he said, disgust in his voice at the allegation.

"That just leaves his past life prior to being syncopated, but alas the syncopators were less than helpful when trying to enquire about pre syncopation.

"Professor, there has to be a reason for his death and, as I just pointed out, I do not believe it was suicide; therefore, he was killed by a person, or persons within or without the syncopators. You say that there is no reason for a member of the syncopators to kill him, so I must look outside them.

"Any assignation prior to joining the syncopators may shed light on his death, but you have refused to co-operate with that element, therefore I must concentrate on securing a conviction with a member and I like you for it. Were the girls some of your friends from university who have lied for you, giving you an alibi?

"Perhaps I should bring them in for questioning, a detailed questioning, break their lie about being, with you. The press would love that story, 'Leader of the syncopators has intercourse with hen party,' they all said that they had you. What a sex orgy that would have been. Now it is down to you, I want chapter and verse of everyone's life," Julie said and walked away, leaving him centre stage.

Julie sent Everet home for the day: she went to the pub and ordered a coffee and sat in her usual place. It never occurred to her that she was positioned to be able to see the bar, all the comings and goings. It was not a conscious thing, it came naturally from her time on the front, she always sat with her back to a solid object and with a good view of the area, to be ready for any action and able to defend herself from attack.

The people on the next table were oblivious to the fact that down the waist band of her trousers, at the back, was a loaded Colt forty-five magnum, again not done consciously, just an automatic reaction; she didn't feel dressed without it. After a period in the convivial atmosphere of the pub; Julie would go home, strip down her gun, clean and oil it, then put it back in her waist band, ready for action, almost subconsciously, she did this every night. At bedtime it rested under her pillow.

She had sat there, not conscious of the people in the bar, yet knew who was in and where they were, her mind was pre-occupied by the murder, trying to analyse everything and put it in some sort of order, make sense of it.

Who was Skins Malone, the person, why did he have to die? He was a very well-educated man and accomplished percussionist, his music may not be in vogue, but that did not detract from his abilities. What part did his bipolar play in the reasoning for his death? Was it part of the reason, or just a fact and nothing at all to do with his death?

"A penny for them?" Jim the barman asked.

"Ha, if only they were worth that much! Out of interest, who was in the bar the night the drummer was killed, with the Professor?" Julie asked him.

"Just the usual crowd, Oh and one of the band joined him after you left, well he seemed to know the Professor and wore those odd-looking clothes, so I presumed he was a member of the band. You know the wing collar and three-quarter jacket in black and a black bow tie, so austere looking, more like an undertaker than an artist," he said.

"Hum again, not mentioned, why?" Julie asked.

"Let me freshen your coffee, it will be cold by now," he suggested.

"Hum, oh, no I'll drink it cold, what is your Madras curry like?" Julie asked.

"It's a good job I know you with a question like that; you are not with us, are you?" Jim asked.

"OK, OK, like Lancashire Hotpot, I'll be glib and say it, no I mean, how hot is it?" Julie asked.

"According to the chef, it is as hot as a Madras Curry, I do not like hot meals, well hot like that, so I have no idea," Jim said.

"I will have a portion and I'll tell you just how hot it is," Julie said.

"I will need him tomorrow night, if you don't mind?" Jim asked.

"Jim, I am not aggressive, I'm a pussy cat, mild tempered," Julie said, smiling at him.

"Who am I to argue with you? Oh hell, I'd forgotten the bikers rally," Jim said, as a group of leather clad individuals entered the bar noisily.

Julie got up, and made her way towards them.

"Good evening, allow me, I am Chief Inspector Julie Ashton and this is my pub, the one I use to relax. Noisy, rumbustious visitors get short shrift, so please, enjoy your evening, but do it considering others, or leave," Julie asked them politely.

"Wow, you are a posh tart. aren't you, ooh, lardy da and all that," the apparent leader said.

Julie gave him a smile, "Please do not confuse being polite with any probability of being weak, or unable. It is required by law that I inform you that my hands are licensed and after the day I have had, cracking a few skulls is very appealing. Now behave, or leave," Julie told him bluntly.

"If I want a pint in here, you can't stop me, I've done nothing illegal," he said, leaning in to threaten her.

"I haven't said you can't; I merely asked you to respect the other guests and keep the noise down," Julie said and turned to go back to her table.

She had felt the apprehension in Jim's voice, so spoke to the bikers. The leader's reaction told her that they were not the type of bikers who were civilised; they were the ones that gave bikers a bad name.

Julie had her curry, but was conscious all the time of the bikers and how good or unruly they were being. They were being contained, but on the edge of being unruly, it was not enough for her to act but one or two of the regulars did leave. She ate her meal and thanked Jim, keeping a close eye on the bikers.

"Can't you ask them to leave? That's the fourth regular who's walked out," Jim asked her.

"They have not committed a crime as yet, so no, I can't, but they very soon will do." Julie said and took out her phone. "Sergeant, send a couple of patrol cars to The Market Hotel and to be there for me," she said.

A few moments later she smiled and became part of the law enforcement group watching the bikers.

"I have told you who I am, now in the interests of road safety, I have asked these officers to join me and we are going to test you to see if you are fit to ride your bikes. Obviously, there will not be any charges, you are not on your bikes, but if you leave and then get on your bikes, well, that would be different.

"You will be arrested for being intoxicated whilst in charge of a motor vehicle," Julie said and tuned to face the leader. "There is more than one way to skin a cat and you should have listened to me. This is my town and you are not welcome. OK Officers, they can refuse to be tested, but once they get on their bikes, they cannot and will be charged if over the limit. We might as well do the job properly, with licenses and insurance. Posh I might be, but you are - well it rhymes with mucked. Next year, bypass Little Hampton," Julie told them.

"What if we are over the limit?" one asked.

"I am sorry, is there a question there, what if? After consuming four pints with whiskey chasers, I very much doubt there being any doubt about the outcome of the tests. About a mile down the road there is a barn and I know the farmer. I am sure he will allow you to sleep the effects off in the barn. All the rooms in here are booked and this is the only pub with rooms. The hotel has a dress code and you will not pass the code," Julie told them and went back to her table, smiling.

"Your coffee, Madam," Jim said, beaming, he knew what she had just done and accepted that she had acted within the law, but punished them for being rowdy without taking them to court, or the police cells.

"You can't do this, I refuse to be tested, you have no right to test us, don't be tested," the leader said.

95

"Thank you, officers, please wait outside by the bikes and as soon as they get on the bikes, test them, rest assured they will be over the limit. Oh and warn the desk sergeant that we will be fully booked tonight," Julie said.

"This is victimisation, bitch, I know the law," the leader said.

"A bar room barrister, excellent, then you will know that I have acted within the law and now I would like to sit back and enjoy my evening. There is no music to relax, thrill and entertain, like the sixties.

"I very often enjoy my meal listening to the strains of the 60's music, tonight I was not allowed that enjoyment because of a loud band of ignorant miscreants. They did not break the law, so I was powerless to act, more's the pity. Now I will relax, listening to the strains of 'The Who,' it is a tape, so following this is Booker T and the 'MGs, with 'Green Onions.' I have heard the tape so many times I know the order, but it never fades into the mundane of modern noise, which I can't really call music," Julie said.

"Fuck you, if we can't ride, we might as well stay and get pissed out of our minds." he said to annoy her.

"Please do, disturbing the peace is a crime and I can act one way or another and I will enjoy my evening. Your best plan is to leave, assuming your rate of absorption is normal, then by lunch time you should be able to ride without fear of arrest, but do not be too confident," Julie said calmly.

"You are a fucking cocky cunt, aren't you?" he asked her.

"I ask that you do not use such vile language, there are other people to consider and as of now you are in great danger of ending up in a cell for the night," Julie said.

"I will say what the fuck I like, bitch, and you can do nothing about it," he said.

"Oh contraire, Jim, will you please ask this lout to leave? His language is vile and he is disturbing me," Julie said.

"I agree, please leave and take your friends with you," Jim said.

"Like fuck and what the fuck are you going to do about it?" he said, leaning in to Jim, threateningly.

"Having been asked to leave, because of being rude and inconsiderate and refusing, I can now act," Julie said.

She took his arm and, in one swift move pushed it up his back, bending him over and pushed him outside. "Do not come back in, or I will arrest you," Julie told him.

He turned around and swung a fist at her. The officers made to join her and she smiled, "Wait," she said, as he ran at her and she side stepped.

His fist flew in her direction as he tried again. She caught it and it was up his back in a second and he was face first into the wall.

"I am arresting you for assault on a police officer. Brown, read it its rights and put it in the cells. I did warn you my hands are licensed, be thankful I was playing with you," Julie told him and went back into the pub.

"Right, he is under arrest for assaulting a police officer and is currently on his way to casualty with a suspected broken nose. I was gentle with him. You have two choices, actually I suppose three, but the first would be insane, knowing now what has happened to your leader. You can take me on or the second is to spend the night in my cells and the most sensible one is to leave and make your way to the barn. I am asking you to avoid this town in the future, fail to do so and I will arrest you. If you can read, get the London Evening News, a back copy and read how I took on six thugs and put all of them in hospital. Do not doubt that my hands are licensed and I break bones. Now be sensible and leave," Julie said.

They got up and left, Julie rang the farmer and made the arrangements for them to sleep in his barn.

Julie went back to her table and Jim brought over a coffee, "Thank you," he said.

"I needed that; sorry, I did antagonise him deliberately, today has been a mess from start to finish," Julie said to Jim.

"No, you didn't, he was the protagonist, see even I know big words," he said and laughed.

Julie laughed with him. "I never doubted it, Jim, but I could have been less antagonistic, he made all the moves and I let him, egged him on, even. I pressed all the right buttons to encourage him to attack me. For that, I apologise, I don't know what got into me, I could have handled it better and I should have," Julie said, adding "The Professor can be very draining, trying to keep up with him and understand what he is saying. It is just being very correct and polite, we do not use it nowadays and to some degree it is a pity, it showed courtesy to one's fellow beings. Like in the houses of Parliament, my Right Honourable Friend is the term they use, even if they hate the imbecile," Julie said.

"I have to agree, there is no respect these days, the youngsters don't seem to respect themselves and there is no respect for authority or age," Jim said.

"It appears to me that with every generation we dumb down a little, but by now we have lost all respect and manners, we are too busy chasing the god Money to be bothered to say please and thank you, or it is computer generated so we don't have to?" Julie said.

"I received a letter the other day, an official one and the guy who sent it couldn't be arsed to sign his own name, it was done by computer. Sorry about swearing, but I was very annoyed; I mean how little effort is needed to sign your name and he couldn't be bothered," Jim said.

"I agree, but your takings are going to be down if you don't attend to your bar," Julie said, laughing.

"Oh, I had better go," Jim said and left her.

Julie went back to thinking about the murder and the information they had, which was not much, the main piece of the puzzle was missing: the reason, the motive.

There was just one thing to do and that was to make the group talk about their past, be it recent, or long ago, somewhere there was a serious enough reason for someone to want Skins dead.

Julie sat there for another couple of hours and changed her drink to a white wine for the last two drinks. Then she went home and smiled as she heard the sound of the bikers in the barn, it would have been loud, but at the far end of the field and with the barn doors closed, it was just audible. She had seen the ghetto blaster on the back of the bike and knew they were not ready for bed and would collect it as they passed the bikes, along with the beers Jim sold them, the party was in full swing.

Chapter 8 - History

Julie woke as usual the next morning; she didn't need an alarm clock but set it every night just in case. She was usually up and switched it off without it going off.

She was showered and dressed and eating her breakfast looking out of the kitchen window at the barn, now silent. She washed up and then made her way across the field to the barn and entered. Two females were up and looked at her, while the rest snored the place down.

"Can't sleep with the noise?" Julie asked them.

They smiled and nodded at her. "What do you think? Shall we wake them, shall I get a bucket of cold water or the hose? Is there a cold water tap on the side of the barn?" Julie asked them.

"You are a nasty bitch, aren't you?" one asked, laughing.

"I can be, the pub finishes serving breakfast at ten o'clock and they will not be fit to ride before this afternoon. By my calculations and from the amount of beer they drank in the pub and then brought back, they will not be fit before say three o'clock this afternoon, maybe later. They may not care, but I have seen what tarmac can do to pretty faces. It is not nice, trust me. It is a long walk home if they are caught over the limit. I will leave you now to consider my advice. Oh, and please tidy up after yourselves. The farmer was kind enough to allow you to sleep in his barn and it is solid, so you would not get wet if it rained, or cold from the wind. Do not leave it in this state, will you?" Julie asked them and left.

Julie was happy that they would tidy up and smiled, most people are civilised, there are just a few hot heads who need controlling. Her first job upon entering the station was to go and visit the leader of the gang.

"Good morning! It does not pay to try it on with me as you found out the hard way. You are free to go, the others are in the barn I told you about, spend the morning with them there and then leave, but do not leave before your alcohol level has gone down, - a lot. Believe it or not, I do not want you in my town, so the sooner you leave, the better, but legally this within the legal limits for alcohol, you have a police caution, now leave," Julie told him.

She went up to the office and smiled at Everet, acknowledging her.

"So I hear, a good night, has it helped you?" Everet asked, smiling at Julie.

"Oh yes, a gang fighter, no bottle, or brains, just mob intellect, he leads them to the fight and then runs to the back. He saw a lone female and had a dozen bikers to support him, with their female partners so twenty-four to one, but singling him out and dealing with him, they cracked up and fell apart," Julie said.

"Ma'am, will we be getting a new sergeant?" Everet asked.

"No," Julie said.

"Oh, so we are now down to just the two of us?" Everet asked.

"No, we will be getting a new Detective Sergeant," Julie said, opening her mail, "This is for you, congratulations," Julie said, handing her the envelope.

"Without opening it, you knew?" Everet said.

"I knew yesterday when I recommended the promotion and it was confirmed, we just had to wait for the letter. P. C. Wilkins is to be the new detective. I hope you help him as much as Collins did you. He is qualified, but will need guidance. Will you be staying at that desk, or do you want Collins' desk? Collins decided that putting you where he was, put you in the middle and oppressed, being between us. It is your decision; you have quarter of an hour to decide and move if you decide to before he joins us." Julie said.

"I am happy here, this is my desk and Wilkins needs to make that desk his own, as I have," Everet said.

"You do realise that puts him closer to the leader and within office dynamics gives him a psychological advantage over you, don't you?" Julie asked.

"Or puts him closer to the teacher, because he needs to be kept an eye on," Everet said. "And they called me a bitch," Julie said," and laughed with Everet.

The door opened and a tall, elegant male entered, "Morning, Ma'am, Detective Constable Wilkins reporting for duty," he said.

"Good morning D.C. Wilkins. This is your desk, D. S. Everet will be your mentor and guide. Do not get settled, we hit the ground running, we have Ivories Wilson in the interview room, you will keep quiet and watch us, listen and learn," Julie said and led them out of the office into the interview room.

"Why have you brought in again? This is persecution!" he said.

"It may have slipped your notice, but the percussionist for the syncopators lies on the mortuary slab. This obvious event may have little or no importance to you, but to us it is very important and we need to find out who did the nasty deed. As a percussionist yourself, we thought you may be sympathetic to our need for, information.

"Did Skins have any enemies, ex-lovers mayhap, or people he owed money to, creditors?" Julie asked him.

"Skins was a lovely person and he would not harm a fly. He had a female acquaintance whilst in higher education, but she left him for another, so any animosity would have been by Skins towards her, not the other way around, as you imply," Ivories said.

"I also asked about money, did he owe money to anyone, especially not the normal type of lender, did he gamble?" Julie asked.

"He was a flower that bloomed and was cut from the plant of life, prematurely," he said.

"We know that, what we want know is why, so you are saying that he did not gamble and did not use drugs and did not have female companionship?" Julie asked.

"Nor male companionship, apart from the syncopators as their percussionist, that is," he said.

"I want to be perfectly clear about this, he was an angel, no vices and therefore no reason to be murdered. You will accept that I do not believe you. Everyone has a vice of some description, some are minor and acceptable, but others are nasty and vicious. An angel I have yet to meet," Julie said.

"Mayhap the choice of your career is the reason, working in the sewers of life," he said, being smarmy.

"Mayhap, then again someone has to clean them up," Julie said.

"Beware that you do not fall foul of the trap they set, enticing you inside," he said.

"I did consider the fact that being a percussionist you may hit the nail on the head, rather than Blowhard next door, who I expected to blow a lot of hot air," Julie said and got up to leave.

"The simile does not do you justice," Ivories said.

"It wasn't meant to," Julie said and they left the room.

"Ma'am, if the drummer is dead, why did you say he was a percussionist?" Wilkins asked.

"A hammer hit the strings of a piano; therefore it is a percussion instrument," Julie informed him.

"Blowhard, welcome to my domain, I hope we have treated you with respect and due diligence. The time you spend here will depend upon the answers you give me. We have unfortunately had a bereavement of a fellow syncopator; it would be advantageous if we were made aware of his past life. In particular any assignations he might have had, or debts he may have incurred, so that is my question are you aware of any assignations, or debts?" Julie asked him.

"I am bound by the Syncopators' Code and will not divulge any failings of my fellow syncopators," he said.

"Great, loyal to the end. It's beef burgers for lunch, enjoy it, won't you," Julie said.

"I must protest at the indiscriminate offer of nutrition, being an animal lover, I do not indulge in digesting the remnants of a fellow living creature," he said.

"Then I suggest you find a way to help us, it is beef stew for dinner. I am fortunate enough to be able to pick and choose what I eat, because I am helping find the murderer of your fellow syncopator. If you want to eat as I do, able to choose, then I suggest you decide which is the most important requirement, food, or your unwritten code?" Julie asked him and got up and left. "Put them in the cells and bring the others in, one of them will talk," Julie said.

An officer entered her office as they did.

"Ma'am, I was interviewing the people in the houses bordering the green and in number sixteen the woman said that she saw a car pull up at or about midnight, she heard the drums start up and was about to complain when she saw the car. The phone is by the window so she was looking out as it pulled up," he told her.

106

"Our first lead, I don't suppose she knew the make, got the registration number, or knows the colour, even, does she?" Julie asked him.

"At seventy-two I doubt she knows the difference between a car and a hatchback, sorry, recognises the difference," he said.

"You did ask, didn't you?" Julie asked him.

"I asked if she could give me a description and she said not, it was dark," he replied and he turned to leave.

"Wait, I am not finished with you, Everet, take Wilkin and interview Blowhard. Go, when he has sat there looking at the burger for a bit. Officer what is your name?" Julie asked.

"Sorry, Ma'am, Tom, Tom James," he told her.

"Well P, C, Tom James, you are with me," Julie said, "Get three more officers and meet me at the front desk," Julie ordered, "Right, you drive; we are going to Brian's Autos," Julie told them.

She got out of the car and could see Brian's eyes light up and he began to rub his hands.

"Brian, being such a good citizen and loyal member of society, I am sure your biggest desire is to assist the police in their enquiries when a crime has been committed. I say this because these good, hard-working officers wish to test drive certain vehicles. I want to test drive the SUV over there, this officer he wants to test drive that salon car. This one wants to test drive the Land Rover and this one he wants a small car like that Fiat 500.

"Now we are all police officers and you know most, if not all of us, and know we will return the cars later in good order and here is fifteen pounds for twelve litres of fuel, you can keep the change. The other option is for me to commandeer the cars with fuel, so you have no objection to us test driving them, do you?" Julie asked him.

"Well, if you put it like that, what about the other officer?" he asked sullenly.

"Oh, he is going to drive this one back to the station and then pick us up when we return," Julie said.

"I am expecting a customer and they want that car," he said.

"I am sure they will be more willing to purchase a vehicle, at the listed price, knowing that there is a prospective buyer test driving, the car. Then again, our mechanic has been lazing about all day and he could call by and check the speedometers and odometers for us," Julie said, adding a smile for his benefit.

"No, there is no need for that, it would be my pleasure to assist you, I am sure the customers I am expecting would like a coffee whilst, they wait," he said, understanding Julie's hint.

"The keys for that car," he said, handing over the keys. "What about that car? It is a much better colour and has had just the one owner," he asked.

"Hum, it does have potential, yes, and just the one owner. OK, how long will it take you to paint it black?" Julie asked.

"Oh, I see, all the cars you picked are black. Does it have to be black?" he asked.

"No, I picked all black ones because I wanted red ones! Of course it does. Officer Crompton, go ahead, and move any and all cars from the front of the stage and make sure there is enough room for us to park on the side away from Number sixteen," Julie told him.

They got in the cars and Julie led off, with them following in convoy, Julie took her time to allow Crompton to clear the space she needed, which was not a big deal, being mid-morning, most of the residents were at work.

Julie parked and then told the others to stay where they were, apart from Wilkins, who followed her to the house.

"Good morning, I am Detective Chief Inspector Ashton and with me is Detective Constable Wilkins. As you can see from across the road; I have several cars lined up, can we go inside, please?" Julie asked the elderly lady.

She invited them in and Julie took her to the window. "I have been told you saw a car park over there the other night, can you see a car that looks the same?" Julie asked her.

"It was dark, I am not sure," she said.

"I appreciate that, but in the street lights the shape would have been noticeable and that is what I am interested in. I brought black ones because it was dark and the car would appear dark, if not black," Julie said, "Look at the front one, was it as tall as that, say, as bulky?" Julie asked her.

"No, it was more like the second one," she said.

"That is great, I thought seeing the cars may help you, now the colour, was it like those cars, or lighter?" Julie asked.

109

"It was like those cars," she said, "Would you like a cup of tea?

"That would be nice, if you will excuse me for a moment? Wilkins, tell them to take the cars back, apart from the saloon and he had a Mercedes. You go with them and bring that one back and park it right next to the stage and hide the one left," Julie told him.

He left just as the lady brought in the tray of tea for them.

"You are spoiling me, biscuits as well, thank you," Julie said, smiling at her.

"Is he not staying? The tea will be cold," the lady asked, concerned.

"He likes his tea cold, don't worry. You saw the car, what time was it, can you remember?" Julie asked, taking the tea from her and thanking her.

"I, well I usually go to bed about midnight, I like the news at midnight, they review the papers, you know? I had just finished watching that when that horrible racket began. I don't sleep that well these days, so I need as much as I can get and with that noise I knew I would not be able to sleep. So I went to the window, that's where my phone is and I saw the car pull up.

"They got out and went on the stage, I saw him speak, obviously I couldn't hear what was said, but the noise stopped and the man on the drums stopped and looked at the big man, that was how I knew he was speaking. Then the man next to him handed the drummer something and he took them but he seemed reluctant, as if he didn't want to take whatever it was. He did take it and adjusted his

110

hands as if putting one in each hand and sat down, then lifted his hands. I was fascinated by now. So, I continued to watch and then he fell, face down on the drums, such a clatter, then silence and the men walked away and drove away," she said.

"I need to be clear in my mind about this, so can I ask you a few questions? it means repeating bits of what you have told me again, if that is alright?" Julie asked her. "The car pulled up and the men got out and then climbed onto the stage. There were two men, or did you only see two men? Could there have been more in the car?"

"No, as I said they got out, there were four of them, two in the back and two in the front," she said.

"I have that now; did all four climb onto the stage?" Julie asked her.

"Yes, but two stood back, just the big man and another man moved forward," she said.

"Great, the big man - was he tall, or big, as in fat say, broad shoulders?" Julie asked her.

"He was both, head and shoulders over the other man, the one with him and twice as broad," she replied.

"The other men, were they say the same as the man handing the item to the drummer, or more like the big man?" Julie asked.

"They were well about the same height as the man with the item, but one was a lot broader and didn't walk, he rolled," she said. Julie smiled.

Julie jumped up and excused herself. "P C James, go and climb on the stage and strut your stuff, just do it, I will explain later," she told him and went back inside.

"Please, come here, did he walk like that?" Julie asked her.

"Is that him? Just like that and about his size, the one next to him was a bit smaller, half a head say, the big man was a good half head taller than him, the man with the item was about the same size," she said.

"Mrs, Jenkins, you have been a tremendous help, thank you for the tea and biscuits. Just one more thing, the car parked over there now, was it that shape?" Julie asked her.

"No, that is angular, it was more rounded," she said.

"Great, I owe you a drink, thank you. P C James, we don't have time to mess about, come on," Julie shouted after him.

"But you told me to," he said.

"If you want to be a detective you need to adapt and quickly. That was then; this is now, hurry we need to get the cars back. I will ask the station to send a car for us," Julie said.

They arrived back in the office just as Everet was entering after the interview.

"Was the woman as useless as the officer suggested?" Everet asked.

"He was, she was a gold mine, the problem was he asked the wrong questions and didn't have Mr Universe. The car was in all probability a Mercedes and a new one. There were four men, two were James's height. One was half a head shorter and the main man was half a head taller. Two were average, one was like James and walked like him, the other was bigger, so we have a muscle-bound thug, two average and one bigger in height and width. They handed him the drumsticks; we have an eyewitness. What about you?" Julie asked.

"Well, he was a gambler and owed money to some not so nice people and some very nasty people. The professor had already loaned him some money, but their cash had run out, they needed this gig to survive until the next one, a month from now," Everet told her.

"I am confused, to break his legs, hands and the like I can understand, but to hand him poisoned drum sticks, why, apart from he owed them money? Killing him will not get them the money, so why?" Julie asked.

"I think the Professor has the answer, but he may not know it," Everet said.

Chapter 9 - Ivories Wilson

"Interesting, do you have any ideas as to how we can get him to tell us what he knows, but does not know he knows?" Julie asked.

"What I mean is, I think it's related to the band, rather than an individual. Losing their drummer, surely, is a big blow to them, far more so than say, the pianist. A brass band say does not have a pianist, but they do usually have drums. I can't think of any band that does not have a drummer," Everet said.

"I agree, apart from a string quartet, the exception that proves the rule, perhaps?" Julie asked.

"Ma'am, thugs are not known for using poison, they tend to beat the person to a pulp so why use poison?" James asked.

"Again, a very good point, I would suggest it was to send a particular message, rather than a general message. The other point is that he was available, was he chosen because he was alone, on stage?

A fight of any description would have been noticed and reported, but poisoned drum sticks were silent and unless they had every instrument in the car the band played then he was, chosen. Sorry, I seem to be arguing against myself all the time," Julie said.

"Not really, they would not need the instrument, just a part of it, a trumpet has a mouth piece, drums have sticks, a saxophone has a mouthpiece, all small and separate; a violin has a bow and so on. I think I am right that only the piano, of the instruments the band plays, does not have a small piece to attach," Everet said.

"Wilkins, check the venues the band has played at this year to see if there was any form of trouble related to the venue, complaints of noise, say?" Julie asked him.

"Everet, we will pay a visit to the Professor to see what he has to say about complaints," Julie said.

Julie and Everet drove to the site of the concert, parked and looked at the stage. Julie was out in a shot and running to the stage, followed by Everet who radioed in for assistance on seeing the white curtain below the stage with a red stain running down it.

Julie took a flying leap, her left foot landing on the middle set of the five leading up to the stage and right foot on the stage as she ran across it to the prone figure. She instinctively took his hand and wrist and felt for a pulse, although she knew instinctively, from the amount of blood on the stage, he was dead.

Julie carefully turned him slightly and saw the gaping hole in the back of his head, his skull crushed in from a very heavy blow from a blunt instrument.

"Forget the ambulance, send for the coroner, there is more brain matter on the stage than in his head," Julie said, with empathy.

She left Everet protecting the scene and went to the motor home to find the Professor.

The sky was clouding over and rain was expected. To protect the scene, Julie rang the local council to get a screen erected over the front of the stage, or at least a polythene covering.

"Professor, I have some bad news for you. Forget the flowery words and lyrical sentences, this is serious. I have just found your pianist dead on the stage, No, do not go; I want to preserve the scene so you will not be allowed on the stage.

"I think you know more than you are saying, I'm not sure if you are hiding it, or do not know that you know? I have asked D. C. Wilkins to find out if at any of the venues you attended this year, there was a problem. You can save me time by telling me if there was problem at any venue. This makes me think it is the band that is the target. So, I may have to put you all in protective custody, you like our cells don't you, so speak!" Julie said.

"I can honestly not think of any altercation, apart from the usual, we do have to practice, how they think we can play the variety of music we do without, practicing, I don't know. We practice during the day, even so we do get complaints about the noise, but they are expected and not serious," he said.

"Apart from the complaints about the volume of you practicing, has there been anything at all that you can think of that could be called a complaint, no matter how minor?" Julie asked him.

"I cannot think of anything, most of the time everything is very amicable. We provide light relief, our music is humorous and people, who do not normally listen to it, enjoy it, but they would not

116

travel to a venue just to hear us. We do have a following, but it is not massive, people who come when we are in town. It is not every venue that we get complaints about our practicing, probably fifty percent. Here for example no-one has complained, although I accept that the lady from over there did mention it and I apologised for Skins and told him that he was not to practice in the night after nine o'clock when the children were in bed," he said.

"So, she came to you to tell you about the volume, when was that?" Julie asked.

"When we arrived, Skins set up and then played for a bit to make sure his equipment was where he needed it. Unfortunately we were late arriving and she asked us not to play so late. As I said, I apologised and told Skins; who also apologised and said he would not do it again. Then the following night, the night before we were to play, he was killed," the Professor said.

"I am not playing games as I said and that counts as a complaint, decry it and downplay it as much as you like, but that counts, now how often does that happen?" Julie asked.

"It doesn't as a rule; you see we arrive just after lunch, so by dinner time we are set up and happy with things. We broke down and arrived late, very late, hence Skins checking so late," he said.

"You say you broke down, what was wrong?" Julie asked.

"Chief Inspector I am but a musician, not an engineer of the motor trade," he said, going aloof.

"If my car will not start in the morning, I can tell you that it turned over, but would not fire, or

117

that it fired, but then died, I don't know why, but I do know what, so, what happened?" Julie pressed him.

"Oh, erm, well it just died, we were driving along and it stuttered, shuddered and then stopped, or is it spluttered and stuttered, anyway it did and I rang my mechanic, who organised everything for us to be picked up and taken to his garage where he got us going again," he said.

"I will need his name and a way to contact him, are you not in a motoring organisation? I would have thought that with an antiquated vehicle like that it would have been advantageous," Julie asked.

"He is my brother and has his own garage, we cannot afford to be told that it will be ready next Monday and he knows this, so he makes sure I am on the road when needed, if we have a session booked for tonight, next Monday is of no use, to us," he told her.

"So, you break down, he has you towed in and makes good the repairs, gets you back on the road, to meet your commitment, erm - engagement?" Julie asked.

"That is how it works," he agreed.

"What about payment? You do not appear to have a couple of hundred pounds put away for a new clutch," Julie asked.

"Correct, yet no, you are incorrect; I agreed to pay him ten pounds a month and we go from being in debt to being in credit and back into debt. He is good and we do not break down that often, he keeps it in good order. When we are not on the road we park it at his place and he trains young lads and they practice on it. It was only six months ago that he had a youngster strip it right down and re-build it, he told me, a de-coke, whatever that is," He told Julie, "Actually he did make an odd comment when we got it back, he said, 'Use the green nozzle, not the black one,' what he meant by that, I have no idea, we do know it is petrol," he said.

"That I do know, he found diesel in the tank rather than petrol, a diesel engine will burn petrol and I have heard that a small amount of petrol will help the engine run better, but never put diesel in a petrol engine it is too thick and will not burn. He was saying that you filled up with diesel by mistake," Julie told him.

"Windrush, he was our designated driver, our usual one was ill, Windrush would not do that, put diesel in, he knows the difference," he said.

"So it was sabotage, has that happened previously?" Julie asked.

"Not until recently, we went to a booking last week, which was not there, it cost us a day's travel there and back," he told her.

"How far ahead are the bookings made?" Julie asked.

"This one was booked last year; we play here every year, that one was two days before the engagement was to take place. We don't have that many that we need a diary, but enough to keep the wolves from the door. We accept that we are a novelty, session players, an oddity, if you like," he said.

"We prefer to know the reason for the death, the motive, it would appear now that the motive is

119

not aimed at Skins as we thought, but the group as a whole, so what or who have the group antagonised?" Julie asked.

"You may think us weird, odd, but we are law abiding citizens," he said.

"It may come as a shock, but murderers do not just murder criminals, they also murder law abiding citizens, but there is always a reason, a motive, as we call it. From what you have just said, the group has offended someone, to have diesel put in your tank and book a, non-existent booking, has anything else happened?" Julie asked him.

"That is impossible, my brother filled the tank before we left and he would not attack the group," he said.

"Did he fill it, or one of his staff?" Julie asked.

"Does that matter?" he asked.

"Yes, it does, he would not do you harm, but a member of staff might, for reasons known only to themselves," Julie said.

"Then he was filling the tank as we arrived, I saw him, she is elderly and is not as economical as when she was new, so we carry a spare gallon or two and it happened after we had put the first gallon in the tank," he told her.

"A gallon would have an effect, but doubtful as far as I know that, it would cause the engine to fail, cough and splutter and clog up the spark plugs, making firing more difficult, hence the coughing and black smoke from un-burnt fuel.

"Come on, professor, you know that an explosion is a flame travelling at over one thousand miles per hour, petrol explodes from a spark and diesel does not. It requires heat and, as I said; I am not a mechanic, but I doubt a gallon in a full tank being enough, to cause it to stop. It may cough, splutter, and make driving difficult and damage the engine. In your case it was more than a couple of litres in a full tank.

"If you continue to lie, or tell me half-truths, I will arrest you. I am not concerned with carrying illegal amounts of fuel, I am concerned with finding a killer before they kill again," Julie said.

"It is in a proper can, a jerry can and we carry enough so that we do not have to fill up anywhere else. I pay him ten pounds a week, not a month and I know he is sponsoring us, we never go into credit," he said and hung his head in shame.

"That I accept, don't ever think that just because I do not have a degree, I am stupid, as I said, I went to the University of life," Julie said.

"I do not think you are stupid, you are a very astute female and in some ways, I envy you. As a professor of law, I did not do physics and did not know that an explosion is a flame travelling at over one thousand miles per hour, fascinating. So is a flame, an explosion?" he asked.

"In essence yes, a flame is a controlled explosion, if you like, it is open and burns more slowly. Take a gas fire, it is not contained, in a vessel, say, it is open and generates heat because of the explosion and produces H_2O, water vapour from the explosion. Now put that gas in a container and set fire to it. It will burn up all at once, creating a rapid expansion of gasses and therefore an explosion, the same flame, but now being released all at once. It creates a rapid expansion of the gasses, called a shock wave which, dependent upon the size of the explosion, can be felt for miles.

"The biggest explosion ever recorded was Krakatoa, the sound was recorded at three hundred and ten decibels sixty miles away and the shock wave was felt one hundred miles away and continued to circle the earth three and a half times before coming to rest.

"The explosives I dealt with were nowhere near as strong as that, but a roadside bomb could shatter a window a hundred yards away from the shock wave, or the vacuum the blast created. Think about it. You blast all the air from a point and there is an equal and opposite reaction because you cannot have a vacuum. A lot of windows are not blown out; they are sucked out, as the air refills the vacuum," Julie told him.

"Fascinating, I could talk to you all day, what," he began.

"I have been here too long; I have a murderer to catch and to do that I need to know why? I want you to discuss with your syncopators any event that may have a bearing on why the band is being, targeted?" Julie asked him and got up.

"I will, rest assured dear Chief Inspector, surely I am allowed to be flowery upon your impending departure?" he asked, looking at her cheekily.

"I shall return, maestro," Julie said, bowing and smiling at him.

"Mayhap, if it is not inconvenient, we could imbibe at the local hostelry and continue this enlightening conversation?" he asked.

"Probably, at a more appropriate time," Julie said and left with Everet.

"Ma'am, where did you learn all that?" Everet asked.

"I have told you, I read a lot, I became an explosives expert for the army and wanted to know what was the biggest ever explosion, what was an explosion, how one is created and the effects, so apart from attending classes, I read up about it. The camp library thought I had taken up residence, because it was not only explosions, but ballistics, as well," Julie said, and laughed.

"They are the same, if not; they are very similar, aren't they?" Everet asked.

"In the sense that an explosion propels the bullet at speeds around twelve hundred miles per hour, hence you never hear the bullet that kills you. It travels faster than the speed of sound, the bang trails well behind it," Julie said, as they drove back to the station, "I want you to take the gigs they performed at and get in touch with the local police to see if anything comes up, go back say six months, no, make it twelve months. They have done something; caused some sort of problem, that the revenge is aimed at the group, so it is as a group that the problem arose," Julie said.

Everet was not as comfortable talking to the Professor as Julie apparently was, so she contacted their agent. She was surprised at the number of engagements they had. She expected it to be one a month at the most, but they were booked every week somewhere, fifty-two local constabularies to contact, it was to be a long job.

They had played from Devon to Carlisle, Newcastle to Cardiff and most points in between.

She decided that the most efficient way was to ask if the group had been involved in any sort of complaint, or contact with the local station on the dates they were in the area. She produced a basic message and then added the dates as she sent it to the various stations.

She knew some of the stations would reply quite quickly, because the booking was quite recent and perhaps still in the memory of an officer from the station, but others would have to look into their records to get the details and that would take time.

The phone rang, "Will anyone be attending the autopsy?" the Doctor asked her.

"It isn't till tomorrow morning, when the DCI will be in attendance," Everet said.

"The DCI asked that I do it as soon as possible and I can squeeze it in, say half an hour, if it isn't convenient then I can leave it till tomorrow," he told her.

"No, the DCI needs to know if the damage was done by a single blow as it appears and if so; what the implement was. She does not believe that any human being could do so much damage without mechanical help. The DCI also needs to know, if he was drugged. I will attend, half an hour you said?" Everet asked.

"Yes, have you attended before, if not, please ensure that you have the waste bin close by and are seated, won't you?" He asked.

"I have, and I will on both counts," Everet said, unsure if she was seasoned enough yet. Julie's advice was sound, but she still struggled with the fact that it was human and being dissected rather than a piece of meat, or animal carcass.

Everet decided that moral support would be a good idea, when James entered.

"Have you attended an autopsy?" she asked him.

"No, Ma'am," he replied.

"Then it is time you did, we are due at the mortuary in twenty-five minutes. The DCI suggested that I think about the body as a lump of meat, which it is and not as a human being. I have difficulty with that, but we do need to attend, so we will. Sit down and have a waste bin close by or the sink," Everet said, hoping she didn't show herself up by fainting.

Chapter 10 - Autopsy

They entered the gallery to watch the autopsy; the coroner was there with the body on a slab and covered. He removed the cover and looked at the body. He moved around checking and then looked up at them in the gallery.

"We have a late twenties male, apparently well fed, who has good muscle tone so active and physically fit," he began, "There are no injuries to the body from any form of struggle, so I would suggest that he was caught unawares and did not know, or see, his attacker."

"Can you assist me to turn the body?" he asked his assistant.

They turned the body over and the gaping wound was now visible, he bent down to examine and picked a bit of bone, out of the wound and then another fragment, until he had several fragments in the kidney shaped bowl his assistant was holding. He then got a bowl containing a paste and smeared it in the hole, filling it and stood back.

He looked up at the gallery, "Nice to see you both still with me. Now we will turn the body again and take a look at the organs," he announced.

The assistant came back and helped him turn the body, he got his scalpel and made the incision a 'V,' from each shoulder and then into a, "Y,' down the chest and opened the chest up, Serious looking cutters were handed to him, to cut the rib cage and remove the front section and then it was the lungs, the stomach, heart and Wilkin's stomach gave up. He was still holding the waste bin, as Everet gave in to her feelings and ran to the sink.

"He appears to have a poor diet, chips and beef burger is not a good diet and small white bits, probably semi digested tablets of some description. I will have them tested to see what they are?" he told them.

"So, he was drugged?" Everet asked.

"Sergeant, I will not speculate, he has taken something that may or may not be tablets, but they are powdery, so they are probably the remnants of tablets. This means that they could be a sedative, or even just a common aspirin for a headache. I will not know, or speculate until they have been tested. Then I will tell you the outcome of the tests, but I will tell you that they were taken within half an hour prior to death, from the absorption. I will also take a blood sample for analysis and then tell you, what they are and if he was drugged, or not," he said.

"When he was found, he was lying in a pool of blood and vomit, could the tablets have been to make him vomit?" Everet asked.

"I do realise that you are... well, not one hundred percent, shall we say, but please accept that until I have completed my tests, I cannot and will not say, it would be very unprofessional for me to, speculate," he told her.

"Is there anything I can tell the DCI?" Everet asked.

"Yes, he ate a beef burger and chips of which there is a small amount left, he vomited and was struck by," he said and with the assistant's help lifted the head and removed the substance he had filled the hole and held it up for Everet to see, "The object was ball shaped, with a spike and that broke and punctured the skull and then the ball crushed the balance in, so a man could have wielded the implement. I will speculate, by saying that it reminds me of a medieval mace, but not one," he said and smiled.

"So it could be, but may not be, probably was, but may not be. Thank you, Doctor, that is very helpful," Everet said.

"We do try to be, a mace has several spikes, this object may have had more than one, but I doubt it," he said.

"So, made for the job, a special weapon?" Everet asked.

"Again, I do not know, but it could have been, more than one spike would make sense, but only one penetrated the skull and there is no evidence of another spike scratching the skull, so probably half the ball was clear of another spike, otherwise there would have been some form of evidence that it had more than one spike, but I cannot be sure," he said.

"Thank you, goodbye, sorry, a ball with a spike would not do that much damage, would it, when held in a hand?" Everet asked.

"No, that was why I used the analogy of a mace, those things were a spiked ball on a chain, now with the additional force from the torque achieved by swinging the ball three or four feet away from the assailant, then, it is possible," he said.

Julie had also had an interesting afternoon, visiting the Professor's brother in his garage and now on her way back.

"Good day, Sir, I am Detective Chief Inspector Ashton and I need to ask you a few questions, if you don't mind. I am sure you know that Skins Malone has been killed and I am investigating, his murder.

"Your brother tells me that you look after his vehicle and that he broke down because diesel was put into his tank, by whom, we do not know. He says he saw you filling it up with petrol, but the spare tanks were already filled and in the vehicle.

"At this moment in time; I am very interested in catching a murderer, carrying too much fuel in suitable or not containers, I am not interested in, just the murder. Do you have any idea how the diesel got into the tank?" Julie asked him.

"Yes, I know exactly how, they put it in, but they did not know. They are very clever people, very clever, but nouce, common sense, they lack. If you open a can, the smell reaches your nostrils and I am sure you would know if it was diesel, or not, they do smell very different. They may be able to tell you the formula for each of them and specify the difference chemically, but put two containers before them and ask them to tell you which is which and I doubt they could do, except by analysis.

"I have two youngsters training up and I stupidly asked one of them to fill the containers for the wagon; that is what we call it. I failed to ensure that he filled them with petrol and, being a wagon, he assumed diesel and that is what he filled them

129

with. Being like absent minded professors, they would not check and just pour the contents into the tank. I am surprised they even thought about that before the tank ran dry, which is what usually happened," he told Julie.

"I see that you own the vehicle, but Skins is a named driver, why?" Julie asked.

"It comes back to what I was saying, I bought it for them and they rent it off me, that way I know they are licensed and insured, they would not drive without insurance, but in all probability, they would forget to renew the tax. This way I know they are taxed and insured. I look after it, so I know the wagon is in good order and safe, they just drive it and make good music.

"Their agent pays me and I give them wages. When they first started, Eugene came to me and asked for a loan. I knew they had done a few gigs, so wondered why they had no money and I asked their agent, thinking he may have ripped them off. It turned out that he had sent them the cheques and they had not cashed them. I found letters from him telling them to cash the cheques, so I met up with him and we agreed that he send me the cheques and I pay them, making me their unpaid business manager," he said.

"So, the fact that they had broken down was an accident?" Julie asked.

"Yes, as far as they are concerned, but it was not done deliberately, it was a genuine mistake, caused by inexperience and insufficient supervision, my fault," he said.

"Can the same be said about the fake booking?" Julie asked.

"No. Ever since they played at Blythe in Northumbria, they have had mishaps. There was the false booking, a tyre went flat, it wasn' t punctured; it just went flat. Someone bashed the side of the wagon, the windscreen cracked; they rang me to tell me that they had locked the keys in the wagon. That is impossible, they would have to have left the keys in the ignition and then pushed the knob down and lifted the handle and closed the door. They are not of that frame of mind to go through all that accidentally, forget to lock it, leave the keys in the ignition, I would accept, but to lock the keys in the wagon, no," he said.

"Quite a list of accidents, have you spoken to the police? It seems to me to be vindictive, as if someone has a grudge," Julie said.

"No, they accept that they are not stupid, but absentminded and therefore that they caused everything, but I don't think they did. Like the doors being locked, they forgot that the back door does not lock properly even if they do go to all the trouble of locking the doors with the key in the ignition. They would first of all have to use the key to lock the back door. A minor detail, but when I pointed that out; it meant that they could still get back in through that door, which they did. See, no common sense, but not stupid," he said.

"Blythe, hum, did anything happen at Blythe that you know about?" Julie asked.

"They did tell me that some female began to convulse by the stage whilst they were on. Several

131

of them have medical elements to their degrees, chemistry, physics and biology, erm, things like that. They stopped playing and jumped down from the stage and began to administer first aid until ambulance men arrived and took her away. Several of the audience had had a bad experience from some drugs being sold, some more serious than others, the police were involved.

If I remember correctly, they pointed out the dealer from the stage, they saw a man going around and not watching the stage. When the police asked about him, they pointed him out; he had not been able to leave again because of the band saying that it was drug related. When asked how they knew, they said that the reactions were consistent with a bad batch of drugs from their chemistry and biology knowledge, telling them their degrees," he said.

"I am trying to remember the degrees they have: if I remember correctly one of them is an MD, a Doctor of Medicine. What is more important right now is that they indicated a drug dealer, the gang would not like that, then again small fry, it would not hamper their dealings that much," Julie said.

"That was what I thought, but that is when things started to go wrong and seem to have got worse and worse, more serious until now with a death. Let me check, I am sure I refused a booking for next week, because they are in court," he said and went into the office.

He came back, smiling, "Yes, I was right, they have a court appearance next Thursday in Blythe, there was more to this, but I'll be dammed if I can remember what it was," he said.

"Don't worry, I will contact Blythe and they will tell me what it is, if there is anything. I am confused though about the accidents, as you said they are all over the country, so the drug dealers must be following them around, which to me seems a lot of work for just a small-time drug dealer. Usually we leave them until we can nail the big fish, the main man," Julie said.

"That, that is it, he is the, hell, b, no, erm, he is related to the main man, his brother, say," he said.

"That makes sense, apart from the fact that if they know who the principal is, why is he still at large and to know that the dealer they arrested, is the brother, say, of the principal, they must know who the principal is. I will make enquiries, you have been very helpful, much more than your brother, which I suppose is not surprising," Julie said and laughed.

"No, you'd be lucky for him to remember this; it is so minor compared to his music and complicated equations and formulas. Their music is like a drug, to them, but at least there are no bad effects," he said, laughing at his brother.

"Apart from two deaths, but I know what you mean. It is a pity that they will not be able to play, this weekend," Julie said.

"Not play? You have got to be joking, their agent has sent four percussionists to be auditioned and two pianists, that was all he could find at such short notice. Didn't you know, the show must, go on," he said and laughed.

"I am sure Skins and Ivories will appreciate that fact, thank you and goodbye," Julie said.

"Goodbye, will you be there, just so that I can look out for you if I remember anything else?" he asked.

"I did intend to go, but I have a murderer to catch, so it all depends on if I have the freedom, to go," Julie said and left him stood in the forecourt as she drove off.

'What is it with the men around here? Don't they have enough single females to hit on? First it was the Professor and now his brother. It's the uniform, Julie, that turns them on and you know it, girl,' Julie thought as she drove back.

Julie used the hands free in the car to ring Everet, "How are you doing with the police stations?" she asked.

"Ma'am, there are fifty-two stations to contact, so I sent a round robin with the dates for that particular station and I am waiting for the replies. I have just got back in the office, so I have yet to check my messages. The coroner called and wanted to do the autopsy now; that is where I have been. He made a form from the injury and it is ball shaped with a spike. He said the weapon is like a mace, but not, the medieval mace, a ball with spikes, but he thinks this has just the one. He found white particles in the stomach which he has sent off for analysis along with blood and tissue, samples.

"Ma'am, it was grotesque, he pushed a rubber solution into the wound and then pulled out the shape of the weapon, covered in blood and brain matter, I threw up, as did Wilkins, sorry if we let you down, Ma'am," Everet said.

"These killings do not make sense, why would a drug baron use poison? they are thugs and gangsters, low lives at best. And then something like a mace and possibly drug him first, why, do they usually like to see their victims suffering?" Julie asked.

"Ma'am, could it be that their victim is suffering? The band as a whole were involved and therefore the band is suffering?" Everet asked.

"You have a good point and I agree it has merit, but to know that Skins or Ivories died a painful death would surely suit their purpose better. It would make them fear when it was their turn. There is no doubt in my mind that it will only end when all the band are dead; this is a vendetta," Julie said.

Julie arrived back at the office and immediately there was a knock at the office door. An officer entered when Julie told them to.

"Ma'am, a forensic report," he said, handing her a buff envelope.

Julie opened the envelope and read the report, then she looked at Everet and smiled, nodding her head in acceptance of the report.

"Now it makes sense; they found amphetamines in his system and a prescription in his possession. We will talk to his doctor as to why he was prescribing them. They also found Valium, a depressant. The amphetamine was taken prior to the Valium, which indicates that he had taken the amphetamine as prescribed and before the depressant, which had not been prescribed, along with a mild sedative.

The killer wanted to make him easier to handle, hence the sedative and depressant. What is also very interesting; is that the keys of the piano had been coated in super glue.

Skins was killed with his drumsticks and now they tried, but failed to kill Ivories with his piano, sedate him, glue his fingers to the keys and then smile at him, making sure he knows he is about to die and whack! But the upper, the prescribed amphetamines, were stronger than the downer and the sedative and they failed, making them act, but not as planned, because he had seen them. They could not go away and come back, he knew who they were, so they had no other option but to kill him where he stood," Julie said.

"He wasn't a small guy and I bet he would have put up a good fight, aided by the upper, he would have been hard to control," Everet said.

"The staged murder failed, Skins' murder was accomplished as they wanted, using his drumsticks, Ivories was botched. We need to separate the musicians from their instruments and believe me, that will not be easy. I want you to send two uniforms to their camp site, I want twenty-four-hour protection for them," Julie said.

"What about the instruments?" Everet asked.

"They are more mobile, the drums cannot be carried by a person, a flute or saxophone can, likewise the piano, one person cannot put it on their backs and carry around. It follows therefore that the murderer can bring the instrument with them, but they could not bring a piano. Find out if Skins had been dosed as well, what was the volume of the dose?" Julie asked.

"Doesn't the report say?" Everet asked.

"Yes, it does, but I need to know the effect of that dosage, I am guessing that it would make the person easier to handle, but not knock them out. They wanted the person to know what was about to happen, which was why the upper Ivories had taken, counteracted the downer they gave him," Julie said.

Everet called the desk and asked the sergeant to organise the protection Julie had asked for, telling the sergeant that if necessary to put them under house arrest, they were to stay in the mobile home.

Julie went to the coroner, and asked him about the dosages.

"The upper prescribed was quite mild; I would say he was a depressed person with low blood pressure. It was meant to stimulate, get him going and quite common in this sort of situation, but to get more details you will need to speak to his doctor. The downer was again not that strong, quite a mild dose, more to impede rather than depress. The sedative, again a mild dose," he told her.

"So, if I wanted to control a person, make them do something they would not want to do, the downer and sedative would make them easier to handle, would you agree with that?" Julie asked.

"Most certainly they would not be out of it, but unable to defend themselves, normally, it was hard to tell, but I felt that they administered a second dose of an upper," he said.

"That makes sense, they made him easy to handle and then brought him back as they were about to kill him, to see the fear in his eyes, but they failed because of the upper he had taken, as prescribed, which countered the downer they gave him, nice one, Doc," Julie said, "How were the drugs administered they gave to him administered?" she asked.

"There was no evidence of them in the stomach, just the upper he had taken, so it follows that they injected him and I did find the site, there were two that led me to believe they had given him the tranquiliser and downer here in the neck and then the upper here in the arm. Then they killed him where he had fallen on the stage convulsing, because of the mixture of uppers and downers, which was also why the indentation was so deep. his head was on the stage, which offered resistance to the blow," he told her.

"That also makes sense, the spike driven in as the head moved, absorbing the blow, but now against the stage, there was no freedom to absorb the inertia of the blow and a much deeper wound. These bastards are sick, thank you, Doctor," Julie said.

Julie made her way back to the station thinking about the crime and methods, trying to find a logical explanation, but couldn't. Whatever happened in Blythe was the lead she needed, but to where?

Chapter 11 - Blythe

She told Everet and Wilkins what she had found out and then went to the mobile home and the band.

"What crime have we committed, Chief Inspector, to have us incarcerated like this?" the Professor asked.

"None, unless you call the music you play, criminal? Personally, I like a nice bit of Beethoven, or Pachelbel, but for light relief I can enjoy Home in Pasadena, say?"

"There is a mad man, or a group of mad men, out to kill every single one of you. I do not have the resources to have an officer attached to each and every one of you, so I have one officer outside and another close by to keep all of you safe. It would not have come to this had you thought about my questions and answered them honestly, with thought.

"Has anything happened to antagonise anyone? Answer, no, yet when in Blythe you were caught up in an incident involving the police, which you failed to mention. So, look upon it as police protection, or as punishment for withholding evidence in a murder enquiry, I do not care, but you are locked in until we find and apprehend, this killer," Julie said.

"This is an outrage, being treated as criminals for assisting the police," he said and turned to a seat and sat down.

"Thank you, now for your information in Blythe and I am sure they are grateful for your help, you were not told to stay indoors. Here, where you withheld evidence, you are. You are not being treated as criminals for helping the police, but for obstructing the police, is that clear enough? Now what happened in Blythe?" Julie asked.

"We were booked to do a three-night tour at three venues, the idea was one night, syncopation, while at another venue they played big band music like Glenn Miller and then at the third venue, it was light opera, Gilbert and Sullivan and we moved around, Blythe, Whitley Bay and Cramlington as the warm up act.

"This particular night we played Blythe, as I may add the main act and in the front row was a young lady. We were actually playing; Home in Pasadena when she collapsed, convulsing. Butterfly, saw this, he jumped down and took control. He is a Doctor of Medicine, but couldn't cope with the demands and opted out. Intelligence and an ability to cope with the stresses of the job are two different things. Anyway, he knew exactly what to do and saved her life, we then were asked if we saw anything and obviously being on stage we overlooked the whole audience and had spotted a man moving about, which is not normal. Having paid for a ticket you usually stand and listen; otherwise, why pay to attend? When attending a concert, you usually stand and listen to the music, or dance to it, not move around from row to row.

"He was too slow and the police, who were already in attendance as protection, shall we say, locked the place down and he was caught. We gave our evidence, made our statements and then he was taken away.

"We also pointed out a man he kept returning to, who was also arrested and they found enough cocaine on him to charge him with distribution.

"Ever since then we seem to have had problems, minor things, but a constant irritation. Like the diesel in the tank, making us late," he told Julie.

"Right; that comes next, it is another reason for punishing you for withholding evidence, I asked if anything had happened and you said no. Yet I know it has, like a broken windscreen, being locked out of your van, flat tyres, need I go on? The only thing that is not connected to Blythe; is the diesel in the tank; that was a genuine, mistake.

I must assume that you have received some sort of threat, which you have ignored, what was it?" Julie asked.

"I, well we, got a note last month, telling us that we must not give evidence in the trial, instead we are to say that we made a mistake and to make that comment now and then, to the police, to drop all charges," he said.

"I see and you chose to ignore it and not mention it when we started to investigate Skin's murder at a house arrest. It will be quite uncomfortable with five of you in this van and I do not care, Ivories is dead because of you and your arrogance.

"They warn you and then make minor inconveniences to your life, which you ignore, so

141

they now make a statement by killing Skins, which again you ignore. So, they kill Ivories and had it not been for us, you would continue to ignore their actions, until you were all dead and rest assured it would be before the trial," Julie said in an angry tone and forceful.

"Then we make this weekend's performance the best ever, we need to practice," he said energetically.

"You step outside this van and you will spend the rest of the time in one of my cells. there will be no performance, this weekend," Julie told them bluntly.

"You would deny us the desire to entertain the gathering, some of whom have travelled from afar to be entertained, by our syncopations. What dire method is this, what abuse of power to deny them of their right to hear soothing, melodious tones that pluck at the heart strings?" he asked.

"It is the desire to keep you alive, to entertain at many more gatherings, rather than not even, at this one. You are grounded, what part of they want to kill you, has not reached that retarded brain?" Julie asked angrily.

"Madam, I and my colleagues are definitely not retarded, to some bizarre and others odd, but we are very well educated and informed people," he said, taking an aloof stand.

"We are not talking about your past but the present time, so perhaps stupid is over the top, but the brain is definitely addled. Now you know why I am not liked from above. I speak my mind and I am capable of defending, my words. The longer you keep secrets, the harder it will be for me to protect you by catching the people who have killed two of your members.

"You made statements about the incident and have you had any further contact with the police in Blythe?" Julie asked.

"Good, how then did they make contact, telling you to withdraw your statements and evidence?" Julie asked.

"They left a note after the van was damaged," he told her.

"Where is that note now?" Julie asked.

"In the bin, the one we emptied last week," he said.

"You threw a vital piece of evidence in the bin and say you are not stupid, how on earth can you justify that?" Julie asked.

"It' was not vital, we read it and decided to ignore it, the show must go on," he said, throwing his head in the air, being aloof.

"Really, I presume you have heard of the 'Temperance Seven,' well, you will soon be the Temperance Five, soon to be four, then three and you decided without any criminal understanding that it was not vital. This is not physics or a chemical equation, some random quantum theory. This is life, your life and the lives of the other band members, how dare you be so cavalier!" Julie said.

"I was not, we decided, not to be intimidated," he said.

"And just how have you fared? Two are dead, how many of them have you killed?" Julie asked.

143

"Pray, Madam, thou knowest that we are musicians, bards of the note, sculptures of the dot and phrase and not Thugees from the dustbin of life," he said.

"Then how did you propose to win this battle, or was it your intention to commit suicide by gangster?" Julie asked.

"Once incarcerated, the battle would end," he said.

"Without your testimony, they would not be incarcerated and they would make sure you did not testify. So, once you were all dead, how would you testify sending them to prison? Believe it or not, it is impossible from beyond the grave to testify. I reiterate, stupid. Do not go out, I will have food sent in and the officers will be armed from now on," Julie said and marched out, slamming the door closed, behind her.

"Ma'am, how did it go, if it is safe to ask?" Everet asked.

"Only just, probably the most intelligent people I have ever met, yet brain dead. They got a note telling them to withdraw their evidence and threw it away. They have had a windscreen broken, tyres deflated and a hit and run damaging the van. And now a death and yet they disregard probably the most important piece of evidence, because they will not be intimidated, they are infuriating," Julie said.

"Then I don't know how to put this, Ma'am," Everet said, knowing Julie was seething and not afraid to speak, but nervous of her reaction.

"Quite simply, wrapping it in cotton wool does not make it any easier to swallow," Julie said.

"There has been an accident and the dealer has been killed. Blythe are now relying on their evidence," Everet said.

"Then we had better make sure they give their evidence, hadn't we? Double the guard and arm them," Julie said and stormed off.

Julie went back to the station and her office, she entered to see Wilkins sat at his desk, reading a novel.

"D.C. Wilkins, so kind of you to attend the office, I do so hope we are not disturbing your recreation. Put that book down and unless you want to be a beat bobby for the rest of your miserable career, you will not bring a novel into my office. Get me Blythe station and the Chief Inspector or above, now," Julie said, making sure he knew she was not happy.

"Ma'am, it is not a novel, it is a biography of London gangs," he began.

"Then listen to me. I wrote the novel in the form of reports and detective work, hence my title, Detective. I have brought down several gangs in Manchester and London, by being a police person and doing my job, not by reading a fictional biography. I did it by being a detective, which is what you are trained to be, but lack experience. The book is based on fact, but then made into interesting reading with a degree of fiction and you are not bright enough to separate fact from fiction, otherwise you would not be reading it as if it were of some help. Detect, that is your job, now do it," Julie said, in an angry tone.

Wilkins did as asked and sat there sullenly until Julie looked at him with that stare.

"I have done as asked, Ma'am, he will ring you back later, Inspector Jarvis is his name," he said.

"I did not ask if he would be so kind as to consider speaking to me, I said; get him on the phone now," Julie said, as Everet entered the office.

"Ma'am, I have organised for armed officers to be in attendance from the start of the next shift.in one hour, there will be two officers at the van and a patrol car will pass every hour," Everet said.

"Now you know why she is a sergeant and not a probationary detective, I asked Everet to double the guard and arm them and what has she done? Everet has doubled the guard and armed them, excellent, now Wilkins, I want to speak to the most senior officer at Blythe now; do you think you can manage that?" Julie asked him.

"Y-Yes, Ma'am," he said uncomfortably.

"Everet, find out if any of the incidents were reported to the police and get the reports sent over, please. That is, if there are any?" Julie asked, doubting that they would have reported the incidents.

"Ma'am, Inspector Jarvis at Blythe," Wilkins said connecting the call to her phone.

"Detective Chief Inspector Ashton here, I believe there was an incident and a band of syncopators gave evidence as witnesses. I need a copy of that file, they are in my territory now and two of them are dead. It was drug related and I

146

believe you arrested a dealer at the scene, who has since died," Julie said.

"Ma'am, I was about to ring you, there was no need to call back, we are very busy here because of the death. It always causes a lot of work when we have a death in custody, as you will know," he said.

"Files and facts I need, excuses, I do not, that death is linked to my enquiry. I am sure it was caused by the same people, so catch my murderers and we catch yours. I am also very busy, so enough of the messing about. I need a copy of their file now, not when it is convenient because of police work, we all have it to do. We can work together to find the culprit, or alone but rest assured your killer is my killer and I will find them, with or without your help," Julie said.

"Have I done something wrong, taking that tone and attitude?" he asked. "I am a police officer and do my job diligently, you ask for a file and it is on its way, because I know you would not ask if you did not need it. I can be nice when I am treated with the respect I have earned, but when I am told to wait, because you are busy. I object, because I am also busy with the double murder of two of your witnesses. An inconvenience it may be, but the same people have now killed three people, so do we share and solve, or are you going to be a prat? Crying in your beer will not solve the case, detective work will," Julie said.

"I will send the files immediately after the call, and by the way, he was not murdered, he just died," Jarvis said.

"I presume you are having an autopsy done and having forensics look at blood and tissue samples. He was murdered, I know it and I have not seen the body, he was about to give up the leader, quite a coup for you, but they made sure he didn't and you fell for it. How long have you been an Inspector?" Julie asked.

"A week," he replied.

"Then listen to a wise old bird for once and take my word, he was murdered. Start an investigation along those lines. Has anybody visited him recently and did they give him anything, Cyanide in a Cadbury's Coffee Cream, is very effective, as is Arsenic," Julie said.

"There was no smell of burnt almonds, so it was not Cyanide," he said, trying to get himself out of an awkward situation.

"Usually there is, but not always and not everyone can smell it. Be an Inspector and check, do not assume, it is your worst enemy," Julie said and hung up.

"Ma'am, would you like a coffee? I was going to make one for myself," Wilkins asked.

Julie smiled, "No I would not and don't you think I am hyper enough? I will have a tea, milk, no sugar," Julie said.

Wilkins asked Everet who said that she would like, again milk, no sugar.

As soon as the message arrived on her computer Julie printed off two copies and handed one to Everet and Wilkins with the instruction to pick holes in it.

After half an hour, Julie asked them to comment, Wilkins was first, he commented on the language used.

"Because you have yet to meet them, I will accept that as a comment, because we have; then it is what we would expect from them. It is in the vein of Victorian genteel English, with old English thrown in, but accurate and pointed, if flowery. Now try to be a detective and find the flaws, as I said, pick holes in it," Julie said.

"How could they see what they say they saw? The lighting blocks out the audience to shadows and heads bobbing about, but not distinctive, so I hear," Everet said.

"That is inside, when the theatre lights go down and the spotlight is on you, but open air it is not as dark and the lighting is not as intense, so yes, they could have seen what they describe as happening," Julie said.

"Then I am having problems," Everet said.

"As am I and that is good, their defence lawyer will have the same problems. What they have said is accurate and factual, if a bit flowery. It is just as I would have expected from such well-educated people with science as a background.

"Any action has an equal and opposite reaction, fact, it is not theoretical and their science degrees are not theoretical, in nature, they are all founded in fact. Add an acid to an alkali of equal value and they cancel each other out, fact, making the substance neutral that is the science they studied, but there are errors.

149

"Be detectives and find the errors. I will be at the Market tonight from seven o'clock and will buy a drink for the first to come to me with an error, I have found four. It is time to knock off, see you in the morning unless you find just one error," Julie said smiling at them, and left.

Julie went home and had a shower and then went downstairs to make her evening meal, then changed her mind, deciding to have dinner at the Market Just as she was leaving her phone rang and she went back to answer it.

"Inspector Jarvis has been on and asked if you would be so kind as to ring him, he is at the station. Do you want the number?" the duty officer asked.

"Please," Julie said and when he had given it to her, she rang the number and asked for Jarvis, "You asked me to ring you," she said when he answered.

"Yes, thank you for being prompt, it is embarrassing, but out of courtesy I wanted you to know. They have found traces of Arsenic in his blood and close examination of the box shows a hole where it was injected into the chocolate, by a very fine needle, which is why the prison officers missed it.

"How did you know it was the coffee cream and how did they know where to inject it?" he asked.

"I didn't, it just rhymed off the tongue, Coffee Cream, but it has a soft centre and therefore easier to inject the poison than say the hazel nut. As to how they knew where to inject, it is very simple, all the boxes of chocolates are identical, so you buy two, open one and measure where it is in the box exactly and inject, ensuring the box is unopened when it is checked, so that it will pass inspection. The slight indentation from the pressure can be masked by a dab of clear nail varnish, or you can take the gamble that it will not be seen. Being sealed, they will not look, too closely," Julie said.

"I owe you one, thank you, it may have gone undetected, or worse still, I may have been for the chop, missing the murder of a prisoner," he said.

"Life is one big lesson, as long as we learn, no harm done, you made a simple mistake, do not let it bother you, learn from the experience," Julie said.

"Oh, rest assured I have, I will query and double check everything from now on, thank you, Ma'am," he said.

"It was my pleasure, I learned a lot the hard way and that is not comfortable, try to avoid it if you can, but it is not always possible, good night," Julie said and left for the Market Hotel.

Julie walked to the Market Hotel, it was a nice night, cold, but with her coat on she was warm and it was not raining, so an enjoyable stroll and her exercise for the day.

She sat at her usual table, there wasn't a sign on it but the locals steered clear of it, knowing that she liked to sit there, watching everything going on in the pub. Julie may read a book, but her eyes were on what was going on. Her order was the same, two coffees followed by two glasses of red or white wine, several customers would talk to her or she would read. She may dine, as she was going to do tonight. It was always convivial, when they spoke, it was not as if they disturbed her, she was glad of the chat.

Tonight it was the file from Blythe, some points she wanted to go over again, always inside the cover, so that she could hide the contents by closing it if someone spoke to her. It didn't bother her that they might see a line or two; it was well out of her area and would mean nothing to a casual glance.

"Jim, good evening, my usual coffee please and I will try your Lancashire hot pot, its years since I last had it," Julie told the landlord at the bar.

"Don't be too disappointed, good mutton is hard to come by and lamb does not have the same texture and taste," he told her.

"Around here, there is plenty of mutton, if you know where to go," Julie said, with a wink.

"Then I am sure you will not be disappointed in the least," he said, smiling. "Bend the rules, but do not break them. Any problems getting mutton, try Hill Top farm, but don't tell the EHO. Your chef will know that," Julie said and laughed.

"I am sure he will, being the farmer's son, as you know," he said, smiling broadly at her.

"I hear that the landlord at the 'Pheasant' is giving away a bottle of wine as a prize in his quiz night. Let him know that he needs to pay the duty on it before Customs and Excise hear about it. French plonk at less than a pound a bottle, why smuggle it in, I'll never know. A word to the wise, with him being a friend of yours," Julie said.

"He offered me some, he had to buy fifty cases to get the deal," he said.

"Then all I can say is, he was done. I was in France last summer and it was on the supermarket shelves at eighty cents a bottle. The French joke about it, saying that the stupid English are the only ones daft enough to buy it, water, acetic acid, flavourings, colourings, and antifreeze, are the ingredients, so they say," Julie said.

"He won't be very happy when I tell him," Jim said.

"He is giving it away because when he sold it, his wine sales fell through the floor, one glass and never again, insipid, acidic and nasty was what I heard. He would save money by pouring it down the drain, come to think of it; he could sell it to the council as drain cleaner," Julie said and went and sat down.

The landlord served her dinner and waited for a second, allowing her to taste it.

"That is Lancashire hot pot, my compliments to the chef," Julie said.

"Thank you, he will be pleased that you like it, but for the next week it will be mutton stew, Fricassee d' Agneau, Mutton casserole, or some such other mutton dish," he said, laughing.

"D' Agneau, is Lamb, apart from that, I like mutton and lamb. It always amazes me that English food is frowned upon, what is wrong with Lancashire hot pot, beef stew, egg and chips; they are tasty dishes and spotted dick, jam Roly-poly pudding and suet pudding to name, but a few," Julie said.

"I agree with you, which is why we have apple crumble and custard for dessert," he told her.

"Do you own shares in a clothing business or something? A second in the mouth and an inch on the waistband and I cannot afford a new wardrobe, but I will have a portion and spoil myself tonight," Julie said, smiling back at him.

She had finished her meal and enjoyed it, sitting back feeling bloated as usual, after having a main course and dessert, but satisfied.

"Ma'am, I have to admit defeat, sorry, I feel I have let you and myself down," Everet said.

"They are not that obvious, more, an item missing," Julie said.

"The arrest was correct and the statements confirmed what the police found, I am lost," Everet said.

"Then shall we see if Wilkins can find one before I tell you. He has just entered." Julie said.

"I have given up, there is nothing, no errors, I even checked some in the Oxford dictionary and there is not even a spelling mistake," James told her.

"No, I didn't think there would be, but the Professor mentioned a name card worn by the dealer, a pass of some description, yet it was not mentioned in the list of the contents of his pockets, where is it? The man allegedly supplying him, was in which corner, at the back?" Julie asked.

Two blank faces stared back, "You did read the documents, didn't you?" Julie asked.

"Yes Ma'am, he was on the left," Everet said.

"According, to whom?" Julie asked.

"Oh, erm, the professor," Everet replied.

"And on the right, according to Skins, neither was substantiated by any other statement, yet they all will have seen him, why was he not mentioned in another statement? The Inspector is new and still settling in, as such he may miss basic details; he would not miss, normally. The girl was in the front row, to which side of the stage?" Julie asked them.

"The left," Everet said.

"Wasn't it the right?" Wilkins asked.

"It was both, attention to detail, Ivories put her on the left, Skins on the right and the professor put her, middle left, or to the left of centre," Julie said.

"And the fourth one, Ma'am?" Everet asked.

"What do we do when taking a statement and there is blank paper left?" Julie asked.

"Put a line through it, to stop anything being added and on Butterfly's statement the page was not crossed off, where it was blank, damn, damn, damn, I missed that. I feel ashamed, missing something so basic," Everet said.

"Good, you should be; I asked you to find four errors, I did not say that the errors were to do with the crime, some were, but not all. Blythe made some basic mistakes, but in their defence, they were being led by a novice Inspector. Who was perhaps more concerned with looking good than being accurate. He had three novice officers on the team. Apart from brewing up, what have you done for me?" Julie asked Wilkins.

"Very little, Ma'am," he replied.

"And yet I think you have done quite a lot, you have watched and learned, hopefully. You have watched us interview suspects and witnesses. You listened to us chatting about the crime, analysing the evidence, take it in and remember and now you have learned that minor details matter. Where is the name card? Why, because it matters," Julie said..

"Ma'am, are you saying that if we solve the Blythe crime, we will solve our crime?" Everet asked.

"I am and I am not, they are using other elements, they have to be, because they have caused problems almost nationwide, but it does all stem from Blythe," Julie said, "I think the orders came from Blythe, but they used local thugs to commit the murders and by local they could have come, from London," Julie added.

"Red wine isn't it, Ma'am? We did lose the bet," Everet said.

"I offered a prize, not a bet, but I must admit I didn't expect you to win. Several times in my past life I managed to survive because I paid attention to detail. As a detective the answer is in the detail, so that is where you need to pay attention. It was more of an exercise in the need to see the detail, as I said, I did not expect you to win the prize. You both read, but do not see," Julie told them.

"Thank you, Ma'am, it has been a good lesson and I will pay more attention. I will read it again to find the flaws you pointed out. Andy, shall we leave the Chief in peace and have a pint?" Everet asked.

"That is the best offer I have had all day and thank you, Ma'am, I will try harder to see the detail," Wilkins said.

"OK, enjoy your pint, oh, excuse me," Julie said and got up. She walked to the bar and looked at a man; he saw her and his forehead furrowed.

"S-Sorry, I was just going, the, erm, the month is not up yet, is it not?" he asked.

"No, it is not, it will not be up until Monday. How is the Pheasant?" Julie asked.

"Not very nice, you should be in there controlling those ruffians, Ma'am," he said uneasily.

"Then they would only come here and to avoid me, this way they stay there and this way, I know where they are, don't I?" Julie asked.

"Y-Yes you do, I am leaving, sorry. M-May I ask if I can bring my wife in on Sunday, it is her birthday and I thought it would be nice to take her out for a meal if I can dine here, That is why I am here to ask, Chief Inspector?" he asked.

Julie smiled, "I will bend the rules for your wife, you may, but behave, no arguing," Julie warned him and went back to her seat and the fresh cup of coffee just delivered.

The Market had always been a nice comfortable pub. Jim the owner looked after his customers and he was well respected. He introduced a ruling that if you started an argument then it was an automatic one-month ban, start a fight and it was six months. Since Julie had arrived, she had left things alone, but made sure the bans were enforced. She didn't threaten the troublemakers; she just looked them in the eye with her stare and they left, sullenly.

Colin Jackson was one such character, a nice, friendly bloke, until he got a few drinks in him and then he became argumentative, which had happened one month earlier. In such a small-town word spread very quickly. No-one needed to tell Julie, she

157

heard about it generally, gossip she would have overheard in the local store, where she bought her groceries, or in the station, from the regulars at the pub, who were on duty.

Colin made his reservation and left, avoiding looking at Julie, but giving a slight nod as he passed her, to which Julie smiled.

Ever since Julie had arrived, this had been her pub of choice and the troublemakers knew this; after a few altercations, they decided that it was more sensible to go elsewhere. She instructed her officers to leave them alone, unless there was trouble.

Like the Pheasant, Julie knew that for him to buy fifty cases, they had to have been smuggled in, he was new and was trying to improve his clientele by offering the wine by the glass, but finances precluded a quality wine. She also knew he was involved in smuggling, but they turned a blind eye to that activity, it was petty stuff and they could keep an eye on it until Julie decided to have a crackdown, when he was arrested and fined and then left alone for a few months.

He was smuggling in about a thousand cigarettes a month, Julie estimated, but not every month. Customs officials were not daft, a farm worker going to France every month, for two days was soon flagged and his contraband confiscated. The owner of the Pheasant was not the brightest spark in the box.

The Pheasant was also the local hostelry for the criminal fraternity, so if anything went missing;

they knew where to check for the criminal, so it served Julie well to leave it alone.

"Ma'am, did you know Harry Bradshaw was back in town? I saw him this morning getting a paper when I was on my way to work," Everet asked her the next morning in the office.

"No, I have not been informed of that, thank you. I presume he is staying at the Pheasant," Julie said.

"I didn't ask, Ma'am, I just saw him leaving the convenience store," Everet told her.

"Take Wilkins and check up on him, date of arrival, length of stay; that is where I am sure you will find him. If the landlord is awkward or obstructive, remind him that I am due to go on the war path," Julie said.

"Yes Ma'am," Everet said.

Chapter 12 - Harry Bradshaw

Harry Bradshaw was a known villain. He began his career with petty shop lifting, then robbery and then robbery with violence, which was when he was last caught and sent down for three years.

Although he was born and bred in Little Hampton, he was wise enough not to burgle anyone in the town. That did not apply to Upper Hampton three miles down the road, where he was caught the last time, trying to rob the post office with an unloaded shotgun.

This was before Julie's time here, but characters like him were common knowledge in the station and Julie had been made aware of him and others.

She also knew that the Market was far too expensive for him to stay there; the Pheasant was the cheapest place in town, which was why she directed Everet to that pub/hotel, being generous with its status. It had been known in the station as a doss house, or flea ridden doss house.

Julie went to the desk and spoke to the sergeant.

"Harry Bradshaw is back in town, so I hear, has he registered here for his probation?" Julie asked.

"No Ma'am; would you like me to check around to find out where he is registered?" the sergeant asked her.

"If you would, please, find out his release date and get me his file, I think I need to know this person." Julie was keen to add him to her list..

"Not personally, I hope he is not a nice person, not at all. Did you know, Ma'am, his mother was a really nice woman and his dad, people who worked hard all their lives.. They were good churchgoers and it was his mother who had him arrested. She could not cope with him and his antics, why he was bad I have no idea, it was the total opposite of his parents. It broke her heart, I still believe that was why she died, a broken heart, the doctor says it is impossible, but I don't believe that," he said.

"In that case I want his file like now, please. What about his dad? is his dad still alive?" Julie asked.

"Sorry Ma'am, he went for a walk slipped, rolled down the hill side, banged his head, and landed face down in the river and drowned just before Harry was sent down, Ma'am," the sergeant told her.

"I want that file as well and, no never mind, I'll get Everet to take me; she knows the area and needs the exercise," Julie said and smiled at the sergeant, who smiled back knowingly.

Julie went back to her office and opened the file as soon as it arrived, it was just the report on the accident, it would take longer to get his personal file out to her.

"Sergeant, where was Harry when his father fell?" Julie asked over the phone.

"I don't know Ma'am, is it not in the file?" he asked.

161

"No, very strange, so he was not in jail, then?" Julie asked.

"No, he was at home, the stupid judge released him on bail, armed robbery and he was released on bail. Judge Warrick has since retired, not before time, he was senile. More to the point he was one of those, 'the poor, poor criminal,' to hell with the victim, everything was about the criminal. Three years for armed robbery and with his record that was the crime, to give you some idea ma'am, I have just sent Pickford's for the file," he said.

"I see, it is that big, is it, well we will have to curtail his activities, won't we?" Julie asked him.

"It took four officers to detain him the last time, Ma'am," he told her.

"I will make a note of that fact," Julie said, and picked up the phone. "Doctor, you did not do the autopsy I am looking at, but I am curious about some of the things in the report, do you have time for a visit?" Julie asked.

"I have an autopsy to perform, but I will be through in about an hour, unless I find something, it should be straight forward," he said.

"I will be there in an hour then," Julie said.

Julie continued to read the report, as Everet returned with Wilkins.

"Ma'am, he arrived on the twenty second and is here indefinitely, he intends to move into the family home, but it needs repairing and he has applied for a grant and support to repair it," Everet told her.

"Did you speak to him?" Julie asked.

"No, he was out, but the Landlord was very helpful, hoping that you may not go on the war path just yet," Everet said, laughing.

"I see, he has just had a delivery has he, well I will leave him alone for a week or two," Julie said.

"Actually, I don't think he has, I think he is expecting one," Everet said, "The wide eyes, and slight shake of the head told me that he didn't want the person entering, so the delivery may have just been made, Ma'am," Everet said.

"Detail excellent and observant, now you have an hour to read that and be ready to ask questions," Julie said, handing Everet the file on Harry's dad.

"And me, Ma'am?" Wilkins asked.

"You are with me," Julie said and picked up her coat, heading out of the office.

They arrived at the mortuary and entered going to the office where the coroner sat.

"Morning, sorry, afternoon, Doctor, I have here a file and I would your opinion on it?" Julie asked, handing him the file.

"First of all, the name is missing and," he began but Julie interrupted him.

"I have taken anything out that may lead you to the victim; that is not the important point, I will tell you the report stated that he drowned as the cause of death," Julie said.

"I presume, which I do not do, but under the circumstances I must, that the victim fell and rolled down a hill. The abrasions are not severe enough for a fall from height, more rolling down a grassy slope with stones. Then again there is this, hum, odd; to do this amount of damage the victim hit their head with some force more like a fall from a height, a total contradiction," he said, frowning.

"Would you agree with me, if I were to say that the blow was the reason for the fall?" Julie asked him.

"That would make sense, hit over the head with a stone and then to roll down the slope would account for the injuries and fracture," he confirmed.

"You may not have noted that he was drowned, does that make sense?" Julie said.

"Drowned, that is impossible, there is no water in the lungs. If he was found in water; he was dead before falling in," the Doctor said and added, "This is not one of my cases, is it?" he asked, shocked that it might be.

"No, you are my second opinion. I was not happy but not being a Doctor, I needed medical confirmation of my thoughts. I felt that the bruises and cuts, principally scratches, did not marry up with the blow to the head," Julie said.

"Exactly, but there was a case several years ago; a man tripped over his own feet and tumbled down a two hundred feet hill side. It was a gradual slope, but steep and covered in grass. He then hit his head on a stone at the bottom, fracturing his skull," he told her.

"Two points, Doctor, this was in this area and we do not have a two hundred feet high slope, this was twenty to thirty feet. The other is a question: what were his other injuries?" Julie asked.

"The bruising was a lot more severe, but the cuts were minor, as in this case. I stand by my decision, this person was dead before they fell," the Doctor confirmed.

"Thank you, Doctor, at this moment in time, I have more questions than answers, but you have at least reduced it by one, but then again added two more, perhaps," Julie said and sighed.

"Good hunting Chief Inspector, can you tell me the name of the deceased?" he asked.

"Yes, Mr. Bradshaw, the elder," Julie said.

"That name does not ring any bells," he said.

"It doesn't surprise me; he died over two years ago, well before you came here. How long is it now since you arrived?" Julie asked.

"Six months, and I have just settled in, I think," he said.

"I have been here about eighteen months now and I am still not settled in, they reckon a decade to be accepted as an interloper and a lifetime to be fully accepted," Julie said and laughed.

"Ma'am, can I ask if…" Wilkins started.

"No, don't," Julie interrupted him.

"Oh," he said, shocked.

"I do not waste time asking if I can ask and then ask anyway, you are a police officer, ask; I only bite stupid people with daft questions," Julie said.

"Erm, well, erm, where are we going?" he asked.

"Almost, 'Ma'am, where are we going?' Is that what you wanted to ask?" Julie asked him.

"Yes, Ma'am," he agreed.

"A concise question, showing due respect for my position, don't you think?" Julie asked.

"Yes, Ma'am," he said.

"Remember it, ask again if you can ask and I will say no," Julie said and added, "We have a murder victim, it is too old to find any forensic evidence, so what do you suggest we do?" Julie asked him.

"C, no, sorry, do we have a suspect?" he asked.

"Almost - keep trying and the answer is; I do, so now what?" Julie asked him.

"If there is no forensic evidence, then the only way to secure a conviction is by a confession, so you intend to question your suspect," he said.

"If I do that, I will alert him to my intentions, so there is something I can do before that, to give me a lever before I accept: they have got away with the murder, what is that, who is involved?" Julie asked him.

"You think he has an accomplice?" he asked.

"No, when someone dies suddenly, who is involved?" Julie asked, slightly exasperated.

"Erm, aren't we involved?" he asked.

"What the hell is wrong with you today, of course we are, who else?" Julie asked him, sounding frustrated.

"Oh, the Doctor," he said.

"Thank you, now please stop and think like a police person, it isn't the doctor as such. He is the coroner, although a doctor may be involved. Who decides how the victim died?" Julie asked.

"The coroner," he said.

"The current coroner was not the one involved in the case, so it would be pointless to ask him, why, he gave a false cause of death so where do you now think we are going?" Julie asked him.

"The one who stated the cause of death," he replied.

"Phew, that was hard," Julie said.

"Won't he just reiterate what the report says and stand by his statement?" Wilkins asked.

"We will have to wait and see, won't we?" Julie asked.

Julie pulled up outside the retired coroner's home and they knocked on the door, when he opened it. Julie introduced them as being police officers and he invited them in.

"Doctor, do you remember the case of Mr. Bradshaw? You put the cause of death as drowning, yet there was no sign of water in the lungs. Why did you say he drowned?" Julie asked him.

"I wondered how long it would take for someone to realise that error. The old Inspector was ready for retirement and I am sure he didn't take the same care he did when he arrived. I said that to alert someone to the fact that he was murdered. My life and the lives of my family were threatened by Bradshaw. He was a nasty piece of work, so I did as he said, but the rest is accurate, he died from blunt force trauma to the skull. The other injuries are consistent with a fall down the slope into the water, but he did not, drown, the Doctor said.

"I have to ask this, are you still in danger?" Julie asked him.

"Yes and no, I am sure my dear that you will understand that my children are well away from here, having grown up. The last left just after he

167

was convicted of the armed robber. My wife, bless her, died six months ago, so there is only me now, so yes, I am in danger, but the people I care for are no longer in danger," he said.

"Then help me put him away, making it safe for you as well. I will not act just yet; I have two other murders I think he may have committed. But I want him where I can keep an eye on him, so will you help me to bring a case against him? I wish to have him safe and sound while I then build the other case, he will not be coming out for a very long time," Julie told him.

"I will admit that I am fearful of him, he is a nasty piece of work; can't you build the other case?" he asked.

"No, it is complicated, it involves another area and when two areas are involved, it takes time to build the case and decide on jurisdiction. The crime I am involved in is in my area, but the instigators are in a different area and I don't want the minions, the lackeys, I want the chief," Julie told him.

"How sure are you that I will be safe?" he asked.

"Don't take this the wrong way, but I will sleep here if I have to, to protect you, he will not get past, me," Julie said.

"My reputation was shot anyway, after the quarry affair," he said.

"I would argue against that, you were not capable of the demands of that situation, because of age, not ability, no-one said you were incapable, just under too much pressure," Julie said, remembering that she was the one who suggested he retire.

"Yes, you did say that and I took it the wrong way, so my wife told me. I bear you no ill will, Chief Inspector, it was time to retire and yes, I want to even the score with him. What do you want me to do?" he asked.

"I will come back tomorrow and take your statement, all I need for now is that you to tell me that under duress, the threat of death at the hands of one Harry Bradshaw, you falsely stated the cause of death as drowning, when it was blunt force trauma by individuals undetermined. Leave it at that and that will be enough for me to arrest him on suspicion," Julie said.

"Then you have it, I accept that I falsely stated the cause of death," he began.

Wilkins wrote it down and he signed it. Julie smiled, "Thank you Doctor, I will now go and arrest him and I am looking forward to that," Julie said.

"You will have back up, won't you, he is powerful," he said.

"Of course, I have Wilkins here," Julie said, smiling.

"I would not have agreed, had I thought you were doing it alone, ring for back up before you enter," he said.

"Don't worry, I am confident, but not overconfident and I know what I am doing," Julie said.

"Ma'am, do you want me to ask for back up?" Wilkins asked.

"No, a show of force will antagonise and inflame the situation. I will ask him to accompany me to the station, politely to assist us with our enquiries," Julie said calmly.

There was the usual knot in her stomach when she entered any lion's den, it had saved her many times, making her more alert and sensitive to the situation, seeing into the shadows.

"Mr Bradshaw, I am Chief Inspector Julie Ashton and I would appreciate it if you would accompany us to the police station with regard to assisting us with our enquiries?" Julie said to him, entering the bar and seeing him sat at the bar.

"Piss off, I'm drinking," he said, without looking up.

"Now that is not very polite, is it? I asked politely, but I only ask once, I am arresting you as a suspect in the murder of one Mr. Bradshaw the elder, you do not have to say anything that may harm your defence later on, when in court. Put your hands behind your back," Julie instructed him.

"Just because you are a bitch and a cunt does not mean I will not thump you, now piss off, bitch," he said.

"By law, I have to warn you that my hands are licensed, now do as I said, or I will make you," Julie said.

He turned and jumped down off the stool and moved in close, threatening her, Julie stood there relaxed, yet every nerve in her body was tingling, every sinew taut. He put his hands up to push her away. Julie put her arms between his and pushed them to one side, brought her knee up into his groin and then followed through with a double handed chop to his back, flooring him. She knelt on his back, pulled his hands behind, and cuffed him.

"Some tough guy you are, bloody hell, you wimp, everyone was telling me I needed back up, ha, like hell, what the hell for, with a pussy like you, I win. I never said I fight fair, I do not, I win. D C Wilkins, help me get this lump of lard to the car," Julie said to the amazed looks of the men in the bar, including Wilkins.

Julie grabbed his collar and began to drag him out of the bar. Wilkins helped her get him in the car and they drove to the station and now he was coming around and they needed extra help, Julie didn't want to knock him out again.

"Resisting arrest, so leave him to recover and then I want him in an interview room. I will collect him, it will save you getting hurt," Julie told the desk sergeant, handing him over to be put in a cell.

He was put in a cell and left still in handcuffs.

Julie went to her office and sat down with a coffee and she read a file on her desk, it was the report on the death of Bradshaw's father.

The autopsy report was as he had told her and she accepted that he falsified the report, because of being threatened. It stated that Mr Bradshaw senior had slipped and fallen down the slope. He banged his head on a stone and ending up face down in the water and drowning, which she did not believe and knew it was not correct.

171

What was shocking, was that the police report backed it up, stating that they found no evidence, of foul play.

The path was three feet wide and the weather was good, it was dry, sunny and a slight breeze.

"Everet, what do you know about the track between here and Valley End?" Julie asked her.

"It has been there since prehistoric times, it has been suggested that there was a stone circle roughly in the middle and that track led to it, probably lined with stones as an avenue. It was wider in the old days because it was the main road between the villages, but through lack of use, nature has reclaimed it and rain has washed some soil down, making it narrower. It has a pebble base and stones with mud or soil; it does not get really muddy, because of the stones, but can be slippery after heavy dew originally two carts could pass on it, but not now," she told Julie.

"So, it is sunny and dry, how does an elderly man slip and fall down the slope?" Julie asked.

"He would have to be on the grass edge and early morning when there had been dew. Otherwise, he must have tripped over his own feet to fall," Everet said.

"I am going to break the ice with Bradshaw and then I want you to take me there, do you know exactly where Bradshaw senior, fell?" Julie asked.

"Yes, Ma'am, as you know, I have followed in my dad's footsteps and he said at the time that it didn't add up. His actual words were that a crime was being swept under the carpet, Ma'am," Everet said, "Can we call at my house, my dad kept his file there, just in case."

"I would like to see that, so yes, his enquiry was not sanctioned, I take it?" Julie asked.

"No Ma'am, he did it in his own time, but he did speak to the Inspector at the time, and he was told to drop it. In those days this was just an outpost, as it were, three, no four officers, the highest-ranking officer was the sergeant. My dad had to go to the main station, to see the inspector.

"Bradshaw senior was a good man, he was well liked and was basically honest; his son however was a totally different kettle of fish. A bully and at thirteen he shot a sheep in the eye, killing it with a slug gun, erm pellet gun. He said he aimed for it, knowing that the wool would stop the slug, but he was not that good a shot, his dad paid the farmer for the sheep and took the gun off his son. Two years later the farmer was found battered and bleeding, everyone knew Bradshaw had done it, but he refused to say so and make a complaint.

"He has terrorised the town ever since, no-one will stand up to him until now, Ma'am," Everet said, smiling, at Julie.

"Thank you for that vote of confidence. What you have illustrated for me is that he is violent and could have committed these murders, which was why I wanted him in the first place, being the local thug, but his dad's death, may be just the lever, I need.

Everet, if you are up for it, join me as I interview him?" Julie asked her and got up; Everet followed her out of the office.

Julie stood to one side as the officer opened the cell, she saw Bradshaw run at the door, and closed it as he crashed headfirst into the door and fell to the floor.

"Oh my, I am so sorry about that, did it hurt?" Julie asked him.

"Oh, hum, erm, oh," he moaned on the floor.

"Here let me help you up, now I do hope we understand each other, you attack and I put you down and as I said, I do not fight fair, I win." Julie reminded him.

She led him, still moaning, to the interview room and sat him on a chair and then sat down with Everet facing him.

Julie set the tape going, and stated who was present and then began.

"Mr Bradshaw, where were you on the night of the twenty second of this month, last Thursday?" Julie asked him.

"I-I am concussed, you stupid bitch," he said.

"I very much doubt that, your head is too thick and it needs a brain to be concussed, I mean, being so stupid, as to run into an iron door, really, Mr Bradshaw? Did you not see the door? It is big enough. I want to know where, you were last Thursday," Julie asked him again.

"Oh, at the shooting range with Albie and two others he brought; I don't know their names," he said.

"Very good, now how do I find this Albie, I need his real name and address," Julie asked him.

"Albert Johnson, I don't know his address, we meet at the pub and the shooting range, where I kick his arse," he told her.

"I see, and then what did you do say, around eleven o'clock to midnight? The range I am sure will be closed then?" Julie said.

"I erm, I was in the pub, Albie and his mates went to do a job," he said, not thinking.

"A job, at midnight, what kind of job entails starting work at midnight?" Julie asked.

"I don't know, do I? I was in the pub as I just said, wash your fucking ears out, bitch," he said.

"Be careful, I have you for resisting arrest, when I asked you to accompany me to the station, a request, but you refused and I had to arrest you, which then led to resisting arrest. Do not dig the hole you are in any deeper!. I can add at any time assaulting police officer and verbal abuse of a police officer and adding those together would mean being sent down for six months, at least. It is far better to co-operate, less painful and avoids prison," Julie said, adding a smile for his benefit. "Now where can I find this Albie?" Julie asked him.

"The pub, he usually comes tonight for a few bevies and then tomorrow night for the firing range," he said.

"There now, wasn't that easier? now what about Sunday night, again between eleven and midnight?" Julie asked.

"In bed, I had, had a skin full, and went home to sleep it off," he said.

"That is not a good answer; you see I was hoping that you would have an alibi, but you do not.

175

You see you have a reputation for being brutal and a man was brutally murdered then and you do not have an alibi, which is enough for me to keep you here and get an extension to keep you here.

"I also want to know where you were when you father was killed," Julie asked him.

"Fucking hell, woman that was two years ago, and he was not killed, he fell, it was an accident; don't you read the reports?" he asked.

"I do, and with a lot of interest. how did he slip when the ground was dry? How did he manage to crack his skull when it is a gentle slope and there are no rocks to bang his head on? How could the cause of death be drowning when there was no water in his lungs? A warm, late summer's day, dry, sunny and a slight breeze, no alcohol, yet he slipped and fell into an icy cold, mountain stream. The shock of this did not wake him and it was not deep enough to swim in. So, he could have stood up, dazed perhaps, but got clear of the water. No, he did not slip, he was murdered and the finger is pointing at you.

"Follow my thinking, will you, you shot and killed a sheep, two years later you beat up the farmer for telling your dad, who took your prized air rifle off you, so you killed him, perhaps you did not mean to, but you did, and I will find the evidence. To avoid further injury, I suggest you be a good boy and accompany me to your nice cell," Julie said, talking down to him, but giving him her stare.

Whether or not he had accepted his fate, she did not know, but he went back to his cell without causing a problem, where she removed his handcuffs.

"If you want to remain with your hands free, do not try anything, you now know I have the upper hand, because I do not fight fair, I win," Julie said, hoping it would sink in and he would co-operate with the other officers.

Julie and Everet now visited the scene where his father, allegedly, fell. XXX

"Everet, are you sure this is where he fell? I mean even in the rain the ground is not slippery, small gravel like stones, are not conducive to a slippery surface," Julie said, studying the ground, and the bank grass top to bottom, "I can't see a stone big enough to cause that kind of damage. Check with the council to see if any work has been done, since the accident. Elderly, and perhaps feeble could slip, but bumps and bruises yes, not a fractured skull," Julie said, thinking out loud.

"Ma'am, he was not young, but a doddering old man, he was not," Everet informed her.

"Did you know him?" Julie asked.

"Not personally, but I did see him in the shop, or walking down the street, he stood erect, and walked solidly to me, Ma'am, he didn't need a stick," Everet told her.

"Find out who was in charge of the case, I want to speak with them," Julie said, and turned to walk back to the car.

Julie knew that any forensic evidence would have been lost after two years, but seeing the scene, she knew that the report was incorrect; there had been, a cover up.

177

Just as Julie was about to leave for the evening, Everet gave her a report, it included the name of the senior officer in charge of the investigation, and that the council had not done any work apart from trimming the verges, the surface had not needed, renewing.

"This gets more and more interesting, we will meet at the office in the morning, and then go and see Sergeant Wilson, to see what he has to say, for himself," Julie told her.

"Ma'am, everyone who has investigated Bradshaw, seems to have had an accident; he is very good at covering his tracks, Ma'am," Everet said.

"Is he now, then we had better make sure we do not have an accident, hadn't we, because I am going to investigate him. I will not order you to assist me, if you are nervous, but I do, ask you?" Julie asked her.

"Then it is about time his rule of terror came to an end, he seems to have a canny knack of being elsewhere, when anything happens," Everet told her.

"Do you know where he was, when his father fell?" Julie asked.

"No Ma'am, it is not in the file," Everet said.

"And when we asked him, it had slipped his mind, conveniently. I do not believe in coincidence, tomorrow, I want every file for every crime, he has been implicated, in?" Julie asked her.

"Ma'am, it goes back some fifteen years, my dad told me to stay away from him, because he was a bad lot. We are the same age, he was in my year at infant school, and then I went to the local girl's college, and he went to the local comprehensive school. I am not ashamed that my parents subsidised my education at a fee-paying school. My Uncle started the builder's yard, and my dad invested in it, he became a director when he retired from the police," Everet told her.

"Then we have a lot of reading to do. Ah, Detective Constable Wilkins, how nice of you to join us," Julie said glibly.

"I went to the archives Ma'am, and I am afraid, I wasted a morning, I had an idea that the group may have been here before, and that drugs were involved, but it appears I was wrong, sorry Ma'am," Wilkins said.

"Then it was not wasted, it saved me having to get that information. They have never been here before, or they were never involved in drugs, which is it?" Julie asked him.

"Both, their names do not crop up in any drug file," he told her.

"Which names, the ones they use now, or the ones they used before changing their names, after the drugs bust, six years ago? Also, we know that they have been here before; they play here every year, so the Professor told us, didn't he?" Julie asked him.

"Yes, Ma'am, the bust was in the next county, so they have the file, and it was only one member of the group who was busted, Skins, for possession, a slapped wrist," he said uneasily.

"Excellent work, so you were aware that they changed their names, and checked both sets of names, excellent work, and initiative. We are now

179

very interested in one, Harry Bradshaw, he appears to be a bad lot, and has caused several problems for the local nick, yet always seemed to be not in, the vicinity.

Tomorrow, get all the unsolved files with him involved, as a witness, or suspect, although I doubt it, include the ones with him, as a victim. I want you to copy his statements, so that I can read them, and I will need to know the crime, and where it took place?" Julie asked him.

"How far back shall I go Ma'am?" he asked.

"Let me see he is twenty-five, so say twenty-five years," Julie said.

"Won't some of the crimes be out of the statute of limitations, Ma'am?" He asked.

"Yes, but I still want to know about them," Julie told him.

Chapter 13 - One Avenue Closed

Julie met Everet, and they drove to the retired sergeant's home, and knocked, he answered the door, and Julie introduced them to him, and they were invited in.

"I was not aware that you were in a wheelchair. How did it happen, if I can ask?" Julie asked.

"You have not told her?" He asked Everet.

"Sorry Ma'am, it was hectic yesterday, we never seemed to stop, and I guess I forgot. He was investigating Bradshaw, and a stray bullet hit him in the lower back, the rifle and shooter were never found," Everet told her.

"Add that to my list, I will get him for every unsolved crime, if possible. I need to know, what happened? As I am sure, you will appreciate?" Julie asked him.

"It is in the file," he said.

"Sergeant, I can read, but I need to hear it from you, files do not tell the whole story, so tell me," Julie pushed him.

"I was taking my dogs for a walk one Sunday afternoon. I heard a shot, and felt a searing pain, and collapsed, Molly, she was a good dog, she ran like hell home, and my wife knew something was wrong, they never left my side, Barney the other dog, stayed by my side until help arrived, the bullet had severed the spinal cord; I am paralysed from the waist down. How does that help, it is in the file, as I said," he told her.

"Some farmer out shooting birds, was it sunny, or raining?" Julie asked him.

"It was a lovely summer's day, I was out in my shirt sleeves," he said.

"How many shots did you hear?" Julie asked.

"One, just the one," he replied.

"What type of dogs are they?" Julie asked.

"Alsatian, why the breed, what has that got to do with it?" He asked.

"Were you walking along, or had you stopped to pick up something, perhaps?" Julie asked.

"What? I was walking the dogs," he said getting agitated.

"In my past life I was a sniper for the British army, and I can tell from what you have told us; that there are two possibilities. I wondered if they were a bad shot, and aiming for the dog, which allowing for the size of the dog, and the kick from a rifle, it is still possible. Allowing for a five degree rise in angle it could be that they were trying to intimidate you, and failed. Even so, to be off by two feet is very bad shooting, and I doubt that," Julie said, "I also have a problem with hearing the shot it is impossible. The speed of the bullet dictates that the sound will not reach you until about three seconds, depending upon distance, after the bullet had hit you. So, two shots, yet you only heard one; why, was that?" Julie asked.

"They did investigate it, but no-one saw anything, or heard anything apart from me, the surgeon gave me the bullet once they had finished with it," he told her.

Julie smiled, "He did, and can I have it, please?" Julie asked.

"I don't know why he gave it to me, or why I kept it, but I did, and I am not sure I want it back, again," he said.

"Everet, when we get back, I want that file. Sergeant, I will do whatever you want me to with the bullet, return it, or dispose of it," Julie said.

He asked his wife to get it from the top drawer of his bed side table; she did, and handed it to Julie.

"A point two, two, a very popular rifle around here, but this was fired from a rifle with a larger barrel. It is too late to get fingerprints from it, too many people have handled it, but it was fired intentionally, it is a premeditated crime," Julie said.

"You are good, how do you know all that?" The sergeant asked.

"There are no striations on the bullet. A crime I solved a year or so back was the same. They pack out the bullet ensuring that it is spinning when it leaves the barrel, and therefore accurate, but there are no striations on the bullet, so it is impossible to identify, the gun. The attack has been thought out. This is a point two, two, bullet, wrap cloth even, around the bullet, and put it into a three, o, three, and it will fire, the cloth will be singed, but the bullet will spiral, and be accurate, and have no striations. I am sorry to say, you were, targeted.

Now we add into the equation, and accept that there will be power loss, reducing the distance the bullet will fly, and ask if it had been compensated for, by an increase in charge. This is important because dependent upon distance, it could have been meant, to kill, making you a lucky man that, is an amateur's mistake," Julie said.

"Our Harry is definitely, one of those," he said.

They left the Sergeant's house, and Julie rang Wilkins, asking him to check Harry's alibi, for the nights of the current murders; Julie did not want to lose track of those.

They arrived back at the office, and Julie looked with a resigned sigh, at the piles of files on her desk.

"I did warn you Ma'am, he has been very, active," Everet said smiling.

"Then it is about time we brought his reign to an end, here you do not get off without a mountain to read, just the same as me," Julie said planting about half the files on Everet's desk.

"What are we actually looking for?" Everet asked.

"Anything dubious, something minor perhaps that I can wriggle until someone squeals, prove he did the deed, or did not, do it," Julie said, and sat down to begin reading.

Two hours later they were still ploughing through the files, and making notes when Wilkins returned.

"Well, Wilkins, what did you find out?" Julie asked glad of a distraction.

"His alibi holds up, ma'am," he said.

"Like, watertight, or iffy?" Julie asked.

"Like airtight, I took a copy of the CCTV footage from the cafe across the street, there is no doubting it is him, but we have him for causing a disturbance. The man in the fracas, is willing to have him charged, he broke the man's arm, and he has been off work ever since," Wilkins said.

"So, he was not at the scene the first night, what about the second night?" Julie asked.

"Not as solid, but solid enough, again from a camera across the street, he is seen entering the pub, and leaving, and there are six locals to testify that he was in the pub, the whole time," James said.

"Ma'am, when his father died; his whereabouts was never listed, it is as if he was not even asked," Everet informed her.

"That is interesting, tomorrow take Wilkins with you, and ask the Sergeant, why not? You two go home, you have both done well today," Julie said knowing that it would not be long before a six o'clock finish would be just a dream, "Sergeant, send officers to the Blacksmiths, and collect one Barry Smith, one Andrew Williams, and one Arthur Jones, and have them put in three separate interview rooms to await me," Julie said, and followed the others out.

She went home, had a shower, and then ate her dinner, and returned to the station, dressed in a blouse and leggings, and she looked evil, her make-up dark, and uninviting.

She entered the first interview room, and for the tape introduced herself, and allowed the interviewee to say who he was.

"I am not willing to be messed about, this is informal, a nice chat, but from my attire you can tell that I am not in the best of moods, a night by the television, or a night talking to three morons, which would you prefer?" Julie asked him.

"Do you want me to answer that?" He asked.

"When asked a question that is the normal, outcome, like I said, interviewing morons, so don't bother, having established that point. Now I believe you swear that Harry Bradshaw was in the pub last Sunday all night, he didn't even go to the toilet, is that correct?" Julie asked him.

"I-I well he may have gone to the toilet; I mean beer has a habit of doing that," he said.

"Yet you told D C Wilkins that he was with you all night. What did you do, go with him, and hold it for him?" Julie asked.

"N-No, I was with him, but he must have gone to the toilet, alone, so not then," he said, now a bit nervous.

"How long was he not within sight, of you?" Julie asked.

"I don't know, I don't time him," he said.

"Officer, put him in a cell, give him time to remember. We do have three empty cells for you to occupy till morning, if needed, to help you remember," Julie said.

"W-wait, I did not time him, but he went as the match started, and only came back, at half time I do remember that," he said.

"I wonder how much more you will remember if; I have you put in a cell?" Julie asked him, cocking her head, enquiringly, to one side.

"Honestly that was the only time," he said.

"So, he was missing for three quarters of an hour?" Julie asked.

"M-More like an hour, they do the match side interviews, and the teams, before the match," he said reluctantly.

"It gets better, now where could he have gone in a whole hour?" Julie asked him.

"The-The house next door she, erm, well, she is cheap," he said.

"Officer, who occupies the house next to the Blacksmiths, find out, as you show Mr. Smith out, will you, good day, Mr Smith," Julie said and smiled, she hadn't lost her touch.

"Mr Jones, thank you for coming in, and helping us with our enquiries. I believe you stated that you were with Harry Bradshaw all night, last Sunday in the Blacksmiths, are you a couple of girls who go to the toilets, in pairs?" Julie asked him.

'I resent that question, we are not girls, so no, we do not," he said adamantly.

"Then how can you say that you were with him the entire night?" Julie asked him, leaning in threateningly.

"OK, so apart from then," he said.

"So, you cannot account for every minute of the evening what about between the start of the match, and half time, was he with you then?" Julie asked him.

"Yes, he was the whole time, apart from when he went to the bog," he said.

"Shall we try again, this time under caution, so that when you lie, I can arrest you?" Julie asked him, and read him the caution, "You do understand that to lie now means a night in my cells, and then an appearance in court, and a fine. How much

187

money do you have to throw away, on a fine?" Julie asked him.

"I-I-I," he began.

"Let me help you, I believe the woman in the house next to the Blacksmiths, is cheap, does that help?" Julie asked him.

"H-How do you know?" He asked.

"I am a Chief Inspector, I know everything. Which do you think he would rather be? Arrested for murder, or as a man enjoying the delights, of a female?" Julie asked him.

"H-He did go out for an hour, and he said it was to dip his wick, a quick fuck, but his girlfriend must not find out. You heard about that man that had it chopped off by his wife, well she is just as able, and vindictive," he said.

"You forget, I am female, and a female scorned, is not pretty sight, and as you blokes say, we do, stick together," Julie said.

"L-Look, you won't tell her, will you? I mean you are supposed to prevent crimes, and by telling her, you will create a crime?" He asked her nervously.

"That depends, his father had a nasty accident a couple of years ago, where were you when it happened?" she asked him.

"It was a Sunday afternoon, I would have been in the pub watching the match," he said.

"That is correct; it was a Sunday afternoon, who was with you watching the match?" Julie asked him.

"The usual crowd, do you want all their names?" He asked shocked that she might.

188

"No, just the ones you sit with, like Andrew Williams, was he with you?" Julie asked.

"Yes, he was, and Barry Smith," he said.

"Anybody else?" Julie asked.

"N-Not that I can remember," he said.

"Is that because they were not there, or because you can't remember?" Julie asked him.

"No, no, I remember because there is usually four of us, and that afternoon there was only," he started, and shut up.

"Thank you, now you have two choices, you can go down for trying to pervert the course of justice, or tell me the truth, either way he is going down, for murder. Do you really want to join him, and him knowing you were the one to help, convict him?" Julie asked him.

"He was not there," he admitted reluctantly.

"Good, now I need you to write it down, if you cannot write; then I will, for you. Now we come to the Sunday following that incident. How many of you were there that Sunday, and remember you have lied already, so it is now up to me if I prosecute, or not. Do not push your luck," Julie said.

"If I tell you, what is in it for me?" He asked.

"I have told you; you avoid going to prison, and that way, we can protect you, fail, and it might just slip out, who told me, and you would not want that to happen, would you?" Julie asked him.

"Just the three of us, but he did not shoot, the copper," he blurted out.

"Then who did?" Julie asked him.

"He is not a good shot, so he asked a friend who brought his own gun, something about using a smaller bullet than the calibre of the gun, I didn't understand what he meant," he said.

"Now to get off clean; I need a name?" Julie asked him.

"I-I don't have a name, but he works at the brick works in the next village, Harry worked there for a bit, and they became friends," he told her.

"Thank you; Officer, please, escort, Mr Jones, to the door," Julie asked him.

Julie went to the ante room, and looked in on an agitated Andrew Williams and smiled, all she wanted now was confirmation and didn't really need that.

"Hello, as you know, we brought in three of you for a little chat; I decided that, if you answered my questions honestly; then I would not need to take any further action. Your two friends realised that I was not joking and co-operated; I hope you are as wise, as they were. I

am very interested in one Harry Bradshaw for the murder of his father and the attempted murder of a police sergeant. I have a statement confirming that he did both deeds and corroboration that means that they both said, he did the deed, so I don't need you to confirm it, but it would be nice. I know you three gave him an alibi, for the Sunday his dad was killed. Yes, it was murder, but the following Sunday a police sergeant was shot and I like him for that one, as well. Nice, a double murder, he will die in prison and then there was last Sunday, it was his style. I might as well have him for that while I am at it and you are the right build for one of the blokes with him.

"Now how good a friend is he? I mean twenty years in prison is a very long time. Can you do twenty years?" Julie asked him.

"I was not involved, neither was Harry, last Sunday, you can't fit him up for that one, bitch. I want my lawyer, I am refusing to say anything, until my lawyer gets here," he said.

"Very well; officer, find our guest a nice cell, will you, and contact his lawyer, tomorrow morning," Julie said, and turned to walk out.

"You can't do that, I have rights!" he shouted at her.

"I agree, you do, as does the victim of a brutal murder,. consider this. I will give you the same rights as the victim. I was special ops; and a sniper and I can bounce you off all four walls in here and not break into a sweat. The same rights as your victim, did you even care about their life? No, well I do not care about your rights, take him, before I lose my temper and plaster this miscreant all over, the walls," Julie said, apparently agitated.

The officer took him by the arm and dragged him to the door.

"Use the end cell that one, is soundproof, fear me, you saw what happened to tough guy Harry, when he messed with me," Julie said, and saw the look of fear on his face.

"What is in it for me?" he asked, bleating.

"Nothing, as I said; I don't need you; I have all I need," Julie said, closing the file and picking it up.

"Harry did not shoot the officer," he shouted from the doorway.

"I have it on good authority that he did, with a man from the brick works," Julie said, as if disinterested.

"Wait; wait, if I tell you, then what?" he asked.

"Very simple, unless you shed more light on the case nothing, if you do then, I won't let it slip that you were the one, who told me," Julie said casually.

"OK, OK, Harry did kill his dad, he wanted revenge for his dad taking away his gun, and served it cold, a couple of years later, I think. But the copper, he did not shoot; that was Darren Jackson," he said.

"Hum, I am not happy at being called a bitch, I know I am, but I don't like being called that, what is his address?" Julie asked him.

"Sorry, about that, he lives at, fifteen, Windmill Terrace, Upper Hampton, but tonight he will be in the Nags Head, it's darts night," he said.

"Nags Head, who, are they playing, The Market?" Julie asked.

"Yes, and he is on the Nags Head team, and it is at home," he said.

"I think a night in our cells would appease my anger at being called a bitch, the only other way would be being prosecuted for perverting the course of justice, six months with Harry in prison. What do you think, a night here, or six months?" Julie asked him.

"I-I agree," he said reluctantly and was taken away.

Julie smiled; she definitely had not lost her touch, three confirmations of his actions, was as much as she could have hoped for.

Julie went to the Market, her local, she had refused to join the darts team, believing it to be unfair and not proper, being a Chief Inspector, but she had supported the team when they were at home. This evening was different, as she entered the pub, there was a noisy reception. Julie went to the bar and ordered her coffee. "Jim, what is going on, the lads seem agitated," Julie asked him.

"Simon has fallen and broken his wrist, he is out of action for the match tonight and it is a grudge match. They won the last time we played, evening up the score. The winner tonight, is in the quarter finals, so it is very tense and we have lost, not our best player, but he was good. As a sharpshooter you will have a good eye. I know what you said and I agreed, but tonight is, well, it means everything. \will you substitute for him. They can't make their minds up who to pick," he said.

"I have business to conduct tonight at the Nags Head, so I planned on going, I can delay my work till after the match, so yes," Julie said.

"Guys, guys, I have your replacement, here you all know Julie, I am sure she will be the best replacement," Jim told them once they quieted down.

"Can you throw a dart?" One asked her.

"I am not too sure; with a gun I will hit the bull's eye every time. Can I use my gun?" Julie asked, joking.

"Here, use these, or are they too heavy for you?" Jim asked.

"I don't know what I should aim for, usually it is the bull's eye when shooting?" Julie asked.

"We play five O one, so the treble twenty is the best, but we finish on a bull's eye, so try, and hit the treble twenty that is the one at the top," one of them said, and giving Jim an odd look.

"Ah, I see that one," Julie said putting a dart in the segment.

"Yes, yes, that's it, now put one to the left and right of that one," an eager player said.

Julie put one either side of it, to the amazement of the team.

"You are on the team; can you do that again?" A member asked.

"Sorry, I was playing with you, I was the squad champion and we won the barrack's title three years on the run, which was why I refused to join the team. They would say you had a ringer, but as a one off I will play," Julie told them.

"Simon will be off for six weeks, you will be with us till the end of the season, won't you?" a member asked her.

"Sorry, I cannot make a promise like that; I may have to work and I will not let you down, so it is tonight only," Julie said.

"We understand, but when you are free; then will you play for us?" a member asked her.

"I will support you when I can," Julie said and they loaded the cars and left for the Nags Head.

They played the best of five games, with four in a team, so one played twice, usually the best player,

194

the previous games were from a draw, now it was knockout games they were playing.

Game one was not Julie and they won that game, game two was again not Julie and they lost that one, game three was Julie's turn and she started with two treble twenties and a treble nineteen. Her opponent looked at her and she cocked her head to one side, indicating luck. He got a treble twenty and then a single one, and then a double twenty. Julie now had three treble twenties and the game went her way after that.

The next game went for the Nags Head and the final game was now between Julie and their star player, Darren Jackson.

He was a well-built man and smiled at Julie as he won the toss and went first, with two treble twenties and a treble nineteen. Julie matched him.

He then threw one that landed just above the wire for the treble, one into the treble and one that slipped below the wire, having hit it.

"Bad luck there, nice grouping though," Julie said, and threw three treble twenties.

He then threw a one eighty and Julie threw two treble twenties and a double twelve, winning the game.

As the game ended and they had their celebratory drinks before them, two police officers entered, and went to Julie.

"Darren Jackson, I commiserate with you for losing, but now I have the pleasure of arresting you for attempted murder. I am arresting you for the attempted murder of one police Sergeant Evans. You do not have to say anything, but anything you do say will be taken down and do not say anything you may later rely on in court that may harm your defence. Take him," Julie told the officers, once she had cuffed him, as a stunned bar looked on.

One of the team came over to her, "Did you have to do that?" he asked.

"Yes, at least I let them play the game before arresting him, I could have done it earlier, when we entered, then they would have lost him and you me. I will go back with my officers, thank you for the game," Julie said and got in the police car and travelled back with them, she entered the Market, while the officers put him in a cell.

While they were arresting Darren, other officers were arresting Harry for conspiracy to murder and for the murder of his father.

Julie was very pleased with the evening and sat at her table enjoying a well-earned white wine.

Chapter 14 - The Trial

Julie arrived at the station the next morning happy and feeling refreshed. She went to her office and saw Everet and Wilkins stood smiling at her.

"Everyone in the village is so pleased, a double whammy for you, we are in the quarter finals and the shooter of Sergeant Evans has been arrested, at long last. I thought I would be late, with everyone stopping me and asking me to congratulate you," Everet said.

"Thank you, it was a team effort, you both helped, don't forget, I just got the pleasure of arresting the slime ball. It is alright cleaning up past mistakes, but we have a double murder to solve, don't forget and this one is current. I do not want our joy at clearing up a past crime to be sullied by failing to solve a current one. Review," Julie said.

"We know that two members of the band had been murdered by presumably the same crew, but by different methods. We also know that they use a piece of the instrument the victims play as the murder weapon, or part of the murder. We know it is related to an incident in Blythe a couple of years ago, when the band, were involved in a drugs case, as witnesses, "Everet said.

"We also know that there are four perpetrators, not necessarily the same four, for each murder and the group were more than just witnesses to the crime. They were involved, accidentally perhaps, but nonetheless involved. We also know that the

197

gang want them all dead, to stop them being witnesses at the trial and that the gang is Blythe based," Julie said.

"Ma'am, just because the band went to the aide of the victim and pointed out the dealer; why do the gang fear it going to trial, surely one dealer less is not critical to their dealings, they will get a replacement, won't they?" Wilkins asked.

"A good point, Wilkins, you would not think so, but it has; so, as you asked, why? We suspect that he is related to the leader and a close relative. We also suspect that he was the supplier to the dealer who they disposed of, as we have said, of little or no consequence, two pence a dozen. This still leaves us with, why?" Julie asked.

"I can only think of a couple of points, one, he is the son of the main person and two, he can point out the main person," Everet said.

"I drew the same conclusion, but I didn't think they would kill the band when they only needed to kill the dealer, a person of little consequence, so it must be closer to home," Julie said.

"So, you think he is related to the main dealer, the gang boss?" Everet asked.

"I do, as you said, a street level salesperson is of little consequence, two a penny and it would be cheaper and less hassle to have him slip in prison. No, he is too important to be discarded; there is a strong link between him and the boss. I have read the statements and Blythe have not questioned him about that, there was no need, they interviewed him about the crime only, because of later events, has that element become apparent.

"Everet, pack an overnight bag, we are going to Blythe; it is ideally situated being a port, for drugs to enter the country. I am sure the local authorities do their best to control the situation, but as a means of importing the drugs are covered, or stopped by the police. The barons find new ways, so it is a never-ending game of catch-up, for the police, up there," Julie said, and turned to Wilkins, "Wilkins, I want you to look into our files and I want you to look for any connection between our local thugs and Blythe?" Julie asked him.

"Ma'am, you are in court in half an hour," Everet reminded her.

"Then you and I have half an hour to pack, don't we? We leave right after I have said my piece," Julie said.

They went home and met back at the courthouse, Julie was called and she went to the witness stand, she gave her name and position and then she was asked to tell the judge about her evidence.

"Your Honour, the path that Mr Bradshaw allegedly slipped on has a pebble coating. The coating is and was not the rounded pebbles, but chippings, with angular edges and corners, aiding a secure footing. On the day in question, it was sunny and dry and it had not rained for two days, so underfoot it was not slippery.

"The slope is covered in grass; without any sign of stones adhering to it, or just below the surface.

"I obtained an exhumation order and sent the body to a forensic pathologist, who stated that, 'the injury was more consistent with a metal object, because of the lack of stone particles in the wound.' When the body was discovered, the area around the injury was covered in blood, but otherwise dry, indicating that the stream had not washed over the head, leaving any stone particles present still, in the wound.

"When a cast of the wound was taken, it was consistent with a metal ball with a spike welded to it, like a medieval mace. I then obtained a search warrant and searched the defendant's house and shed. I found a metal ball attached to a chain and took it to the forensic team to examine, they found blood under the joint where the head met the chain and it was confirmed to be that of Mr Bradshaw. The indentation of his skull was consistent with being hit by such an object. The defendant's hobby was to make medieval weapons and armour; so it would not have been out of place in his home," Julie said, and went silent.

"Are you a forensic scientist?" the defence asked her.

"No, I just reiterated the forensic report, which will be given in evidence at the trial and the scientist will be available for questioning at that point in time," Julie said.

"Your Honour, this is to assess if Mr Bradshaw should be sent for trial and held in custody until the trial, as we are requesting. This is not the trial, as my learned friend appears to think," the prosecutor said.

"Your Honour, how can I cross-examine scientific evidence if a scientist is not available?" the defence protested.

"Can you produce the scientist?" the judge asked the prosecution.

"I can, Your Honour, but as the Chief Inspector said, this is just a preliminary hearing, where the available evidence is stated, to justify holding the suspect until the trial. The report has been made available to the defence and yourself, scrutiny of the evidence contained within the report is for the trial, not this hearing. Because of the strength of the evidence, we feel that there is a strong chance of flight and ask that the defendant be held in custody until the trial, Your Honour," the defence argued.

"I have to agree, the report stands for the moment, examination of the report will take place at the trial, I am sure, continue." the judge said.

"You are quite a formidable female, are you not, Chief Inspector? My client suffered a minor concussion when you arrested him; excessive violence was used in his arrest, how come?" he asked.

"I told him that I wanted to ask him a few questions about his father's death. He refused and took a swing at me, attempted assault. I defended myself and told him that I was arresting him for the attempted assault of a police officer and arresting him for the murder of his father and to come with me. He was dazed, I admit, so we helped him to the car and into the station where we called for a doctor, as is required. I then reiterated the caution, prior to questioning him," Julie said.

"I have two witnesses that state that you entered the bar and sneaked up behind him and hit him with both fists on the back of his neck, banging

201

his head into the bar, they say that you were the aggressor," he said.

Julie didn't say anything. "Your Honour, please tell the Chief Inspector to confirm or deny, the allegation?" the defence lawyer asked.

"Your honour, I did not hear a question, just a statement, factual or not," Julie said.

"Did you sneak up on the defendant and hit him?" the defence lawyer asked her.

"No, I did not," Julie said.

"Then you are accusing these men of lying?" he asked shocked at the idea.

"Yes, I am," Julie replied.

"You swung a foot into his groin, really Chief Inspector, is that part of apprehending a suspect?" he asked.

"I did not, he took a swing at me; I ducked and hit him in the solar plexus and then his back just below his neck, winded and dazed, he was easier to handle for my officers, not being as, to use your words, formidable, as I am," Julie said.

"So much violence to apprehend one man, over the top, wasn't it?" he asked her.

"You Honour, am I on trial here? I ask because I do not have a defence lawyer present, which I am entitled to. Then again, he is guilty and the defence lawyer has to try and get him off. We dotted every 'I' and crossed every 'T'.

"In nineteen ninety-five he was accused of robbery; the charges were dropped. In two thousand and five, he began his reign of terror.

"Four officers were sent to arrest him, two ended up in hospital with facial injuries, including a broken nose and cheek bone. In two thousand and ten he put another three in hospital. In every case no charges were brought, these are now out of time, past the statute of limitations, but the local police force feared him and he got away with murder, nearly.

"The officer investigating the death of his father was shot in the back and is paralysed from the waist down and that is the second charge. He conspired to have the sergeant murdered and in three days' time, I will be back with the man who shot him and he will tell you that it was orchestrated by that man," Julie said, ignoring the judge as he tried to control her.

"Another outburst like that and I will hold you in contempt of court, do you, understand me?" he demanded.

"I apologise to the court, Your Honour," Julie said, but she knew she had got her message home and smiled inside.

"I have here three witness statements and I ask that they be withdrawn, because they were obtained under duress. You did threaten them, didn't you, and having seen how capable you are, they made a false statement. Isn't that correct?" the prosecution asked her.

"I did threaten them with a prison term, yes; they lied under caution, which is, a criminal offense. You really should check up on your law you know. I said that I would not prosecute them if they told me the truth. If you are now saying that they lied to me, then I will have them arrested and charged with perverting the course of justice. I presume you will make a statement to that effect, won't you?" Julie asked him.

"You do not ask the questions here, I do," he said.

"Well?" the judge asked, looking directly at the defence lawyer.

"Sorry your honour, well what, if I may ask?" he asked.

"Are you accepting the testimonies as fact, or are you going to make a statement that they are, false?" the judge asked.

"Erm, I need to think about it, can we say, tomorrow?" he asked.

"Are you asking for an adjournment till tomorrow, then?" the judge asked.

"Erm, yes your honour, to give me time to consider the statements," he said.

The judge banged his gavel down ordering an adjournment till the next day.

"You fucking useless cunt, I said get me off!" Bradshaw shouted and took a swing at his lawyer.

He ducked and the officers pounced, Bradshaw threw them off and took a swing at them, Julie stood in the witness box looking on as a fracas began, one officer down. Julie turned to the judge.

"Your Honour, may I assist the officers, allowing for the fact that I am formidable and it will not end, gracefully?" Julie asked him.

"What are you waiting for?" the judge asked, fear in his voice.

"My hands are licensed, go quietly, or I will get involved," Julie shouted.

Nothing happened, so she picked up an officer and moved him to one side and smiled at Bradshaw, who took a swing at her. She ducked and rammed her fist into his solar plexus. She then swung an upper cut to the jaw no-one saw her move, or the miss, by her fist, allowing her elbow to connect with his jaw and he lay silent on the floor, on his back.

"I do so hope you do not feel that was excessive use of force, Your Honour? May I ask that the adjournment be for two days? We are about to leave for Blythe, on another case, Your Honour, and to get there and back in time for the hearing tomorrow morning would be impossible. Plus, the defendant may still be in hospital," Julie asked the stunned judge, still sat in his chair.

"N-No my dear, definitely not, did you kill him?" he asked nervously.

"No, he will sleep it off, but he may have a broken jaw. Everet, call an ambulance please, and get two officers to escort him to hospital, once he is shackled," Julie organised and then turned to the defence lawyer, "I suggest you persuade him to plead guilty, then I won't have to organise protection for you when you lose. I presume also that you now accept he is guilty and I use sufficient force, not excessive force. One officer is battered and bruised and the other is joining him in the ambulance. I suspect a broken cheek bone; you did hear it crack, didn't you?" Julie asked him, and walked away.

They drove to Blythe, Everet had informed Blythe that they were on their way and the reason for their visit. It was a long drive and they took it in turns at the wheel, once they arrived, they informed the desk and the local Inspector joined them.

"D. S. Everet will have told you why we needed to come. The case of the drug related death at the music festival is related to our two murders. Of that there is no doubt, so we need to find that connection. I have my D C looking for any connection between the thugs we know about and drug gangs up here. I want to look into your case with a view to the actual link. We have received a copy of the file, but I need to visit the scene and speak to a few people, not to interfere, but to find the answers I need," Julie told him.

"I have to admit that once they start talking about the chemical compositions of the drugs, I am lost at that point and I need a translator," he said and laughed.

"I am with you there, talk to me in English, please, which was why I asked a doctor friend of mine. Apparently, there are some components that are hallucinogenic; others mellow, so the taker feels as though they are floating on air. But it is very addictive and they miss-mixed the batch which led to heart failure. Unfortunately it was not quick or painless, hence the convulsions. He estimated that she would have been in agony for a full two minutes before death, and nothing they could have done would have saved her," Julie informed him.

"I did know most of that, but some of it is new such as, there was nothing they could have done to save her, that makes me rest easier, knowing we did everything we could do. I have a new bit to add to the puzzle, they were manufactured in Germany and smuggled into Brussels and then here. I have been on to the German police and they are investigating it as well. It was on their radar, but they have not had a death, as yet. The guy selling the drugs is not speaking, I get a funny feeling that he is not English," he told Julie.

"Then perhaps we can help, Everet speaks French and German. Her mother was French, so she learned it at home and took German at school and I speak Arabic so how about we try tomorrow? I also speak reluctant," Julie said.

"What kind of language is that?" he asked.

"It has been developed over several decades; you grip the miscreant by the throat and plant them heavily against the wall, usually banging their head in it. This has the automatic response of registering that their safety is at stake, and they find a way to converse. It has not been accepted as a way we interview, but I have had good results by the practice, usually by the threat of doing it, rather than actually having to do it and they seem to find a means to communicate," Julie said.

"Chief Inspector, I cannot condone violence in any form," he said.

"You don't have to, I will not lay a finger on the creep, but they will know that I am capable," Julie said, smiling at him.

It was late, so after the initial meeting with the local inspector, Julie and Everet left the station and booked into a local hotel.

They had dinner, a couple of drinks and then an early night, Julie was up as usual, without the alarm she had set, just in case and joined Everet for breakfast.

Then it was off to the police station and the interview room. Julie stood in the ante room watching him with the local inspector.

"You intend to rattle his cage, he seems very calm to me, as if he is in control, not us," the Inspector said.

"He does indeed; it is almost as if he believes he will not be going to prison. Have you offered him any sort of deal?" Julie asked the inspector.

"No, we didn't see the point; we have him bang to rights on this one and he will not tell on the others involved, in fact he would not speak without his solicitor present. You are wasting your time, Chief Inspector," he told her.

"Am I? We will see about that, won't we?" Julie asked him and led the way into the interview room.

"Hello, I am Chief Inspector Julie Ashton and with me is Detective Sergeant Everet. What a lovely day it is, the sun is shining, there isn't a cloud in the sky and we are off to the beach later. What a pity you will be stuck in here, even after such a short period of time, your skin has taken on the pallor of not seeing the sun.

"You can if you wish have your solicitor present, but this is not an interview, this is just a chat. You see we come from a town south west of London, called Little Hampton and a neighbouring town called, Upper Hampton and it is the scene of a double murder.

"The murder is of two of the band that witnessed your actions and slowly but surely they are being eliminated from testifying at your trial. This will not happen, because I am protecting them now.

"Once you have been convicted, I will haul your miserable backside down to my domain and then I will have the pleasure of interviewing you. Look into my eyes, they do not lie. The judges love me, because I dot every 'I' and cross every 'T'. The prosecution loves me, because I hand them a rock-solid case. The defence hate me, because they know they are on a hiding to nowhere. I am not a person who is held by rules, I make my own and I hate little scum bags who kill innocent young ladies.

"Ones who poison them with illegal substances, keep looking, know them, they change as my temper changes from a caring glow to an evil red as my mood changes from being nice to hate, and I hate you, even now. But I am being watched by the nice Inspector, so I will not touch you here but later, now you know I do not make false promises, or threats. The next time you get a visit, ask them what happened to Harry Bradshaw and Darren Jackson, they both decided to try and take me on, to stop me from arresting them. Bradshaw won a trip to the local hospital and I am here, fear me.

"We are going to the beach now, to sunbathe until after lunch, when with your solicitor present, I will interview you. You have to decide if you want to be interviewed here, under the inspector's protection, or at my station." Julie asked, leaving him in no doubts as to what was in store for him if he didn't co-operate.

They left the interview room to see a sour faced Inspector.

"You can't threaten a suspect like that and to tell him that you will beat him is absolutely forbidden, how the hell did you get to be an officer? this is incredible," he said, aghast.

"What I say and what I do are two different things; he will need a clean pair of underpants, we will be back at one o'clock, please have his solicitor present and then we will find out if I made an impression," Julie said and they left the station.

Julie was not joking, they went to the beach at Whitley Bay and sunbathed and then had a relaxing lunch, before returning to the station.

Again, they stood in the ante room watching, as he told his solicitor what had happened, his solicitor made notes and looked shocked at the comments being made.

Julie entered the interview room with Everet and sat down, she started the tape and stated those present, and then smiled at the prisoner.

"This morning we had a little chat, well, to be precise I spoke to your client explaining a few of the facts of life," Julie began.

"So I hear and I am appalled at the comments as to the violent nature of your conversation." His solicitor interrupted.

"If you don't mind, I was speaking and it is rude to interrupt. I am here now to say that I will not need you to join me. I had a phone call whilst I was resting on the beach on this glorious day, to the effect that Mr Jackson has now admitted the crime and made a full statement. In it he stated that you were the instigator of the murders and this means that once they have completed their investigation and you have completed your time in the local prison. I will be then taking you to my patch to face charges of conspiring to commit murder. I can wait, what will it be, about five years for dealing, would you agree, Mr Solicitor, first offence?" Julie asked him.

"If they get conviction, on dubious statements and un-substantiated evidence," he said.

"I take it you have not heard, in a video taken by a member of the audience, you can see quite clearly him - dealing. This is important, because it is the dead girl he was selling the drugs to. Oops that makes this case now murder, so let's say ten years before he faces another ten years, may be more, being a second offence. You may even be old enough to get your pension when you come out, good day," Julie said and stood up.

"You are bluffing," he said.

"Mr. Harris, call my bluff if you like," Julie asked him.

"Oh, I am, bitch," he said.

Julie smiled and opened up her laptop, "I will of course make a copy available to your solicitor. But first, I make the rules here; you give me something in return for me showing it, to you.

"The member of the audience which you may have seen, then again perhaps not, you were too busy supplying and dealing in a deadly drug. You were also very lucky that only a few people had

211

taken the drug when she collapsed. The police were able to save the ones that had, by quick action, or stopped them from taking, the drug. Their actions saved you from a mass murder charge. I want the name of the supplier. It is that or attempted, mass murder that will get you twenty years before you join me," Julie said.

"I wish to speak to my client," his solicitor said.

Julie and Everet left the interview room and stood outside in the ante room, watching.

"Ma'am, I didn't know we had a video of him, dealing," Everet asked her. "Shush, Photo shop is brilliant and when you have a local Sergeant who is a marvel with computers, anything, is possible: that was the message I got on the beach. He had just sent me the video. Sergeant Hastings worked with me on another case in London and saved the day with his abilities and friends. We cracked the case using a computer. I asked him a couple of days ago, when I decided to come up here," Julie said.

His solicitor came out and invited them back in.

"Do we have an agreement? I show you the video I have and you tell me the name of the main dealer?" Julie asked.

"He agrees, reluctantly and you drop the mass attempted murder charge?" His solicitor asked.

"I cannot promise that, but I can say that once he has served his time, I will not be waiting at the gates to arrest him again," Julie offered.

"He agrees," his solicitor said.

"I want to hear it from him, do you agree?" Julie asked him.

"I agree," he said reluctantly.

Julie opened up her laptop and ran the video. It showed a view of the audience and a clear shot of him dealing and the buyer turned to look at the camera as she turned away, there was no doubting the evidence.

'I have held up my end, now it is your turn. Remember you are twenty-two, twenty years for attempted mass murder and then another twenty for conspiring to commit again, mass murder, the murder of seven members of a band," Julie reminded him.

"Hilary Harris, supplies me, I do not know who supplies her," he said, sullenly.

"What is your connection with Hilary, your lover?" Julie asked.

"Yeah, we, well, we, she's good in the sack, the kitchen table, the, well, every room in the house. I get her as a bonus for selling the most in a day. But I do not know who she buys from, honest," he said.

"How many of you are there, what is she, a nymphomaniac?" Julie asked.

"I don't know, she just likes it, there are seven of us, five girls and two lads," he told her.

"I presume she is not a lesbian, so it is fifty, fifty and you get the best pitch?" Julie asked.

"I suppose so, I've been with her the longest," he said.

"How soon can I have the copy?" his solicitor asked.

"I give the same respect to a scum bag as they give their victims, you can have a copy, but photo shop is an excellent tool, as long as you are capable of using it," Julie said and ran a copy off on a disc for him, "I keep my word, there we are, a copy of the video showing him dealing, it will not be used in evidence, but there it is, for you," Julie told them, then she smiled a, 'got you' smile and left after closing down the tape and the interview.

They went to the Inspector who smiled at them, thinking he had won and Julie handed him the tape, smiling back.

"There we go Inspector. Hilary Harris is the dealer who supplied him, he does not know who supplies her, but she does. I'll leave it with you. Oh, and can I have a copy of the interview tape, please, Hastings has more work to do," Julie said.

Chapter 15 - Stretch

Julie and Everet decided to go home; it was only early afternoon, so they drove back, stopping off for dinner at a service station and arriving back mid evening.

Julie dropped Everet off and then went home feeling very pleased with their trip, she now had an angle to break the two, they held.

Julie began her day doing research and found out that Hilary Harris was her married name; she was Darren Jackson's sister.

Taking Everet; they went to the interview room where Bradshaw was waiting.

"What is it about you that makes me feel you have nothing to do with the murders of the band members? You now know that I have you for conspiracy to murder the police Sergeant and for the murder of your dad, but that is where it ends, for now. Then again, I also feel that you know more than you are telling me about, Darren Jackson," Julie said.

"What's in it for me, if I help you?" he asked.

"I could reduce the charge from conspiracy to murder, to malicious wounding and put in a good word for you to help reduce the time spent inside. Like suggesting twenty years, with time off," Julie suggested.

"What about life, with time off?" he asked.

"No way, shall we try manslaughter for your father, because it was not premeditated and malicious wounding, fifteen, no time off, you will do twenty-five if I throw the book at you, take it, or leave it," Julie said.

"You have the ball for the pianist, with his fingerprints on it and the victim's blood, but you do not have the first one, or the next one. The drummer, he did not do it, but he did organise it. The sticks would not kill him, but the injection under the tongue would. I want more for the name," he said boldly.

"Everet, charge Mr Bradshaw with withholding evidence, added to the murder and conspiracy charge; let's call it a nice round thirty years. Do not play games with me, you will lose, big time," Julie said and got up to leave.

"OK. OK, he brought in a gang from London and they are to do another one this weekend," he said.

"How and when is it to happen?" Julie asked him.

"I do not know that, all I know is that he has been on the phone to the gang and he has booked them for this weekend. It was all done over the phone, so even he does not know who they are," he admitted.

"Everet, charge Mr Bradshaw with the manslaughter of his father, Mr. Henry Bradshaw and conspiracy to wound the Sergeant. Wait, we have his phone records, all the calls were local ones. How did he book them?" Julie asked.

"He has two phones," he said.

Julie left the room and Everet charged him and then the officer returned him to his cell.

"Wilkins, we don't have much time left to book Jackson, we now understand that he has two phones, which is why we found nothing on the one he had on him. The uniform officers did the search, take a couple of them with you and this time, find that phone! Do not return without it, take the house, workshop and car apart, brick by brick if you have to, but find that phone," Julie ordered him.

Julie considered her next move and, as Everet entered the room, she smiled. "We are going to his workplace; he is a blacksmith and is employed in an iron works making wrought iron fencing and gates. I presume he will have a locker, that is where we will begin," Julie said.

"Ma'am, won't we need a search warrant?" Everet asked.

"No, not if we ask the boss, the lockers belong to the firm and he will not want several visitors doing inspections, will he?" Julie asked, smiling at her.

It took them half an hour to reach his place of work and ask the owner for permission to enter Jackson's locker and have a look around. Julie was looking confused as they left the foundry.

"I was sure he would have left it there because it is not a normal place to search. Where else may he have hidden that vital piece of evidence?" Julie asked of no-one in particular.

"A mobile phone is not something you leave lying around; usually you keep it to hand. Had it been drugs, then his locker would have been searched, but a mobile?" Everet questioned.

217

"A mobile used little, his main one he had with him, as expected, but this one, unlike a drug phone, which is in constant use, this was for a job say, or two, so not needed to be to hand, where else has he been?" Julie asked and then her eye opened up and she smiled. "She is apparently cheap. Don't you find it odd that a day before a murder and on the day of the murder: he is being entertained by a female who is cheap? It isn't Jackson, it's Bradshaw who organised the murders, he is the link. Jackson shot his father for him, but Bradshaw is the link with the London gangs," Julie said.

"I had not thought about it like that, even at fifty pounds he would have paid her a hundred, which is a lot out of a week's wages, for a worker on basic pay," Everet said.

"He does supplement his income by shoeing horses," Julie reminded her.

"Not at any of the proper stables. People short on cash use him and take their chances, shoeing a horse is not about slapping a metal thing on its hoof. That would be like saying that a podiatrist just cuts your toenails, there is a lot more to it, than that," Everet said.

"Like I said, I am a ballistics expert, not a country girl. So, tell me?" Julie asked.

Everet explained to Julie that a Blacksmith who shoes horses, is like a podiatrist, he shapes the hoof and looks for diseases of the hoof and treats them, giving her the abridged version.

"Oh, so it isn't just a case of slapping a bit of metal on and nailing it to the hoof, then?" Julie asked and laughed.

218

"Good grief no, the shoe has to be the right size, the edges to the hoof have to be removed, it has to be shaped, he has to check for foot rot and various other things that can go wrong," Everet said, shocked.

"Like I said, give me a gun any day, reliable and solid, as long as you look after it," Julie said.

"So is a horse, as long as you look after it. There is nothing like a hot throbbing animal between your thighs, clearing a five-bar gate," Everet said, remembering the days she went on the hunt with her dad.

"We are still taking about horses, aren't we?" Julie asked.

"Yes, we are Ma'am, if you are free on Saturday, come to the farm and I will take you riding," Everet offered.

"I might just take you up on that, the last time I went riding it had a hump on its back, and did its best to throw me off and that was just getting up," Julie said, laughing.

"A camel of course, Afghanistan," Everet said.

"Actually, that was the last time, previous to that I rode horses, I became friends with a landowner out there and we went riding quite often. His dad was dead, killed by a roadside bomb, he was my age, the closest I have come to making that fatal mistake, getting married, but he was expected to join the government, being a rich landowner and I was a sergeant in the British army. He became a civil servant with expectations and I was moved to Iraq as a lieutenant. The last I heard, he is now in the government and married to a local woman and I have no regrets. Can you honestly see me bowing down to a man?" Julie asked.

"No Ma'am, I can't, that's the house, Ma'am," Everet pointed out as they neared.

"Are you sure; I was told that it was next door, not four houses away?" Julie asked,. "I thought he was a ten second wonder, leaving as the half time whistle sounded and back for the second half, but to walk so far? It amazes me he had time to undress. He walked from the bar across the car park, down past two pairs of post war semis and managed to undress and then do the business; get dressed and walk back in quarter of an hour?" Julie asked.

Julie turned into the pub car park and walked to the gate then down the rear of the semis and into the garden of the fifth house and checked her watch.

"I am ex-army and walk at the regulation pace, four miles an hour and it took me almost a minute to get here, so that is two minutes here and back. if we then add from the bar to where I started. We are looking at two minutes, which leaves just thirteen for his entertainment. It is possible, but it has to be, wham, bam, thank you Ma'am, for it to be possible," Julie said, considering the time scale. They walked around to the front and Julie banged on the door, there was no reply. She banged again, this time opening up the letter box and shouting that it was the police as Everet banged on the door.

"Nip around the side, I suspect you will see a male running, perhaps pulling his trousers up, as he runs," Julie said and banged again, impatiently.

"Alright, alright, I'm coming," a voice shouted. Julie raised her eyebrows in acknowledgement of the comment.

Everet arrived back smiling, letting Julie know she had been right, the woman opened the door and she was smiling, showing Julie she was right.

"Good afternoon, I am collecting for the police benevolent fund - perhaps in your case, time might be appropriate. Now, I am Chief Inspector Ashton and I was wondering just how much you charge, per quarter hour?" Julie asked her, smiling.

"I do not, what I do, is not illegal and you can do nothing about it, now fuck off, bitch," she said, and began to close the door.

"I think a visit to the local police station may be necessary, unless you invite us in and answer our questions, because aiding and abetting is illegal," Julie told her.

"W-What, aiding and abetting, what the hell are you talking about?" she asked.

"Like I said, inside, or the police station, you choose?" Julie asked.

"You had better come in," she said, calming down a bit.

"I have you as an alibi for a crime and we are just getting around to asking you if you were preoccupied with one Colin Bradshaw on Sunday last, between the hours of eleven forty-five and midnight?" Julie asked her.

"I-I don't remember, if he says he was here, then he was," she said.

"I don't suppose you keep a record of who comes and goes, do you?" Julie asked.

"No, I do not," she replied.

"But surely you remember him; I mean isn't it usually an hour, they book for, he was very quick, being here for less than quarter of an hour?" Julie pressed her.

"I do not know a Colin Bradshaw; you are not that naive, surely? They do not use their, real names, Chief Inspector," she said, mocking Julie.

"In that case I will need you to identify every person who visits you, down at the police station. No names, just by their appearance and then I can see if you pick out Mr Bradshaw, it won't take much more than say, twelve hours, we can pick you up at six o'clock tonight," Julie said and began to rise.

"Wait, wait, I, well erm, is he a blacksmith say, or a farmer; I do get a lot of farmers." "Last Sunday you say, a big bloke, I remember him, a quickie, yes," she said.

"So, he was here, good, that makes it official, arrest her for aiding and abetting. What did he want?" Julie asked.

"A quickie, a hand job, twenty quid, that was all he wanted. What is this about aiding and abetting?

"He did not have a hand job, as you put it, he used a phone and I want that phone. I am inclined to forget the aiding and abetting that carries a two-year sentence, for a first offence say, as long as you give me the phone, otherwise we will continue this down at the station, when you will be charged," Julie informed her.

"I wonder if Mrs Wilkinson knows what her husband does on a Friday afternoon?" Everet asked her, "I understood he went to the market."

"What about that for an idea, your clients are no longer safe? I can reveal all their identities down at the pub. I will put you out of business and prosecute you," Julie said, putting pressure on her, "I can get a search warrant as well. Does the income tax know about the income you have, what about VAT, it is a service you are providing and the environmental health?" Julie said, turning up the pressure.

"OK, OK, I'll get it, he did come, as you said, but he just used the phone, all I heard was, 'Good, I will let them know,' and then he left," she told them.

She left them, then returned with the phone and handed it to them.

"Why do you have the phone?" Julie asked her.

"I don't know, he asked me to keep it for him and he gives me a tenner a week to hold it for him. Anything else he pays for separately," she told them.

"When did he give it to you?" Julie asked her.

"He said he had a big job coming up, it was about a month ago, he asked me to look after it for him," she said.

"When is he due next?" Julie asked.

"He's booked for this weekend, tomorrow at midnight again, I can have a client here, upstairs and he will come in and leave without me seeing him like last Sunday. I was not telling lies; I did not see him last Sunday," she said.

223

"I will have it back to you before then, do not tell him that we have had it, for your own safety," Julie warned her.

The technicians at the station took down all the numbers in the phone and traced the numbers where possible, most were throw away phones, ones used by drug dealers, as she had expected. The technicians then placed a bug in the phone to trace calls and listen in. The court order was not that easy to get, but Julie managed it on the grounds that it would provide vital proof of evidence already obtained.

She then took it back and handed it to the woman, and thanked her.

"Everet, I hate this part, we cannot arrest him, we do not have the evidence and the time allowed for us to detain him is about to expire. We know that there will be another attempt this weekend and can do nothing until the weekend and then just watch, be vigilant, and hope we can stop the murder," Julie said, frustrated.

Just because there was nothing they could do decisively; that did not stop them finding clues to add to their growing collection, but they were just the titbits, there was nothing juicy coming through. Nothing Julie could get her teeth into. Yet she would be the first to say that even these clues were important and began to paint, a picture.

What she wanted more than anything was the link to the Blythe connection and that eluded her. There was no apparent link between the people involved in these deaths and the reason up in Blythe.

Everyone knew why the members of the band were being killed, to stop them giving evidence in a murder and attempted mass murder enquiry, yet there was no viable connection. To know something is not good enough for the courts, you need proof and that was Julie's problem, she had none.

"Ma'am, we have a problem," Everet said down the phone Saturday morning, disturbing Julie's day gardening, a hobby she had started since moving into the country.

"We do not have problems, we have challenges; problems may not be solved, challenges can be, surmounted, so what is the challenge you are asking me to surmount?" Julie asked cheekily.

"Sorry, Ma'am, we have a challenge, which I believe could be a problem when you hear what it is. Stretch is not in the camp, he has gone Awol," Everet told her.

"Absent without leave, is he? I apologise, that, could be a problem.. where are you?" Julie asked her.

"I told the station to ring me before you Ma'am; you have not had a day off in four weeks, it was stupid, I just wanted you to have a chance to recharge your batteries, sorry," Everet said.

"I appreciate your considerate actions, but life is not fair and does not consider my welfare, thank you. The problem, when did he leave, who let him leave and where did he go?" Julie asked.

"I have yet to ask those questions. I am just about to leave and thought that you needed to know, this is not a minor detail I can handle for you, Ma'am," Everet said.

"No, it is not, there may be some serious arse kicking to be done, I will pick you up, I'll be with you in quarter of an hour. Ring the station and find out who was on duty, guarding them," Julie asked her.

Julie went upstairs, had a shower, got dressed and left within the quarter hour, minus make-up. Julie picked up Everet and they set off for the site where the band were supposed, to be staying.

"Well, who was on guard duty?" Julie asked as they set off.

"No-one, there was a big accident on the motorway, several cars and lorries involved and officers were being called in from the area to assist, because of the march in London. The area is under manned and your order was countermanded," Everet told her.

"Was it? I want to know who countermanded my orders and it had better be a super, or above?" Julie said.

Everet rang the station to find out and it was a Chief Inspector from a neighbouring area. Julie said and did nothing. Now was not the time for an internal battle, which it was, as she saw it.

"Professor, I was led to believe that you and your band were intelligent, as such, what part of 'do not move from here because your life is in danger,' did you not understand?" Julie asked him as they arrived.

"My dear, dear Chief Inspector, do not worry yourself so; 't was a tragedy beyond our limits. Stretch is from a musical family, they are all engaged in musical performances, his very skilled sister has had an accident. She has broken her arm and may not be able to play professionally again. Empathies are justly required and visitations on her are also required to empathise, this is a tragedy of immense proportions for such a musical family," he said, smiling, for her benefit.

"I see, and it is indeed a tragedy and the death of your Double Bass player is not, is that what you are saying? He will not suffer a broken arm, he will die. This is just a means to get him away from protective custody, which he has acceded to, like a fool. Do me a favour, do not think and allow me to think for you. What is his sister's address?" Julie asked him.

The Professor gave her the address and she rang the local police station to get an officer around to the address as soon as possible.

"Ma'am, we are short staffed, there has been an incident, it could be an hour before anyone is free, Ma'am," the desk sergeant told her.

"Sergeant, take an officer from the scene and send them to the address *now*, a life is in danger *now*, so do it. I will speak to your Super for clearance, but send the officer now," Julie ordered him.

Everet rang the Super and passed the phone to Julie when he answered. Julie told him the details, her actions and the reasons and asked for his support. He said that she should have asked him first, Julie said that time was vital, the officer needed to be there before he left, wherever he was, it was that critical and she apologised for usurping her position.

He accepted her argument and said that he would support her request.

Julie now paced up and down on the grass in front of the van the band were living in, anxious for news.

"Ma'am," Everet said, handing her the phone.

"That was a waste of time, she has not broken her arm, she is currently rehearsing at the Albert Hall, for tonight's concert by the Philharmonic Orchestra, Vivaldi, I believe," he told her.

"Super, has the officer seen her, spoken to her?" Julie asked.

"No, he went as you asked to the house, her husband told him." The Super told her.

"Please, find out, make sure she is safe and then find him and put him under house arrest, no, take him into safe custody. She is the bait to get him away from safety. I am faced with seven highly intelligent, stupid individuals. Daniel may have got away with it, but these guys will not, walking into the lion's den is ill advised at the best of times," Julie said.

"I am short staffed, I need every officer," he argued back.

"I am an hour away; otherwise, I would do it myself, even though I am short staffed. Are we not supposed to protect and serve? Well, that is what I am asking. Ring her, find out that she is safe and then keep your eyes open, look for him," Julie said not getting desperate, but making it appear that she was.

Another ten minutes passed before the Super rang back to tell Julie that she was already in the auditorium for the dress rehearsal and did not have her phone with her.

Julie, exasperated by not being listened to, got into her car and put the siren on and raced to London and the Royal Albert Hall, where she entered, showing her Warrant card, and then went into the auditorium and up on stage. She spoke to the conductor, who was very annoyed at the interruption and said so. Julie smiled at him.

"Music is life, but lives are more important. I apologise for the interruption, but a man's life is at stake. I need to speak to your orchestra." He stepped down, allowing her to take his podium, "I am sorry to interrupt the excellent music I heard as I approached the stage, but a man's life is in danger, and I believe his sister plays in this orchestra. He has left police protection, to see her, because he believes she has a broken arm. Can the sister of Stretch Jones, not his birth name, who plays with the Vantage Syncopators, please join me in the auditorium, thank you," Julie said and thanked the conductor before leaving the stage and sitting in the auditorium.

It took a minute or so for the woman to join her.

"I see you do not have a broken arm, do not go home alone, stay indoors. I accept that you have a performance tonight, so please get someone to take you. I will try and arrange for an officer to stay with you," Julie told her.

"Do you think my life, is in danger?" she asked.

229

"I don't know. he left our security because he was told that you have broken your arm, which clearly you have not. It was a ruse to get him away from the protection I was giving them.

If he is now with them, then you will be safe, but if he isn't then they may decide to injure you and use you to get to him. They want him, not you, but they will have no compunction about using you to get him. I will try and use my influence to get an officer to stay with you, unless the Director will give you protection for a couple of days," Julie said.

"Excuse me, what is going on?" a man in a suit asked them.

"I am Chief Inspector Julie Ashton and this lady's life, or wellbeing, may be in danger. I am not from this area, so I can't order a bodyguard for her, but I will ask," Julie informed him.

"As an important member of the Orchestra, I will ensure her safety," he said formally.

"I thank you; we have information that another member of the band we are protecting will die this weekend, so it will be just until Monday. A member, this lady's brother, has left our protection and has travelled to London, believing she has been injured, has he been in contact with you?" Julie asked her.

"No, he has not, when did he leave?" She asked Julie.

"That I don't know, the Professor saw him at ten o'clock, he took the phone call soon after that, so between ten o'clock and ten thirty, is the best we have," Julie said.

The director looked at his watch, "It is now eleven thirty," he said.

"He will have had to use public transport, so he could still be on his way here. What time did you last have your phone with you?" Julie asked.

"That would be about ten o clock, we wanted an early start this morning, so we were here for ten o'clock and then on stage soon after, tuning up, so no later than, ten fifteen," she said.

Julie pulled out her mobile phone, "Everet, check if anyone got the train into London and what time, it was due to arrive in London; I presume at St Pancreas, but check and check the busses?" Julie asked her.

"How did you let him leave, if his life is in danger?" she asked.

"I can only say that we did not, but the reason is as yet to be investigated. Thank you again for your help and I am sorry to have interrupted your practice. I now need to be at the station for when he arrives, hopefully; if he comes here, please let me know. I will not object to you tying him to a chair to make sure he is here when I arrive," Julie said.

"That will not be necessary, security will hold him for you," the Director told Julie, smiling.

"Thank you, see you in a bit, so that you will know he is all right," Julie said and left hurrying to her car and again under the siren she dashed to the station to be ready for his arrival, hopefully?

She parked outside and left the blue lights flashing so a traffic warden would know it was a police car and hurried inside to the manager's office.

She was asked to enter and she showed him her warrant and told him the reason for her being there. Everet had rung as she rushed to the station to tell her he caught the ten fifty-five train and it was due in at eleven fifty-five. The manager found the platform and Julie ran to the exit just in time to see the passengers leaving the train.

The manager arrived a little after her and told the man on the gate that he was to do as she said.

"There, that is the man I want," Julie said, pointing out a man in odd clothes, making him stand out.

Julie was by now fuming and she allowed her annoyance to show. He approached the gate; she grabbed his collar and dragged him to the nearest wall and she planted him against it.

"You idiot, brains; where the hell did you leave them, hey?" she asked him, her hand on his throat, but not choking him; her eyes were what told him she was not happy.

"M-My sister needs me, do not try and stop me," he said more from bravado than anything.

"You do not leave the camp, never, unless I say you can, you tell me of a problem, and I will sort it. You do not have the brains to sort it. A member of the band will die this weekend unless you do as told. I have just left your sister in the dress rehearsal and she is not happy about being dragged out of the rehearsal to speak to me. It was to be told that her brother is an idiot and may be dead, which understandably, she was not happy about.

"The conductor is not happy about me interrupting his rehearsal, all for an idiot, a stupid

232

idiot. You do as I say, or I will put you in a cell and I am not happy about being taken away from protecting the group to find one idiot!" Julie told him, her eyes digging deep into his mind as she starred at him, angrily.

"I have called the police, let go of him, madam," a voice said behind her.

"I am the police; now do you want me to put the handcuffs on? I will put you on a lead if I have to, you do not leave my side, is that understood?" Julie asked him.

"Y-Yes, Chief Inspector, I am sorry for all the trouble, but my sister is hurt," he said.

"No, she is not, have you not been listening to me? I have spoken to her at the Royal Albert Hall, which is where we are going," Julie told him.

"I need to know she is safe," he said.

"The director has organised security for her, the only problem is you and you are my problem, which I will solve any way I have to, in a cell, or with your friends, it is up to you," Julie said forcefully.

Julie turned her head to her right and looked intently at four men several yards away, they saw her and made to leave.

"Those men, they are here to kill you; don't ask me how I know; I know from the way they watch, they stand, their essence. The waves they give off, call it a sixth sense, apart from the fact that three of them had shoulder holsters. Now do you believe me?" Julie asked him.

"If you say so. I could not see a shoulder holster, but you know what you are doing, I am sure," he said.

"You do not see the holster; if you did the police would arrest them, it is in the baggy side where the holster is, the extra cloth, to hide it. The arms are not as close, to make room, for the gun," Julie tried to explain.

"If you say so," he said.

"Look, my arms are relaxed as normal, now put a magnum forty-five under the arm and the arm has to give it room," Julie said, putting her gun under her arm to show him, "Now do you see? It tends to make them walk ape like; that is the only description I can offer," Julie added and put her gun back in her waist band.

Julie led him out and into her car and then got in the driver's door.

"Can't I ride up front with you?" he asked.

"No. the child locks are on in the back; that way you do not escape me, put your seat belt on, now," Julie told him.

"You said you were taking me to my sister, this is not the way," he said.

"Obviously, the black cruiser behind us, is I think, the men wanting to find something to get to you, like your sister, so we are taking the roundabout way, now put the belt on, it will be safer, when I accelerate," Julie said.

"How, how, do you know?" he asked.

"It is the only vehicle that has blacked out windows and has followed us from the station, although we have gone around in a circle, now we lose it, hang on," Julie said, she slapped the siren on and hit the accelerator.

The next two corners were handbrake turns, the next road was a nice straight road, and she pressed down hard on the accelerator. Julie was glad that her friend had souped up the engine, the acceleration was frightening. After half a mile, she saw them dropping behind her, unable to keep up. She did two more handbrake turns and then she did a handbrake turn to face the opposite way. She ended up by the curb, sirens off and on the opposite side, she smiled as they sailed past the road she was on and pulled out, going back towards the city centre.

She kept checking her mirror just in case they had seen her, "Not very comfortable when you are being thrown about in the back, is it? Next time, do as I say and put the seat belt on," Julie said.

She rang the Albert Hall and asked if they had an underground car park, they told her there was one and she asked to be allowed to park in it, she was told the barrier was open, she arrived, and entered the car park, and they closed the barrier behind her.

She parked and let him out, and led him up into the auditorium and to his sister, who was with the orchestra on a break. He now wished he had not rushed, as she gave him a big telling off for not doing as he knew he should have done, speak to Julie.

Julie watched with interest as this diminutive lady tore a strip off him, all six feet six inches of him, hence his name, she didn't come up to his shoulders, but she ruled the roost, as it were.

Whilst this was going on, Julie rang the police station and reported the car, giving them the registration number and asked for the name of the owner and address.

"Ma'am, the details you asked for, the car is owned by a known gang member, one Gavin Richards, who reported it stolen at ten twenty this morning, Ma'am," the officer told her.

"Thank you; I did rather expect that to be the case. Can you do me one more favour? Does he have any connection with one Darren Jackson, one Colin Bradshaw, or anyone, up in Blythe, Northumberland?" Julie asked.

"Ma'am, I can't help you with that, but I do know CID, are interested in him, the word is, it is drug, related," he told her.

Julie smiled, wanting desperately to tell him that he has helped her and how much she hates the word, can't.

"Thank you. Who is in charge of the investigation?" Julie asked.

"Inspector Harrison, Ma'am," he told her.

"Thank you, I will be ringing him later, give him that message and that I think our cases may be linked," Julie said and hung up.

The rest of the drive back to Upper Hampton was far more sedate, and comfortable back to the camp site, where Julie parked up and let Stretch out.

"Can we get this clear, please, I do not care if I have to chain you to the van outside in the rain, or snow even, you, do not leave this van without my permission. I do not intend on spending my next day off chasing a moron around London for the fun of it. Two months since I last had a day off and you lot ruined it. It will not happen again, the next time you will be in cells until the court hearing. Do I make myself clear?" Julie asked them.

"We, we needed," The Professor began for them.

"I do not care, there is no excuse that can fit the idiotic move you made, you tell me, and I will sort any problem," Julie said bluntly.

"What if it is a problem you cannot sort," The Professor asked, adding a smile.

"I will sort any problem, I do have a brain, fists and a gun and there is not a problem one of those things cannot sort out," Julie said, making sure it sank in.

"I will make sure they do as you say, Chief Inspector, and can I apologise for the un-necessary interruption to your well-deserved rest day, it was selfish and inconsiderate of us," the Professor said.

Julie turned to leave and then noticed that she was the only officer present, Everet was just entering a house across the road.

Julie took out her phone and rang the station telling them to send an armed officer to the site.

"Ma'am we do not have one to spare, they are still busy at the accident," the desk Sergeant informed her.

"Then get one back, now! This is my patch and they ask me to borrow officers - you take your orders from me. I did not tell you to send any officers, get one back now and get them armed and down here within the next half hour, or you are in trouble. If anyone argues, you tell them to contact me; your stripes are hanging on a thread. On Monday I will be speaking with the Chief Inspector who told you to countermand my orders. You do not have the authority, only I do, now do we have an understanding?" Julie asked him.

"Yes, Ma'am, sorry Ma'am, I will have an armed officer in attendance with the half hour, Ma'am," he said contritely.

Julie smiled, he obeyed an order as he was supposed to do, but it is polite and necessary to ask the superior officer and not to act irresponsibly by taking officers without knowing the circumstances at that particular station being known.

Chapter 16 - The Professor's Brother

Julie was now faced with a major problem; having seen the men at the train station; she knew that the lives of every member of the band were in danger. It may only be one member, but which one? Just because they had targeted Stretch did not mean that the others were safe. Having tried to get him and failed, they could now target anyone of the others.

After the incident, taking the officer away from the band; Julie decided to make sure the officer knew the situation.

"P C Tomlinson; listen to me and listen carefully. I will repeat it until you are sick of hearing it, because it is so important. You stay here no matter what, or who says differently, you take your orders from me and no-one else. Told to leave your post by the Commissioner, you say, yes sir and then ring me and I will deal with the Commissioner, but you do not leave, your post unless I say so. Now do I need to repeat it, you come under my orders and no-one else's. I will deal with anyone who countermands my orders, you do not move, unless I say so," Julie said, making it absolutely clear, "I am now going home to have a shower and change, if you are not here when I get back, expect to be writing parking tickets; is that clear enough?" Julie asked him.

"Yes, Ma'am," he said.

"Right, you lot," Julie said, going into the van, "I presume you will need to practice with the new members? That can take place between six o'clock and eight o'clock tonight; I will be back by then and tomorrow we can discuss when I get back. After this coming weekend you are moving to a new venue, for their concert, great. That means you are no-longer my problem but for the next week you will do as I say. I will wish you all the best, it has been interesting being with you but I will be glad to see you go and look forward to your return next year, by which time all this will be memory," Julie said, smiling at them and turning to leave.

"Chief Inspector, you do know that we do have a venue to follow on, but it is local, and we usually stay here for that engagement. The amenities are much better here and it is within travelling distance so we tend to stay," the Professor said.

"That could pose a problem, it is not in my area, which means inter-force co-operation. I would be responsible for you whilst in this area, but they would be responsible whilst in their area, making it difficult to organise, for once couldn't you stay in that area?" Julie asked hopefully.

"That is a problem, you see the stream here, where we get our fresh water, is crystal clear and free of nasty organisms but the stream over there is not, there must be a factory up stream, which divests itself of its waste into the stream, why drink ninety percent pure water when you can have ninety eight percent pure water, with added natural minerals, which makes it better quality. You did not think that we did not use our qualifications, did you?

"The dear Doctor Jones does test the water weekly and it is better for you than the water via your tap," The Professor told her.

"That is very interesting, but does not help me. Now if you will excuse me, I need a shower. The water may not be as pure, but it is a lot warmer from my shower than that pond," Julie said and left them.

She collected Everet and they went back home, they travelled in silence as Julie thought about the next couple of weeks until the festival in the next town, the next area for policing, Upper Hampton was on the border of the two areas.

For Julie there were two problems, firstly she would be responsible for their safety whilst in her area and she would now have to organise for their safety, whilst in the other area. Her problem was that she did not get on with the Chief Inspector for that area. He was a stickler for the rules which Julie, far too often, circumvented. Her view was that all's fair in love and war and she was at war with the criminal fraternity.

"Everet, get some rest, we are going to be busy, they are going to be staying for another two weeks. We know there is a connection with Blythe, but who with? Tomorrow I want you and Wilkins to dissect the names on the phone, names and addresses and criminal records of any and all of the names on it. Take Bradshaw to the house and collect the phone; do not let him know we already have the information, protect our witness. Make him think we are super-efficient; give him an hour and

241

then ask why he has the numbers. What service do they supply, most will be drug related, we know this, but I want him to say so, use the murder to frighten him to say and admit to supplying drugs. I will be on guard duty, but obviously reachable, by phone," Julie told her.

After her shower, Julie got dressed in warmer clothes and then went back to the site and smiled, seeing the officer standing there like a sentry, his rifle at rest, but available and stood close by the van, but not next to it, allowing him a view around the area.

"Well done, Tomlinson, good vision and cover if needed, ex-army?" Julie asked him.

"No Ma'am, just a good listener," he said.

"And observant, I hope?" Julie asked.

"Yes Ma'am, the band have made two trips to the pond for water, the lady from the house two down on the right, brought them a dish of food, it smelled like a stew, Ma'am," he said to prove his point.

"Made your mouth water, did it?" Julie asked.

"No Ma'am, I am vegetarian," he said.

"Nobody's perfect," Julie said and laughed, he smiled at her joke. "I am now going to take the band on stage, I want you to check the area and then take up a position stage right and I will go stage left. The backdrop is only plywood, so keep an eye on it. We will take it in turns to walk around the back," Julie said.

Julie went to the van and collected the band, leading them to the stage. She smiled at the officer and he obviously did not know what 'stage right' meant, so Julie took that position. It didn't matter who was where, as long as they occupied the opposite corners of the stage. Julie looked at him and decided he was not about to move, so she left and did a tour around the back, as the band started to play.

It was not her style of music, but she admitted that they were good and she allowed herself a few dance steps to the music, whilst she was around the back, but never in front of a subordinate; she smiled at the thought.

Ukulele Lady was blasting out as she turned the corner to the far side and then stopped, Julie ran to the front, fearing the worst.

"No, no, no, it is like this, now try again and keep up, from the top," the Professor was saying to the new piano player.

Julie wondered what he had done wrong; she did not notice the mistake.

She returned to her corner and looked back behind the stage.

Five minutes later the officer took his turn to walk behind the stage, while Julie found her foot tapping to Home in Pasadena.

Tomlinson joined her at the front. "Ma'am, do you have a gun? I just wondered; would you like my side arm?"

"I do have one, don't worry, it is just not visible, but I am armed," Julie told him, "Ah, Ah, you never walk in front of a performer, down the steps and back into you slot," Julie said, stopping him from walking across the front of the stage. She looked at the Professor and smiled at the look he gave, Tomlinson.

By eight o'clock the band had had enough and the Professor was happy with the performance, for the day. He knew they had a week to perfect the performance with the new members and Julie was happy with Tomlinson, he seemed to be alert and awake to the situation.

Julie also realised that visibility was reduced around dusk, which was why she had put the eight o'clock time limit on the evening.

"Tomlinson, you did well tonight. When the next shift appears; make sure he, or she, knows the dire consequences of failing," Julie said, giving him a look to make sure the message sank in.

Two deaths on her patch were two deaths more than she would tolerate, there was not to be a third.

Julie went home to bed and planned tomorrow when she would need to pay the camp a visit during the day, but most of her Sunday would be free.

The day went as expected, she visited the camp at each change of officer and made sure they were aware of her requirements and then returned to her garden. She also spoke to the Professor during her first visit.

"I will be coming and going today, practice as much as you like during the day, but no later than eight o'clock tonight, as dusk falls, I want you secured in the van. I will be back tonight for the final period," Julie told him.

His contrite and subdued manner told her that Stretch had told them about his day in London, and her driving as she escaped the gang after him and it had the desired effect, if unwanted.

In the evening Julie arrived to see a different officer on duty, she started by checking the van, something the officer may not think about. The far side was obscured from his view and anyone could sneak up and plant a bomb under it, so she as usual made sure. She did not think that would be what they planned, but she always needed to be sure and so she checked.

Her next job was to check under the stage, just a cursory look, but it put her mind to rest, and then she joined Johnson on stage, again they took turns in walking the area around the back of the stage until eight o' clock, when she looked at the Professor, who called it a day.

"We played well tonight, the new members are settling in well, don't you think?" he asked her, as they walked back to the van.

"I have no idea, to be honest, but you all do seem to be making good music and conversing well," Julie said.

"Is this not your genre of music, dear Chief Inspector?" he asked.

"The only music that is not my genre is the modern, bang, bang noise they call music. I may not buy a record of this genre, but I enjoyed listening to you tonight and I am warming to it. It is fun, rather than serious that does not mean you do not take it seriously, it makes me smile," Julie said.

"Then we are succeeding, it is not classical, serious music, it is meant to be lighthearted and fun, which is why we appear so serious, it is to balance the session," he told her.

"I was not around in the fifties and sixties but my father was and he played that style of music, not many females born when I was, no, I will not give my age away, but I can sing Buddy Holly songs, the Rolling Stones, Elvis, The Beatles, you name the band, if you are old enough to remember, I am sure I will have heard of them," Julie said.

"Like Squeeze Box?" he asked.

"By The Who, that one?" Julie asked and smiled a cheeky smile at him.

"You know your stuff, let's try a golden oldie, a TV show shown in early nineteen sixty, I think sixty-one, about and Au pair in Brighton, the theme tune was by Aker Bilk, name that tune?" he asked with a flourish.

"Aker Bilk it can only be one, Jeanne, renamed, Stranger on the shore, I have the forty-five, from my dad's collection" Julie said.

"That is cheating; do you have many of his records?" he asked.

"I do actually, I am an only child so I got the lot, when I moved here; I had to get a van to bring them down, there were so many, Vynal and Bakelite records, I don't suppose you have any 78s, in the van, they may not survive a journey," Julie said laughing.

"No, but I do at home, well, it is my brother's place really, but he keeps all my records, while I am on the road," he told her.

"He seems a nice guy looking after your van for you," Julie said, with a smile.

"Not him, my other brother, there are three of us, me, the brother who looks after the van and my youngest brother, he is an investment manager and lives in the same town as the one looking after the van."

"You didn't tell me you had another brother, does anyone else know that you have two brothers?" Julie asked, her acute sense of danger being aroused.

"Apart from the band no, it isn't something I tell people, I mean living with your mum has a bad connotation, but living with your brother, well?" he asked.

"Does he know about the incident?" Julie asked.

"No, we told no-one, apart from the one looking after the van," he replied.

"OK, I have access to many things, so I know you changed your name, but does anyone else know; your previous name?" Julie asked, weighing up the dangers.

"Not that I can think of," he said.

"I'll leave it at that for now and sleep on the problem, see you tomorrow, good night," Julie said.

"What is the problem?" he asked.

"These people will get at you anyway they can, even by killing your brothers. I have to decide if their lives are in danger, as long as they do not know you have a brother, they are safe, but if they find out; then they are no-longer is safe. I have had a car keeping an eye on the garage and that brother, but I did not know about the other one," Julie said.

247

"I will risk my life, but I will not endanger anyone else's, I will not give evidence as long as they are in danger. The rest of the band have the right to give evidence, or not to give evidence, it is their decision," he said and turned away.

"Now you listen to me, as long as these swines can do as they please, we are all in danger. I protected your double bass player, didn't I? I will not allow anyone else to die, if it is at all avoidable," Julie said, frightened that his evidence may be lost.

"And if it isn't, I will not take the risk; you cannot ask me to put my brother's lives in danger. I can choose if I want to put my life in danger, but I will not make that choice for them. I withdraw my evidence," he said adamantly.

"What does your brother do for a living?" Julie asked him.

"Her works for a bank, as an investment manager, as I told you; he is a highflyer," he said.

"Then he can work from home using a laptop, or tower and I will have an armed officer in the grounds, or house. Your testimony is vital to the prosecution and for us to get the murderer of your band members; who will have died in vain if you withdraw," Julie said.

"Then we both have something to sleep on, don't we?" he asked.

"Yes, we do, the difference is that I will do my job and protect you and your family, will you do your job?" Julie asked him.

"I always do, my job is to entertain, not fight villains," he said and entered the van.

Julie went home considering her options. It was a sleepless night, as she went over and over the evidence. Julie knew that the best way was to put the murderers behind bars and the dealers, but she, rather the Blythe Police, needed his evidence to do that. His was the evidence that saw the dealer dealing and able to identify him, others saw bits, but not as much, which could be overturned by a good defence. A good defence lawyer could overturn their evidence, his was the evidence that saw everything clearly, although at the time he did not know it. Their combined evidence would put the dealers away for a long time.

For Julie, Monday morning broke bright and early, showered, dressed and on her way to the station before the streets were aired, as the desk Sergeant said, as she entered. She agreed with him and went to her office.

She shuffled some papers, undecided, and frustrated, she would be blamed if he withdrew his evidence, yet she knew that her actions were the right ones, he deserved to know the truth.

Julie left her office and went for a walk, hoping the early morning fresh air would move the clouds obscuring her thoughts.

It worked, she heard her father telling her that if in doubt, go to the action and where was the action? His brother's house, speak to his brother, get his opinion, circumvent the problem.

Happy, she went back, got into her car and drove to his brother's home. She arrived at eight o'clock and parked in the drive of the one million plus house set in its own grounds The Professor was right, he was a highflyer.

Julie rang the bell, "Good morning, I am Detective Chief Inspector Julie Ashton," Julie said, showing her warrant card, "I am investigating the murder of band members with your brother's group. May I come in; I'd like to have a chat with you?" Julie asked.

His brother invited her in and offered her a coffee. They ate breakfast and Julie apologised for the intrusion,." I don't know if you know what is going on?" Julie asked.

"My brother is a law unto himself, he has a brilliant mind and spends his time playing that outdated music for a pittance," he said.

"Each to their own; I say. I like him, he is a challenge and I like that and he makes me think, when we chat, but that aside, do you know about the court case?" Julie asked.

"What on earth has he done now?" he asked angrily.

"Nothing, he is helping the police in a drugs case, he is on our side, nothing for you to worry about, he is, as I said, helping us. The problem is that the gang are threatening him and he is being forced as it were to withdraw his evidence. He now fears that they may try and use you, to make him withdraw his evidence. I am here to ask if you can operate from a hotel room, until the trial. It will be on my patch: that way I can offer you solid protection." Julie asked him.

"You said it was drug related, so gangs are involved; that is correct, isn't it?" he asked.

"I will not lie, yes, it is. His life is in danger, two members of the band have already died, he is willing to take that chance, but he is not willing to take that chance with your lives, which I understand. I will protect you; you have my word. I will be dead before they get to you and I am too young to die," Julie said.

"But that will mean us living in a hotel, for how long?" he asked.

"The trial is set for four weeks' from today," Julie told him.

"Have you seen this, sorry I didn't know we had company," a pretty woman said, entering the dining room.

"I am Julie, forget the title and a police officer," Julie said, holding out her hand to the woman.

"My wife, Susan," he introduced her and then Julie with her titles.

"Sorry, but it is incredible," she said, putting the television on as they showed Julie screeching around corners from CCTV cameras.

"May I explain, I have been vetted as Royal security. When I was in the army and trained to get the royal family out of danger in the event of an attack? I used those skills to keep Stretch safe, can you see that black utility vehicle about three cars back? Watch as it falls farther and farther back," Julie said.

"It was you driving?" his wife asked, shocked.

"Guilty M' lord, wow they got that, nice, my instructor would be pleased with that manoeuvre. He tried and tried, but I just could not get it right. The idea is to move from this side of a dual carriage way to the other, facing the right direction and allowing the police/security services to close the gap while you speed off. I changed it and stopped the car as if parked, allowing them to sail past me and it worked, Stretch is safe and sound, if a little shaken," Julie said.

"And how many lives did you put in danger with that ridiculous driving?" his wife asked.

"The idea is not to put any lives in danger, it takes skill and nerve, but no-one was in danger apart from Stretch, by those killers. To use my gun would have put more lives in danger. The last thing you want is a fire fight on the streets of London. My aim is good, but is their aim?" Julie asked.

"Can I see your gun?" A teenage boy asked.

"No, it is not a toy, it is to protect and used for that only; I can draw it if I need to and I do not need to, so no," Julie said.

"What is it?" he asked.

"Time for you to go to school," his mother said.

"It's a Colt Magnum forty-five," Julie said.

"Like Dirty Harry?" he asked.

"No, his was a revolver, mine is an automatic, carrying a lot more rounds than his. Now that is as far as I am willing to go; I need to talk to your Mum and Dad and you need your education, it has been nice talking to you, maybe we can talk more later?" Julie asked.

"If you will excuse me, I need to take him to school," Susan said and left them.

"So, do you think our lives are in danger?" Winston asked.

"If he does withdraw his statement then no; and if they do not know he has brothers. The only problem is, how will they know he has withdrawn his statement prior to the trial? So, the simple answer is, I do not know and want to err on the side of safety.

Can you have a month off from work, or work from a hotel room for that month? Here I will have to ask the local police to protect you. Doing what I would like you to do, I, would be protecting you, which I would prefer. I know my abilities and I do not know those of the local police. I am sure they would do their best to protect you, but I prefer to be the one making the promises, promises I can keep," Julie said.

"The simple answer is yes, I can; the bank would give me the time off, or as you say, allow me to work from home, as it were. My wife is a housewife so it would not pose a problem for her. My eldest son is at Oxford and I would not want to interfere with his education problem and, as you saw, my youngest is at school, another problem. Their education is very important, how do you propose to address that problem?" he asked.

"To consider those problems, I would need to know what your eldest is studying," Julie saidd.

"He is studying forensic science," he said.

"Then a month with a forensic scientist would be advantageous for him?" Julie said.

"I suppose it would be, but he would fall behind with his studies," he countered.

253

"Not if the university gave him the work they were covering, how far into the course is he?" Julie asked.

"I will not hide it from you; you have been honest with me, so I will be. We are old fashioned as it were, and had to get married, but we loved each other, and have a loving relationship, so it was not a problem. He is in his final year. There is like a twelve-year gap between my eldest, and youngest sons," he told her.

"In that case, I am sure the experience would do him good, I have a friend at the local forensic laboratory, he would be getting valuable experience, and he would be able to study. As for the youngest, I could enrol him in the local secondary school," Julie said.

"He goes to a fee-paying school; just not as a resident, he comes home each night. He is in the top class, and you want me to send him to an inferior, secondary school. He will never make up for the time lost," he said.

The phone rang, "You will have to excuse me, it may be the bank, I do have appointments this morning," he said, and answered it, "It's for you," he said, handing her the handset.

"Yes, OK, I am on my way," Julie said, and made for the door, at a pace.

She did a hand brake turn in the drive, and shot off, leaving a stunned looking Winston stood at the door.

She raced to the school using the satnav, and screeched to a halt across the gate, she jumped out, and ran up the drive, gun in hand.

"Now we do not want to have bodies lying around, do we, especially in front of the children?" Julie asked.

"Tell that cunt that he does not give evidence, or this brat dies," the man holding their son said.

"That is not going to happen, put the gun down, or I will fire. You must be desperate, to try and kidnap a child in broad daylight, and you have failed, now do as I say, or I will, fire," Julie said, and a man popped up from behind the car, and he pointed a gun at Julie, she did not hesitate, and shot him between the eyes.

"I do not miss; let him go now that is your third, and final warning," Julie said.

The man was obviously shocked that she did not hesitate killing his partner, he seemed to hesitate and think, but slowly he lowered his gun, and let their son go.

"On your knees, hands on your head, you lot keep back," she ordered the officers about to run in.

"Armed officers," a voice shouted.

Julie put her hand in her breast pocket, and showed her warrant card, "Armed police officer, Chief Inspector Ashton, now you put the cuffs on him," she ordered the lead officer, keeping her gun on the criminal.

She watched as the officer put his cuffs on the prisoner.

"Read him his rights, and take him away, I want him booked with attempted kidnap, attempted murder, scuffed shoes, and being an ugly sod, throw the book at him," Julie said, in disgust.

255

"An ambulance is on its way, Ma'am," An officer told her.

"I think it is too late for that, he needs the coroner's van," Julie said with irony.

"It wasn't for him, Ma'am, it was for them," he said indicating Susan and her son, who seemed oblivious to what had happened, and was probably looking forward to school, and his newfound fame.

As expected, there was the sour faced authoritarian approaching her about to read the riot act for discharging a gun in school grounds.

"Madam, before you say anything, remember there was going to be a body here, it was him, or me, now, you decide if you would rather it be the body of a law enforcement officer, or criminal, lying on the ground?" Julie asked her, before she had time to speak.

"You did not tell him to drop his gun, you just fired?" she said angrily.

"How many times have you looked in the eyes of death? Until you have, do not judge, he was about to fire. I have been trained, and know the signs. His mistake was that he thought I was police trained, and aiming for the body, which was protected by the car. I am army trained, as a sniper, and aim for between the eyes, check if you like, it will be central. I make no apologies, he was about to shoot, and I stopped that. Now if you want, I can give you the name and address of the Commissioner of Police, and you can tell him how I killed a criminal, who was about to shoot either me, or a child. I am not happy that it was in front of children, but I ask the question why, were they not taken inside, to protect them?" Julie asked her bluntly.

"You are a cheeky young lady, to ask me that. The staff protected the children, and do not say that they were not protected," she said astounded that Julie implied it.

"Then we agree to disagree. I now need to speak to his teacher," Julie said, and turned to the nearest officer, "I want two armed officers to protect Mrs Coulston, and her son until I return," Julie told the officer, and began to walk to the school entrance.

She was being followed by the head teacher, who seemed agitated.

"This is his classroom, and Miss Smith is his principal teacher," the head told Julie.

"Hello," Julie said and made the introduction, "As you have just heard, or seen Mrs Coulston's son is in danger, I am going to protect them, but it will mean that he cannot attend school, so I need his work for the next month. I have yet to decide the best way to do this, I suggest you get a week's work, and then if I collected you on say Saturday morning, you can check his work, and give him the next week's work, and a tutorial, say?" Julie asked her.

"He is a bright child, and I am willing to help in any way I can," his teacher said.

"I do have a sway with the landlord of the pub/hotel, if you would like I could pick you up on Saturday morning, and bring you back on Sunday night. Say a morning's work with the rest of the time as a holiday, food included" Julie offered.

"How can I refuse an offer like that? I presume you want to leave now, so give me your E-Mail address, and I will send the work to you," His teacher said, smiling, an uneasy smile, her nerves still raw from the events of the morning.

"Good, I will arrange it," Julie said, giving her, her E-Mail address, and left her to collect Mrs Coulton, and her son.

They drove back to their home, and after Mrs Coulton had given her anguished, and distraught account of what had happened, Julie made to speak.

"It was great dad, she pulled her gun, and bam; she shot the gangster between the eyes, no hesitation," His son told him, which only made matters more difficult, for Julie.

"At that age they do not know fear, just the excitement, it was not real for him, the kidnap was, but the gun was once removed, to him, it was Dirty Harry taking out a bad guy. I have now made my decision, I am taking you into protective custody, you can spend it in a cell, or the hotel I mentioned, I do not care, all I care about is you all being safe. I have arranged for him to do his schoolwork by a teacher from his school, so he will lose nothing. This is no longer your choice, I now take the decision, and you are with me one way, or another," Julie said bluntly, making sure he knew that he had no option.

"Then I don't suppose I have a choice, I have rung the bank, and told them," he said, adding, "They want to know where we are going, apart from that, I will work from the hotel room, if there is anything I need to do," he told her.

"I told you, a hotel near me, and that is all they need to know, this is not, a holiday. To contact you they have to contact me first, and to do that, they will need my mobile number, here it is," Julie said writing it down on a piece of paper.

"They will need to know the address," he said.

"Why, as far as they are aware it is a hotel in Timbuktu," Julie said.

"This is a bank, not a seedy place of business," He argued.

"The biggest crooks of all are bankers, but they do it legally, how, don't ask me, twenty nine percent on credit cards balances, and zero-point zero one percent on credit balances, there is one hell of a discrepancy there," Julie said, "You tell them, nothing," she added.

"Then don't owe anything, pay the balance off at the end of the month, and then it is, free money," he said.

"I do, but I do know people, who do not, and have problems, in a rural area, money is not as freely available as in the city, and if we all worked in the city, who, would produce the food, we eat? There is no point in having millions in the bank, if you are starving to death, can we say we agree, to disagree?" Julie asked, and made to move.

"I admit you have a point, farm workers are probably the lowest paid workers, and find it hard to make ends meet, as do pensioners," he said.

"I would not object so much if it were not for the fact that they are advertised, as a panacea, a cure all, for all your fiscal problems, when they are, the

259

problem. Now are you ready to leave?" Julie asked him, ending the discussion.

"You seem to have a down on bankers, of which I am one, so later perhaps, we can continue this erm, conversation," he said.

"I very much doubt it, there is nothing you can say to justify the actions of bankers, they bow down to the god, money, and I do not. I believe people are important; you do not, only their money is important, and how you can separate it, from them. Now we are leaving, end of conversation, you will not change my mind, they are a necessary evil. It is like, erm, I like say the Beatles, and you like Beethoven," Julie said.

"But if you haven't heard Beethoven, how do you know you don't like his music?" He asked her.

"Susan, are you packed, we need to leave. Hello, yes, I am busy at the moment, I will be back in an hour, have you done as I asked, good, tell me when I get back. Pardon, who the hell told them? You ring the inspector, and tell him that I have it under control, and as soon as I get back, I will confirm that I have. Please, tell him that it will not be for the next hour, and not to panic. I did expect that, again contact them, and tell them that I will make contact, this morning," Julie said into her phone.

They loaded the car, and then set off, an hour later Julie was stood in the bar at the pub booking them in, apart from the eldest child, who they had contacted, and told him to get the train down.

Julie looked on as they booked in, and took out her phone, "Everet meet me at the pub, you'll have to walk unless you can cadge a lift, and bring PC Jones down with you, armed," Julie said.

"We normally have a suit, I don't suppose there is one here," he said disparagingly.

"You know, you are cleaver, no they do not, it is your choice, a bullet in the back, or suffer without a suit? I know what I would choose, and be grateful that I was being protected, and my family. Thank you, Jim, I would prefer number seven and eight, they have a lobby for my officer, and one is a double, the other twin beds, if you can do that for me?" Julie asked.

"I was going to give them eight and ten; ten is the biggest room we have, and has a comfortable area, as Mr Coulton asked," Jim said.

"Jim, I do not care about comfort, just their safety, and splitting them up means that my officer has two separate areas to watch, put them in the rooms I said, unless they are occupied," Julie said.

"Shall I book a table for seven, as usual, for you?" He asked.

"No, make it seven thirty, and for five, that way my officer can have something to eat, whilst we eat. One more thing, if anyone rings to speak to them, they are not here. Tell them to try the Plough at, let me see; now?" Julie asked as she decided which town, to find the pub they were in.

"What about saying, no asking them, to try The Plough, at Hampton-by-the-stream?" Jim suggested.

"Yes, that is a nice place, and far enough away, not as nice as here though, Jim," Julie said.

"Flattery will get you anything you want, almost," he said, and laughed with Julie, "Andrea, watch the bar for me, whilst I show them to their rooms, please?" Jim asked a waitress.

"Jones, they are in seven and eight, no-one enters, without me, I mean that. I will escort the chamber maid, each morning, OK, no-one," Julie said.

"Yes Ma'am," he said, and left them.

"Now we go to the band, and tell them, you drive, I have phone calls to make, remember it is my car, and it is not scratched, and you cannot afford the pain associated, with scratching it," Julie said.

"I do have my advanced test, Ma'am," Everet said.

"That's as may be, an F1 racer would have a problem accelerating with it, nought to sixty in three seconds, is fast, too fast for a novice, you are honoured," Julie said.

"I have no idea how fast F1 cars are," Everet said.

"Nought to sixty in say two point four seconds, so they would not leave me standing that is for sure. A friend of mine is equivalent to say Q, in bond films, and he took the production engine out, and then worked on it, he bored it out, and tuned it up. The only reason it is not as fast as a racing car is, the weight. I did not ask exactly what he did; he has my new car at the moment. His hobby is with a racing car team, amateur, and this will be one of their cars when he has amended things, to make it legal, on the track," Julie told her, as they set off.

Julie made the calls, telling the inspector at Blythe that she was about to talk to the Professor, having put his family in protective custody, and about the attempt to kidnap, their son. She then rang the chief Inspector at the local station to the school, to explain her actions, that was an awkward call, and she expected repercussions.

Julie didn't have to wait long, before the repercussions began as soon as she hung up, her phone rang, and it was her Super.

"What the hell do you think you were doing? Who the hell do you think you are, Dirty Harry at the OK corral? This is England not the American wild west," The Super shouted at her.

"Yes Ma'am, may I speak, you were not there, I was, and I made a judgement call. If you had been in combat situations as you know I have; you get to know when they are going to shoot, it goes beyond the threat, to action. You now have to decide if you wanted me on the floor bleeding out, or him. I will not back down; I protected my charge, and my own life. I suppose you now have to decide if I did the right thing in protecting my charge, or if I should have allowed them to kidnap a thirteen-year-old boy, and kill him. He had seen their faces, so they would have killed him. As I said Ma'am, you were not there," Julie said, in her defence.

"This is not over, Chief Inspector," The Super said, and hung up.

"Ma'am, what do they expect, the gangsters had guns, what other action was available, to you?" Everet asked.

"To die, and save them a problem, they do not realise that since the sixties, my dad's days in the force, England has become the current, OK Corral, all villains now carry a weapon. Knife crime has reached epidemic levels; thieves carry a gun in case they are surprised, when thieving. It is a sad fact Everet, crime and punishment has passed, it is now kill, or be killed.

To even attempt to kidnap in broad daylight, they have to have guns, to pull it off, and be prepared, to kill. Cynical perhaps, but as I said, you were not there, I was, and looking down the barrel of a nine mill Glock. Intelligent policing has its place, I do not dispute it, but unfortunately, brute force also, has its place," Julie said.

"I suppose we need a balance, and acceptance of both elements, a time to think your way out of a situation, and a time to act, unfortunately the line between them is very, very thin," Everet said.

"And don't I know it; I had about one second to decide if he was going to shoot, or if I could talk him out of it. You would be dead, but because of my training, I knew the answer. He would have shot you whilst you thought about it, as with most of the other armed officers there. They have not seen the dead eyes, fixed and staring, no brain activity, just the cold stare, of an unfeeling psychopath," Julie said.

"I accept that, to talk someone down they must have feelings, we all think everyone has feelings, but as you said a psychopath, lacks them, hence psychopath," Everet said.

"Drop it now, we are here, and I don't want to upset him, before we have to, I want him on my side," Julie said.

"Professor, I gave you my word, and in case you did not believe me, join your brother, his family, and me for dinner at the pub, tonight," Julie said.

"After a very distressing event," he said.

"I never said that there would be fun all the way, the main thing is they failed, and I kept my word, you, your band, and your family are safe, and I will keep my word, as long as you do, and testify," Julie said.

"Seven o'clock, for dinner?" He asked.

"Seven thirty, I need to make sure everything is in place, I trust my officers, but I like to see that I am right, and have every angle covered. Would you like me, to pick you up?" Julie asked.

"Not on your life; Stretch told me about your driving, I would prefer to arrive safe, and sound," he said, but had a smile on his face.

"In that case I had better collect you, when I inspect the officer on guard duty," Julie said, laughing back.

"I will look forward to that, my second choice of career was, as a racing driver," he said.

"You stick to singing, and playing the trumpet, and let me do what I do best, keeping you safe," Julie said, smiling at him.

"From what Stretch told me, you do not have a production engine under the bonnet?" He asked.

"No, twin carburettor, twin cam, and bored out from a twelve hundred to a two litre, or the engine taken out; and a new one put in, courtesy of a very good friend, and a general who has a soft spot, for me. It is not for general use, you need a one five

265

two dash sixteen stroke alpha seven eight four, to be allowed to drive it, which you do not have. See you at seven," Julie said.

They got back in the car, Julie now in the driver's seat.

"Ma'am, do I have one of those, if I do, I never knew it?" Everet asked.

"I had two options, upset him by telling him I was not prepared to let him drive, or make up a requirement; he was not outside, when we pulled up, and saw you driving it, so I invented a requirement, and saved face. Now, what about the interviews with, Bradshaw and Jackson, what did you find out?" Julie asked.

"As you suspected, most of the numbers were about him dealing in drugs, supply and sales, most were incoming, which were from buyers, two were not incoming, but outgoing, and to suppliers. Most of them were short as we would expect, arranging a time and place for the sale of the drugs. With a duration, of about ten seconds, one was odd in that it was an outgoing call, most of the time, then it changed, and came in. That one lasted for five minutes, and then an outgoing one, again longer than usual, with another call incoming one that was again longer, than usual.

Bradshaw admitted that it was to persuade him to find someone to take out a member of the band, and he suggested Jackson, but apart from that, he was not involved, he just suggested a name," Everet told her.

"What did you offer to help him tell on, Jackson?" Julie asked.

"Immunity from the dealing," Everet said.

"Full immunity, or up to the date, in question?" Julie asked.

"I said that we would not charge him with the dealing charges we already had, against him," Everet said.

"Good, he is still dealing via the gang he is associated with, so we can still charge him with dealing, allow me; that pleasure," Julie said.

Chapter 17 - Charges

"Good afternoon Harry, I see Detective Sergeant Everet offered you immunity from prosecution, up to the date you assisted us, wasn't that kind of her? There is one small detail, it is no-longer that date, and I know you are still trading in that crap, via your helpers, so Wilkins, read Harry the charges, and his rights, and charge him with dealing in class A drugs," Julie said, and made to leave.

"You-you can't do that, we had a deal," he shouted.

"Yes, we did, which you broke, by carrying on dealing, I kept the word of a fellow officer, any dealing prior to the date you assisted us you are immune from prosecution, but after that date, is another thing. To be free of these charges, which you now are aware that it applies to, are up to this date, only. You will make a phone call to this number, and tell them that the police did not have enough evidence to charge you, but the band, are now under police guard, and they are still going to testify, and it would not hurt to make sure they know what a bitch, I am.

Please, use my name, make sure they know who, it is, they have to kill, to stop the band from testifying. One more thing, I am a detective chief inspector, and I must be worth more than an obscure band member, so let's see how much I am worth, to them," Julie said, "You will also tell me where the

268

drugs are, so that we can close you down, or face thirty years, an old man, you will be ancient, when you come out, if you do come out, alive. Shall we see how intelligent you are; new name, and identity, or prison, your choice?" Julie asked.

His face dropped, he knew she would do as she had said, and he also knew that what she had said was true, with his record, and the severity of the charges he was facing, he would die in prison, it was do as told, or die in prison.

He made the call, and gave Wilkins the address, and names of his dealers and suppliers. For the area, he was a big fish, but in the scheme of things, he was small fry, but with connections, and that was what Julie wanted, one of his suppliers was the connection she wanted, and there were only two of them.

"Everet, I know it is not very likely, but let's do the job fully, I need an address for these two numbers, and a name, if possible?" Julie asked her.

Julie went back to her paperwork until she got a phone call, the one she was not afraid of, but was not looking forward to getting.

"I have decided to suspend you until after the enquiry. Detective Sergeant Everet can take over in the interim," the Super told her.

"Is she also expected to put her life on the line, by telling the gang out to kill the band that she now, controls them, and is protecting them, personally? You do know she is not an armed officer, and has not taken the course even. Everet is a good officer, but has never fired a gun, in defence, or killed a human being, which I am sure you have not, and do not know how, it feels? To have the guts to squeeze the trigger, knowing you have ended a life. If it did not hurt, I would stop, fearing I was becoming one of them, and enjoying the power over life, and death. I have never killed any animal that was not going to kill me, vermin, or for food, never, including this morning.

Everet, I have been suspended, but I will protect you, armed as necessary, and they cannot stop me.

I quote article seventeen of the special services orders, any member of the special services is required to protect any serving officer, member of the royal family, and serving politician in her majesty's government, or other serving officer. You are a serving officer, so it is my duty, to protect you," Julie said, and hung up.

"Ma'am, is that a regulation?" Everet asked.

"It should be, to stop pompous idiots from interfering, we are so close; I can feel it, but I need to make them make the move. There are two gangs, which one is the one, we need to close down. The other one we can leave to the local boys, but one is out to kill seven members of a band, to stop them from testifying, and that, I will stop," Julie said in a determined manner.

"How, if you are suspended, Ma'am?" Everet asked.

"I am still allowed to go out to dinner with friends, am I not?" Julie asked.

"Yes Ma'am," Everet said.

"I am still allowed to go, and pick the ones up that have a problem getting to the restaurant, am I not?" Julie asked.

"Yes, Ma'am," Everet said.

"Then that is what I will do, it is time to go home, and I suggest you also, go home, not that you need me to tell you, now you are in charge," Julie said, smiling cheekily.

At seven Julie arrived at the band's van, and collected the Professor, after she had completed a circuit, checking everything was in order. She hoped that the emphasis had now been moved from the band to her. It was something she had used in the past, relying on her keen sense of a threat, a sixth sense she had developed, but she also realised it was not infallible, so there was always a strong risk, and threat to her life, but that was what engaged, the sixth sense.

Julie noted the car in her rear view, it was not the type of vehicle used around here, but could be a visitor, so she clocked it, and noted its presence. Unlike London, where she could use side streets to check if the car was following her, here there were no such moves to make, one road in, one road out, was the norm.

"You seem otherwise engaged, if I may say so, Chief Inspector?" He asked.

"I am, as usual, I am preoccupied with the safety of my charges. Did you see the Hedgehog by the side of the road? Did you notice I moved over to make sure I avoided it, no, why? That is because you are not in, protection mode. The bush we just passed moved right, when the wind is from the left, because the deer stood back there, brushed past it, but it could have been, a sniper. Not a very good one, to be honest, a poor one, but everything is because of something, and I suspect every movement, and that is why I am here, and not in the ground," Julie told him.

"I for one am glad you are here, I never did thank you for saving my nephew, seeing just the bad, and not what you did, the risk, and skill you showed. Sorry," he said, and smiled at her, Julie smiled back.

"I did my job, and now I will again, around this bend the road is dead straight for about a mile and a quarter, I see you have your seat belt on," Julie said, with a smile.

"Oh hell, Stretch told me, what that means," he said gripping the door grip with white knuckles.

"There are no corners here, so it will just be acceleration, no handbrake turns, I hope you cope with G forces, we will hit about three," Julie said, as she dropped into third, and slammed the throttle to the floor.

Julie noted that he did accelerate, but it was not an attempt to keep up with her, more of a chance to accelerate, because the road was straight.

An easy long left into the straight before the town, and then into the car park, where she sat watching for the car to go past, which it did.

"Just making sure, how many people were in the car?" Julie asked him.

"Let me get my breath back, and I have no idea, why ask me?" He asked.

"I just wondered if you were being observant, two, a man and woman, the man was driving, and the woman was not young, not old, but say, fifty," Julie said.

"What colour, where her knickers?" He asked, being glib.

"Come on, I couldn't describe them, I hardly saw him, that is not the point, it is to see the probabilities, the possible dangers, and they did not pose a danger, from what I saw. The point is that at this time of night, when visitors are about to dine, a car not from the area, asks a question. Are they a threat? The answer is no, question, and answer satisfied, we can now eat," Julie said.

Julie did get a phone call from Everet, who informed her that Everet should do something about the lunatic drivers, around there, who thought they were on Brands hatch racecourse. It was her uncle, in the car behind them, arriving for a few days visit, Everet, did not inform him who it was in the car, or why.

They had a very nice meal, and then Julie ran him back to the van, and returned home.

She entered the cottage, and looked around, wondering if she could survive without the excitement of her job, every nerve tingling as she checked, and double checked the safety of her charges, facing down villains, ready to shoot, if necessary. The challenges of getting the evidence to put them away, and yet she knew she acted right, he was going to shoot, she had no option.

Instinctively she knew the kidnapper with Simon, would not shoot, a child, how, she could never explain it, but she knew, just as she knew the other one, would shoot her. Was it in their eyes, the one with Simon had life in them, the one facing her had dead eyes, cold, lifeless eyes, focused, without emotion?

Julie went to bed, and slept for the first time in a week, the tensions of protecting the band eased, the one good thing to come out of this was that the Super had been obliged to send reinforcements, to protect the band, and the pub, there was now an obvious, and real threat, which she could not afford, to ignore.

After breakfast Julie, went into her garden, and began weeding and breaking up the soil with a hoe.

The hairs on the back of her neck began to stand on end, a sure sign of problems, she watched out of her mind's eye allowing time for the person to walk the length of the cottage, and appear around the corner. She fell flat on the ground, her gun in her hand, pointing it at, the Super.

"Really, Chief Inspector," she said.

"Sorry Ma'am, I knew someone was coming, but who it was, I had no idea, and you did not say anything, so I assumed the worst, and protected myself. I have set myself up as a target, and being suspended will not stop them, they do not know, and anyway they want me dead, so it is not safe here, for you, Ma'am," Julie said.

"With reactions like that, I feel perfectly safe," she said.

"Can I offer you a coffee, just because we do not see eye to eye, does not mean that I should not be civil," Julie offered.

"Thank you, yes that would be nice," she said accepting the offer.

"Officially, you are suspended, it is procedure when someone is shot by a police officer; I am sure your name will be cleared, but until it is, you are suspended.

Unofficially, thank you for taking them on, I commend your actions, instinct is something I envy. I am a pen pusher, I know this, and I rely on officers of your calibre, to keep everyone safe. Drugs, have become a big problem, even around here, which was why I asked for you. Knowing your, erm, disrespect for authority, your cavalier attitude, because I thought that was what was needed, to bring it under control, and from the latest reports, I was right. Bradshaw behind bars, he has run the last two inspectors, ragged, always being, one step ahead of them. How, is what I want to know?" She asked Julie.

"It is not always the best way to hit a wall head on; a pincer movement works better, sometimes. I took the side of least resistance, his girlfriend, whilst Everet was checking phone records. Faced with the facts, he had no other option but, to surrender, Ma'am," Julie said.

"Brains and skill, what a combination, I won't say beauty, it might give the wrong impression," she said, a broad smile on her face.

"Ma'am, I know you are straight, as you know I am. A good figure, nubile, and well formed, has blinded many a Taliban terrorist, just long enough for me to pull the handgun from behind my back,

275

and shoot them, between the eyes, in war, anything is allowed," Julie said.

"That is what this is to you, a war. No wonder you are in so much trouble, or get into, so much trouble. This is peace time, not war time," the Super said.

"Tell that to the gangs, who carry guns, and use them only to be told they have been naughty, and not to do it again, instead of sending them down, for life. We are too soft on criminals, so their mum and dad divorced, I have worked with several police officers whose parents were divorced, and they did not turn to crime, so why is it allowed as an excuse, in our soft courts. You did the crime, do the time," Julie said angrily.

"I agree, you will not get any argument from me, about that," the Super said, "We are still in unofficial mode Julie, I am asking you to take on the job of protecting, the band?" The Super asked.

"I am sorry Sandra, but I cannot accept that, to protect them we need to find, and put behind bars the gang, in Blythe, they, are the key. The line goes from Bradshaw to two telephone numbers in London, and then, up to Blythe, break the chain, and they will just get a new one. We have to break it at its strongest point, Blythe, they are pulling the strings," Julie said.

"And making yourself a target; does what?" The Super asked,

"Brings them to me, and away from the band, for now, and gives us a line to follow. The concert is this weekend, and then they are here for the next two weeks, so we have just one week, when I am not in charge, of their safety, before the court case. Or from the other side, we have three weeks, to end this," Julie said.

"I cannot sanction this, even if I did, it would not make a difference, would it?" Sandra asked her.

"No, it wouldn't, I have taken them on, not the police, they see it as personal, I pose a threat, and the police do not. What does that say, for the police?" Julie asked her.

"Again, I can't argue, it just shows what a formidable woman, you are. What I will do, is give you D S Everet, and her access, to us, and you have my, phone number. I will also try, and get the suspension lifted, because I agree, we have to close down, Blythe," she told Julie.

"Thank you, Sandra, and now Ma'am, if you don't mind, I want to get that side of the garden weeded, this weekend," Julie said.

"Pushing me out, are you, Chief Inspector?" The Super asked, laughing.

"The longer you stay the more danger, you are in. I doubt them coming today, but I need to be ready in case they do, and to be ready for tomorrow. Don't bother trying to get the suspension lifted, after they have been; I will be back, suspended. Four armed men, and I shoot to kill, I do not ask them to lay down their weapons: I shoot to kill," Julie said bluntly.

"I can have you put under protective custody," The Super suggested.

"What, and spoil my fun? I will try, and save one of them, to be interviewed, as long as I do the interview, it isn't pretty, so do not ask how, I

277

interviewed the Taliban, but he will, find out," Julie said.

"I have to say, do not say anymore, the unofficial period has ended. Thank you for the coffee, and good luck. Now I will take my leave of you," the Super said.

"Not so fast, go upstairs," Julie said, her hairs standing on end again as a warning, "Don't just stand there go, as I told you, down," Julie shouted, and dove down the hall, to a rifle, and then there was the bang, as she fired, and the Super dropped to the floor.

Julie was up, and off down the corridor, three shots through the door, and she turned into the lounge area, another two shots. The Super moved to the edge of the door frame into the lounge as two shots rang out in quick succession. She was just in time to see Julie fire at the front window, and then roll over, to fire at the back of the room, and then click.

An arm came into the room, a gun leading it, Julie was up, and grabbed the arm the person it was attached to, flew into the room, and landed on the coffee table breaking it, as he began to recover Julie was on him, there was the crack of bones breaking, and he lay still.

Julie had a new gun in her hand now, from the dresser on the side of the room, and two more shots rang out, but this time the silence that usually followed, was broken with a cry of pain.

The Super cautiously entered the kitchen, where she found Julie kneeling over a wounded man, as he cried out in pain.

"Who sent you?" Julie said, and did something that ended with a cry of severe pain.

"I will kneecap you, who sent you?" Julie asked.

"I will not say, he would kill me," he said.

"Then you have a dilemma, I am here, and very happy to oblige him, your legs are useless now, the bullet broke your spine, but the pain from knee capping, is excruciating. I am offering you a new life, a new identity in a wheelchair, or excruciating pain, and then death. You choose," Julie said.

"I-I," he said,

Julie pointed her gun at his knee, and cocked the gun for effect,

"T-Tommy, Tommy Hatshaw, he sent us," he said.

"Where will I find him?" Julie asked.

"Blythe, I am a dead man," he moaned.

"Keep your nose clean, and do as told, and you are not. Sandra, call an ambulance, will you? You listen to me, and listen good, do not move, they may be able to remove the bullet, and you will walk again, I lied, but it is very close, so do not move," Julie said.

"What are you, a doctor?" He asked.

"No, a ballistics expert, the half charge round will from that range tear through the belly, but only rest against the spine, a full charge would go right through you, and into the cupboard behind you," Julie told him, and turned to Sandra, "I lied again, but he will pose you no problem, until help arrives, as long as he believes what I said, there is a box of Tampons up in the bathroom, use one in the wound,

279

to halt the flow of blood. I had better not be here when the troops arrive. It would be nice if the bodies had been removed, before, I get back," Julie said, and smiled.

"I will not try and stop you, as I should do. You are suspended pending an enquiry, be careful, I want you back on duty, as soon as possible," the Super said, and smiled back.

She heard Julie's car start, and got the tampon, she inserted it into the wound before help arrived in the form of Everet, and an ambulance, moments later three police cars, with four armed officers rushing into the cottage.

"D S Everet, I am asking you, it is not an order, you can refuse to do it, but D C I Ashton has gone to Blyth, to bring this matter to an end, and she is alone. I want you to follow her, and try and persuade her to come back. I will get the local police, and in London, to bring the two people you suspect in, for questioning," the Super asked her.

I am on my way, I'm not arms trained, apart from my dad, on the farm, so, can I ask you, to show the officers where the injured criminals are?" Everet asked her.

The super smiled, and left Everet, who now collected the automatic from the side, once it was tucked in the waistband of her trousers she left, heading north.

Julie, was not in a hurry, they would still be there tomorrow, and although Julie was good, she was not invincible, and had been shot, a flesh wound, but it needed attention, and a hospital was out of the question, too many questions and delays, but she knew what to do.

She was not a fool, she knew, she had invited the attack, and as she had suspected, they were cowards. They had sent more than one person to deal with, one person. Six was the number she had allowed for, to eight. She had several scrapes and bruises where she had thrown herself on the floor prior to firing; these were just par for the course. The loss of fluids from the wound was what had her, concerned.

She pulled up in the first service station, and attended to the wound, it was not as bad as it could have been, but it was a wound that needed attention. A through and through, but in the fleshy part of her side, she washed it, and applied a large dressing with antiseptic on the dressing, then went into the cafe, and ordered a coffee, and a large and small bottle of water. She took three sachets out of her pocket, and put one in the small bottle, and two in the large bottle for the journey.

Julie's phone rang, and she answered it, "Ma'am, where are you?" Everet asked her.

"Alone, as I like it, why?" Julie asked.

"The Super thought you might need some help, I am leaving the M25, and entering the M1, it might be nice to share a car, company?" Everet offered.

"Thank you for the offer, but I stand a better chance of succeeding on my own, instead of protecting you," Julie replied.

"I will have you know that I won the gun clubs challenge two years on the run, in rifle and pistol, and I have used a twelve bore clearing vermin from

281

the barn, and that is what we are doing, isn't it, clearing vermin?" Everet asked, and Julie smiled.

"Yes, it is, but we have to do it legally, so before we put a lump of lead in the vacuum between their ears, we have to ask them to surrender," Julie told her.

"Also Ma'am, it will give you a witness to the fact that it was self-defence. Do you have a name, and address?" Everet asked her.

"I have a name, but not an address, as yet; I intended to get that whilst I was up there," she said, hiding the fact that she had been shot, and needed a day to recover, stop the bleeding, and replace the blood loss.

"See, obviously, you need me, Collins was my colleague, and friend as well, Ma'am. I am supposed to bring you back, by persuasion, but the Super is not daft, she knows all too well that I would not, be able to. She knows we are a team, and why struggle with half a team, when the whole team is ready, and willing?" Everet said, trying to persuade Julie to wait for her, and join forces.

"The whole team has not dived, and ducked behind rocks, avoiding bullets in a fire fight, and lived to talk about it. I left England with a squad of twelve good men and women, and came back with six, there, but for the grace of God, go I. Three were killed by shrapnel from a roadside bomb, when a follow up squad, drove over it, how we missed it; I will never know, but obviously we did, and the other three to snipers, who did not live to tell the tale, we lost fifteen personnel that day," Julie said.

"Wouldn't it be easier if we talked face to face with a hot steaming coffee, before us?" Everet asked.

"What makes you think I am not? Meet me at Scratch Wood, I am in the cafe by the car park, and sat to the left of the door," Julie said.

It wasn't long before Everet entered, and looked to her left; Julie sat, and looked at her as she seemed confused, unable to see Julie.

Julie got up and went to her, "Sorry, I forgot you have not been trained in common sense, and you want to, join me? Well lesson one, the person speaking usually states the side they are on by sight, hence my left, your right, you have a lot to learn. How do you know that it was your right? Because you always sit with your back to a wall, or solid surface, it stops the Taliban from sneaking up behind you, and slitting your throat, so I would be facing, the door, obviously," Julie said.

"I accept, I have not been trained in avoiding attack from behind, but I am a good shot, and can create a distraction, at least, while you take out the targets," Everet said.

"Everet, I appreciate your concern, but, and if you repeat this to anyone, I will have you. There is a hole in my side, I pushed the Super out of the way, and that split second, cost me a bullet, it isn't bad, a through and through, but had I been alone, then I would not, have been shot.

I saw him, and realised the Super was in the way, so by the time I had pushed her, he squeezed the trigger, as I pushed her, I fired, and he will not be firing a gun again, but a split second is all it takes to squeeze, a trigger.

Drop the handgun with just four bullets in it, and pick up the rifle resting by the door out of the kitchen, and three into the door, he was framed in the glass so no mistake. Drop the rifle, and collect the handgun on the hall stand; one out the front window as he passed, and then drop, roll, and take out the one framed in the kitchen door. Eight bullets left and four down, the next one was a belly shot, I needed one alive to question. The next one was again framed in the glass, this time, on the back door. Yes, I had glass put in all doors, so no-one could sneak up on me, your dad said it would be cold, but I am alive, because I insisted. Six down, and two running for cover, and to report back, he will be expecting us," Julie told her.

"So, what is the plan?" Everet asked.

"To kill him, you do not live, if you threaten my life, if not, he will only come back in the future, so I end it, now. Apart from that, I don't know yet, I need information, like an address, and to case the place, see how many men come and go, and when the best time is, to attack," Julie said.

"And I presume to get medical attention for the wound?" Everet asked.

"A day at least in hospital, a day or more answering question at the station, and then they have time to organise. No, we attack when they are not, organised," Julie said.

Chapter 18 - Recovery and Plans

They left Everet's car at the service station, Everet told the police they were doing, and the local station collected it, being a police car.

Julie took the wheel, and they set off heading north all the way up to Newcastle, before they turned off the M1, and headed for Blyth.

By the time they reached the hotel Julie had chosen, not in Blyth, but close by, she had drunk both bottles of water with the salts in to replenish fluid, and mineral loss.

Everet insisted on changing her dressing, and checking the wound.

"Do not say I need to go to the doctor, or medical help, we do not have time. I am here to arrest a villain, not fill in papers. It missed every artery luckily; otherwise, I would have had to go to the hospital. It is clean, I made sure of that, and I have applied antiseptic cream so it is just a matter of keeping it clean, until I have time to address, the problem," Julie said laying down the law.

"I am here to help, not dictate, it is your life that is at stake, not mine," Everet said.

"That sounds like you are going to interfere, and tell me it is worse than I think it is. How many bullet holes have you seen, I have seen dozens, and it is as expected, from a nine millimetre, so don't say it," Julie said, while Everet dressed her wound.

"I am saying nothing Ma'am, it is neat and tidy, who, stitched it up?" Everet asked.

"Who do you think, I refused the doctor, and hospital, so that leaves you, and you didn't do it so, who else?" Julie asked.

"I am not medically trained, but I would say you did a good job," Everet said.

"I would say efficient, I closed the hole, only. Now I need rest, so come for me at seven for dinner, and then tomorrow you can do the leg work, and find me that address, here is the name?" Julie asked, handing Everet a piece of paper.

"Yes Ma'am," Everet said seeing Julie's eyes closing, from fatigue.

Julie again went to bed after dinner; she needed as much rest as possible to allow healing to begin. After breakfast, Everet set out for the local council offices, to enquire about the address for the name, Julie joined her for lunch, and then they went to Julie's room, where Everet told her the addresses she had been given.

"Do you know what they are?" Julie asked.

"Yes, Ma'am I do, this one is a large house, set in grounds, I presume his, or her home, this is a warehouse, I presume for storage, as is this one, on the docks," Everet told her.

"So, if they have a warehouse on the docks, she imports, do we know what?" Julie asked.

"Coffee, and crockery," Everet told her.

"What an interesting combination, not coffee and sugar, crockery, I caught a gang separating cocaine from pottery, a few years ago, and coffee has a strong smell, intended to hide, class A, drugs. But a well-trained dog still picks it up. We used dogs to search for explosives; I wonder how

286

Damian is doing, he lives up here, try this number for me please?" Julie said handing Everet her phone, as she winced, and lay back.

"Ma'am, what's wrong, do you need a doctor?" Everet asked worried.

"No, definitely not; I have nothing to do, and feel the pain, but once we get going, I will feel nothing, until it is over," Julie said.

Everet made the call, and handed the phone to Julie, "Damian you old dog, how the devil, are you?" Julie asked, as if she was not injured.

"Yes, yes, I am a bitch, I promised to ring, and didn't, I have been rather busy, catching villains, which is why I rang. I need a sniffer dog for drugs, class A, do you have one?" Julie asked, "Back ground smells, well pottery, and coffee, yes, I know, I will need a well-trained dog for those items, and so I rang the best trainer, I know," Julie said, "You do, what will it cost me; dinner tonight, when you deliver it, it is a deal, see you at seven well, ten to, say," Julie said, and lay back handing the phone to Everet.

"Ma'am, I don't like how you look, are you," Everet asked concerned.

"We have an agreement, you do not interfere, or you go back. I am fine, just in a little pain, as expected; I have been shot, now do not mention it, again," Julie said.

At ten to seven sharp Damian arrived with the dog, and handed it to Julie in the car park.

"There we go; I need it back for the weekend. You'll like her, she has attitude, and that was why I called her, Julie," he told Julie.

"Are you saying that I have, attitude?" Julie asked him, laughing.

"I wouldn't dare, Ma'am," he said, and laughed.

"Well Sergeant, for your information, I do not, but I do admit to being a bitch when upset, so we will make a good team, does she attack, as well," Julie asked.

"I do know you, you would not be asking if it was authorised, so yes, she does. Do you have a name?" He asked.

"Yes a Tommy Hatshaw, have you heard about him?" Julie asked.

"Him, the local lot have been after him for years, but just can't get him, witnesses die, and evidence is lost. We talk about the long arm of the law; well, his is a lot longer, from what I have seen. He is as black as the ace of spades, and that is just his soul, if he even has one, do us a favour, don't catch him, end it for us?" He asked her.

"Damian, not in front of D S Everet, she is going to apprehend them, like a good police officer, well, whatever I leave behind," Julie said.

"How many kills to her name?" Damian asked.

"Zero, but she is going to create a distraction, to help me do the business," Julie said.

"Then I suggest she takes the dog, it seems placid, but when the shooting starts, she will chew the arm off anybody pointing a gun, at D S Everet, like I said, attitude," he told them, and offered to help.

"Madam, we do not allow dogs in the hotel part, and especially in the bedrooms," a woman said, approaching Julie.

"Detective Chief Inspector Ashton, and this is a police dog, trained to sniff out drugs, would you like me to ask it to check your premises, for drugs; I can do? Shall we start with the guests in the dining room?" Julie asked.

"Do you have a search warrant?" She asked.

"I am staying here so, invited in. I do not need, a search warrant, apart from the fact that your sign says dogs, welcome," Julie said.

"We put the dogs in the outside rooms, not in the main building, and you are in the main building, because you did not have a dog when you arrived. Had we known you were bringing a dog, we would have put you in the annex," she said.

"Then after tonight we will move into the annex, not a problem, I would prefer, the annex, but I am tired, and need my rest tonight, so can we agree to that?" Julie asked.

"There is an extra charge, for the dog, another fifty pounds, per night, as advertised," she said.

"Does that include meals?" Julie asked glibly.

"Most certainly not, the furniture smells, and has to be changed, more often," she said, looking down her nose at Julie.

"Then add it to my bill, now if you will excuse me," Julie said, wanting to get away.

She stepped to one side, and Julie went to her bedroom, and lay on the bed, and fell asleep, she woke with the dog on the bed, next to her.

"Attitude did he say, off, go on, get off the bed?" Julie asked the dog who just looked at her with soulful eyes.

Julie sat up, and winced holding her side, Julie the dog, barked at her.

"OK, OK, I need a pee as well, give me a minute," Julie said to the dog.

She got dressed, and she took the dog outside, and then back to the room where she put her make-up on, and then went down to breakfast, joining Everet at the table, and Damian.

"I didn't expect to see you, here," Julie said.

"You know me, I look after my dogs, you mean nothing to me, but Julie does, so I want to make sure, I get her back," Damian said.

"Damian, how many dogs have I lost?" Julie asked him.

"There is always a first time, and he is not to be trifled with, there will be twelve guards for you to deal with, and your assistant is as much use as a chocolate tea pot, and you know it, you need me. No disrespect Ann, but I know what she is capable of, and you would be a hindrance, you have Julie the dog, she will protect you.

Now the plan, you do have one, don't you?" He asked.

"I thought I would begin by closing him down, hence Julie, a visit to the docks first, a forty-five, and a dog, no search warrant, that way I get the evidence, to get, the search warrant. I am a stranger to these parts, and need directions. How was I to know they were drug dealers? The fact that my dog was trained to search out drugs, and got off the lead, was an accident. But she found drugs, and then all hell let lose, it was self-defence, my lord," Julie said.

"I see you have all the excuses ready, good, but why were you carrying guns, an armed squad was not, called out?" Damian asked.

"I am an armed officer, and while on duty, I am armed, my lord," Julie said.

"OK, I accept you have the gift of the Irish; she can get out of a situation no-one else can. How did you get that officer to send someone else, to clean the latrines?" Damian asked.

"Quite simple, you see I was not in the army, I had retired, because we work to the Gregorian calendar, which used the birth of Christ as the start date, and seeing as he was born in six B. C. The year was not twenty fourteen, but twenty, twenty, which meant that I had left, seeing as I was leaving in April twenty, twenty, and it was May, so I had left the army," Julie said.

"What happened?" Everet asked.

"He reported me, and I did two weeks guard duty, but I did not clean out the latrines. Besides, guard duty was a doddle, being an officer; I sat there, and ordered the privates about, which, was what started the officer's revenge, in the first place. We were of equal rank, but he had seniority, and tried to order me about, which I objected to. He was a prat, and probably became a general," Julie said, glibly.

Slowly the dining room emptied, until just Julie's table was occupied, and covered with used crockery.

"Excuse me Madam, breakfast has finished, and we need the table so that we can reset it, for lunch?" A waitress asked them.

"I need a table for say half an hour, can we use that one?" Julie asked indicating the one in the corner.

"We need to clean the room, ready for lunch, Madam, there are tables in the lounge you can use," she said standing her ground.

"They are coffee tables, and too low, I need a table this height, like I said that table in the corner, would be fine, you carry on doing whatever it is you need to do, and we will be out of your hair, in half an hour," Julie said keeping her cool.

"I will have to ask the manager," the waitress said.

Julie knew that bending down so far, could open the wound, and she needed to avoid that, at all costs, it was too soon to start bending and stretching.

"What do you need it for, Julie?" Damian asked when they were alone.

"I need a destination to ask for," Julie said, as if he should have known.

"What about Whitley Bay, it is a couple of miles down the road?" He asked.

"You have been out of it for far too long. I want to go into a warehouse, as if I had arrived, and they were expecting me. So, it needs to be a warehouse, and I need to know what goods are in there, so that when they say I am in the wrong place, and that it is down the road, it will give Everet here time to slip the lead, and Julie can find what we really want, it is called, subterfugion," Julie said.

"Is that a word?" Everet asked.

"I don't really know, it comes from subterfuge, to hood wink, have I just invented a new word," Julie asked, laughing.

"Madam, the Manager asks that you vacate the table, we have our work to do, and we are open for lunches in an hour. We have the floor to vacuum the tables to polish, and set ready, and the waiting on staff need to have a break so, please move, and vacate the table," she said friendly enough.

"Now do you see why I prefer women; men are just not devious enough. I need a warehouse, so that I can go in, and look around, before, being stopped," Julie said.

"Give me a minute then, go into the lounge, and order a coffee, you look as though you could do with one. Ann, will you get Julie please, allow her to get to know you, pet her," Damian said.

Julie and Everet did as he suggested, and he joined them a moment later, his phone to his ear.

"Sorted, a ship has just docked, and is off loading crockery into his warehouse, alongside it another ship is also offloading a variety of items, including crockery, but for a different warehouse, if we hurry, we can get the tail end of the crockery for his warehouse, but the containers for the other will be being offloaded, so that is what we want to see, the other warehouse," Damian said.

"She also has the luck of the Irish," Everet said laughing.

"Madam, excuse me, but there is blood on your blouse," she presumed the manager said.

'Hell, ok Everet, you need to put a new dressing on it, now you know why I did not want to sit, at those tables, the wound has opened up," Julie said.

"Ma'am, do we have time? I mean we don't want to miss the boat, literally, what if I got you a fresh top, I will be quicker, you can go to the car, and open it up, and start it," Everet suggested.

"Do that, there is a T shirt, as well," Julie said.

"Do you want me to call the doctor?" the manager asked.

"No, I don't have time, come on Damian," Julie said, and they set off for the car.

Half an hour later they were on the docks, and looking around, like strangers would do, but Damian knew exactly where they needed to be, so he directed them, gently.

Julie entered the warehouse, her hairs stood on end, a quick glance showed her where most of the workers were. A man approached them, from out of the gloom, and he had a gun under his jacket, which Julie spotted.

"What are you doing in here, this is private property?" He asked.

"We have an appointment to inspect the new lines being delivered, Julie Ashton; you are expecting me, aren't you?" Julie asked.

"No, we are not expecting anyone, hey keep that dog under control, catch the bugger, it is not allowed in here," he said angrily.

Julie the dog, ran around sniffing until she liked what she could smell, and sat there, indicating the drugs, and looking pleased with herself.

"That is the case I want," Julie said, and made to go to it.

"Now listen bitch, you are not allowed in here, and get that mutt out of here," he said angrily.

"Detective Chief Inspector Julie Ashton, and that is a K nine, she hunts out drugs, and she has just found a case. I wonder how many more, she will find, now you can save time, by telling us, which ones have the drugs in," Julie said.

He approached her, and as he did, she grabbed his arm, and twisted it up his back banging his head in the nearest case, and removing the gun from the holster, with her other hand, keeping a tight grip on him. A shot rang out ricocheting off the floor, Julie twisted, and shot him; he fell off the walkway around the warehouse, and then she twisted again, and pointed her gun at another man.

"Don't try it," she said, another shot rang out, and another guard fell from the walkway. Julie turned to see Damian pointing his gun at the walkway.

"I didn't know you were armed," Julie said.

"I was not, it is Ann's gun, but now I am," he said, and smiled.

"You that side I will take this side," Julie said, as she lowered the man to the floor, face down in handcuffs.

"Julie, heel," Damian said.

"That is too close for comfort, who do you think you are ordering about, Sergeant?" Julie asked laughing, realising it was the dog not her, he was talking to.

Julie got to the top of the stairs just as quick as Damian, adrenaline now killing any pain, a quick check of the clip, and then a look at Damian, who was ready with Julie the dog, ready to pounce, Julie, nodded, and they burst into the room at the same time.

Julie saw the dog fly through the air, as a shot rang out, followed by another, and a scream of pain.

She was by now in the office, and looking at a twelve bore, so she didn't hesitate, her shot echoed the one from Damian's gun.

Another shot rang out followed by a thud as it slammed into a case, Julie, the dog with attitude, cleared the railings, and landed on a stack of boxes a short run, and then she flew through the air, landing on one of the men with an automatic rifle, who had just entered the warehouse, he was screaming as she ripped bits off him.

Julie was out, and she fired, as she took a dive onto the landing, taking the other gunman out. Damian called Julie off, and it went quiet, for a moment until the screech of the sirens broke the peace, and armed officers entered the warehouse, shouting orders. Julie sat down on the stairs and rested, until an officer ran up to her, shouting for her to lay down her weapon.

"D S Everet, tell him before I blow his brains out, for god's sake," Julie said wearily.

"Excuse me that is Detective Chief Inspector Julie Ashton, a registered, armed officer," Everet said, showing them her warrant card.

"Sorry Ma'am, are you alright, your shirt is red, I presume with blood?" The officer asked.

"It has opened up a lot more Ma'am, you need attention," Everet said.

"Damian, where is this other warehouse, I can be attended to, after I have finished my job," Julie said, "And I want a search warrant for it, now do it. Everet, get me the Chief Constable," Julie said.

Everet rang the number, and handed the phone to Julie.

"Morning Sir, D C I Julie Ashton, you have probably heard about me, and in not a good way I accept, but the point is you have the head of a major drug distribution set up, up here, and I am going to close it down. The question is, are you going to help me, or not? I need the armed officers sent to clean up after me at this warehouse, where we found boxes of drugs. Damian is getting a search warrant for the other warehouse, and Tommy Hatshaw is going to jail, if he surrenders, if not, a wooden box, and to be honest I do not care, which?" Julie asked him.

"Do you know to whom you are talking?" he asked her.

"I take it my reputation has yet to reach, Northumberland. Obviously, seeing as I asked my sergeant to ring you, I do know, yes, now do I get them, or am I alone. With them there will be less mortality. Without them, I go in shooting, one against twelve; I go in both guns, blazing.

Damian, Everet, Julie and I, have just arrested one, sent one to the hospital and left, what is it?

Eight for the coroner, haven't we, Julie?" Julie asked.

"Woof," Julie said, as Julie stroked and petted her.

"Two for the hospital, the one in the office did as told, so he is not as badly chewed," Damian said.

"Sorry amend that, eight dead, two hospitalised, and one, arrested," Julie said calmly.

"I do not believe it, who the hell are you, some sort of demon?" He asked shocked.

"I have been called that before, I am fast, agile, and deadly, preferably, I arrest villains, but if they shoot, then they die. Now I am rested enough to get the rest of these swine, so do I get these officers, or not?" Julie asked cold.

"I will assign them to you, for two days, but that is all," he said.

"I'll send them home tonight, don't worry, Damian, have you got the search warrant?" Julie shouted handing back the phone to Everet.

"Yes, I just need to collect it," he said.

"Take a squad car, and go, hurry, I want a tea break before we tackle, the head boy," Julie said.

"Ma'am, let me redress the wound, please?" Everet asked her.

"You four from the squad cars, take charge here, armed officers get ready to follow me," Julie said, her adrenaline still running high, as Everet attended to the wound.

"Ma'am, it needs re-stitching," Everet told her.

"I am out of thread, so stuff a tampon in, if it is bad, otherwise, leave it covered," Julie said determined.

"Ma'am, I really think you should seek medical attention," Everet said.

"My adrenaline is running high, every nerve is tingling, my senses are acute, so this is not the time to back down, now is the time to strike, while I am at peak performance, slap a dressing on it," Julie said, with determination.

Everet obliged, realising that had a senior officer been present, Julie would be on her way to hospital, but she was the most senior officer there, and she was not going to back down.

They went to the next warehouse, and Julie spread her troops to cover all exits, and then burst in. It was executed like an army raid, the van drove through the front doors, followed by Julie, and her section. They were as expected, ready for the attack, and fired as the van burst into the warehouse. Julie, and the officers returned fire, this time Everet was not left out of the action, looking after a prisoner, she fired back missing her target, Julie smiled at her nervousness, the cause for the miss, but Julie having taken out a gangster to the right now shot the target Everet, had tried for.

A sharpshooter on the range, cannot necessarily kill, to avoid it, they tend to miss their target, not on purpose, but psychologically, they will swear they had the target in their sights, how they missed, they will never know, Julie did know, a nervous twitch.

Julie had seen it too often, on the ranges they cannot miss, a bull's eye every time, in the field they cannot hit a barn door, something to do with the sanctity of life, it soon changed when the bullets really started flying, and they accepted it was kill, or be killed.

It was short lived, the gangsters soon realised they were on a hiding to nothing, and surrendered, it is funny how just a dozen men, and four or five not in uniform, appear to be everywhere, at the same time, far more than the actual number.

The gangsters were by now secured in the van sent by the chief, to transport them to jail. Julie gathered her troops, and smiled at them.

"Two down, one to go, and this one will not be as easy, he believes he is above the law, and invincible. Expect causalities, his main force will be there, and they will not back down. Our only hope will be to hit with force, and not stop, I do not care how old the house is, or how historic. We drive into the house guns blazing, a mini tank with a fifty calibre, would have been nice.

How on earth the local cops allowed him to get the weapons, and set them up; I have no idea, he sits in a fortress.

The plan, I will use stealth to reduce the perimeter defences, along with Damian, on my mark you will drive in, do not hesitate; go for it. Hit the front of the house as if you intend to drive right through. Inside there will be six officers," Julie said, and indicated the officers, "The others will make their way around the back, and when all hell breaks loose, you hit the back. Our information is that he has a safe room; great; that way I get him, he will not be going to prison.

This is not a gang, it is a syndicate, a nationwide syndicate, controlling most of the crime, in Britain, and they have no morals at all, get in the way, and they will kill you, they are sick, sadistic, Bastards.

You take us here, and stop, Damian, and I will then make our way to the house, on foot, you wait until my mark, while you six are waiting, the others get into position here, and again, wait for my mark. I am eagle one, the van is eagle two, and you are eagle three," Julie organised.

"Ma'am, you do realise the van is just a production vehicle, it is not reinforced for smashing down houses of stone, don't you?" The sergeant asked her.

"I do, that is why Damian and I, have arranged a new van for you, on loan from the army, crash bars, and reinforced, but it does have to go back. The army do not know, they have leant it to us, the motor pool sergeant is a good friend of Damian's," Julie said smiling.

"Won't he be in trouble?" An officer asked.

"Only if they find out, apart from that we served together in Afghanistan, and she is due to retire in two weeks, so what can they do sack her, when she is about to retire, anyway?" Julie asked.

"A dishonourable discharge, instead of an honourable one," he suggested.

"Army assists police in bringing down a major crime gang, and punish sergeant, for helping police. I don't see that happening, they would not survive the publicity. Especially when I get involved, and all the facts come out, like how the local police turned a blind eye, to the gang's activities. It is big enough to bring down the government. We bend rules, we do not break them," Julie said.

"Sorry Ma'am, I was just," he began.

"Don't, you asked, and I told you our thinking, end of story, and now focus. This will not be pretty, or easy, you need to be focused, we are outnumbered, but we have right on our side, make it work, for us. Do not go in half hearted, or half cock. We hit them hard, go in determined and challenging. Forget the half hour debate to get them to surrender, drop your weapon or I fire, they do it or you fire, no second chances; that will only get you, killed.

They have dogs, I love dogs, but in this case, they are a weapon, shoot them, arrest as many as possible, but it is kill, or be killed, remember that," Julie told them.

Chapter 19 - Attack

Julie left the group with Everet and Damian; they made their way to her car.

"Everet, don't, I am fine, I feel nothing. Damian, I'll take the far post, you take the nearest one. Everet, when we stop, you stay with the car, I am trusting you with it. Do not get it scratched, pull the transporter in behind you and wait for my signal, apart from letting eagle three, move out. When I signal, you wave the transporter on and follow it," Julie said.

"I won't let you down this time, Ma'am," Everet said uneasily.

"Have I said you let me down? No, I have not, because you haven't let me down. I missed the first time; it is because you accept that life is sacrosanct and cannot kill. When a bullet just misses you; that will change, your life is also sacrosanct and you will defend it," Julie said, "You should also know that Damian is a Special, he is not a police officer, but he was my Corporal and he can, and will, do the job. I don't know if any of the others can, slit a throat; the stealth part," Julie told her.

Julie reached under her seat and pulled out a knife with a long blade, which she passed to Damian, and then pulled out a second one, for herself.

"I like it when you provide the equipment, it is always perfect, a nice sharp blade, honed to perfection," Damian said.

"Everet, you are base," Julie said, pulling over.

Julie got out with Damian and went to the boot where she pulled out two automatic rifles and a handgun. She handed the handgun to Everet.

"It has fifteen rounds, do not use automatic fire, use single shot, you will empty the clip in two seconds, if you use automatic," Julie warned her.

They set off at a fast walk before disappearing into the wooded area beside the road. Everet settled down to wait for the transporter, which was due in fifteen minutes at the most, giving Julie time to get into position to avoid a long wait.

Damian and Julie used the mud to cover their faces and broke twigs to act as disguise. At the wall surrounding the house, Damian stayed back as Julie sneaked along the front, close to the wall. As she was about to pass the gate, Damian made his move and scrambled up the wall, he smiled at the stupidity of leaving the decorative edge, giving him foot and hand holds to climb the wall. At the top he peered over carefully. The sentries were not facing his way and he jumped up onto the platform, and slit one throat and turned to stab the other quickly.

"Sparrow hawk to eagle leader, position one secured," he said and propped the men up to look as if they were still guarding, while he stayed low.

Julie was by now up her corner and about to leap. She was just as efficient slitting one throat and then stabbing the other man, before he realised what was happening.

"Eagle leader to eagle one and base, time to move," Julie said.

They did not reply, there was no need, Julie watched as they moved up the road accelerating and then turning hard into the gates that crumpled without much effort.

Julie had placed a small charge on the gates hinges as she passed, blowing the hinges as the transporter was about to hit them.

Julie and Damian now concentrated their attention on the grounds; the house knew the attack had begun from the noise of crashing through the gates.

Julie and Damian shot two dogs as they ran at the transporter and then two of the men patrolling the grounds.

Julie had told Everet to stop at the gate and now that the transporter was inside and heading for the house, Julie and Damian climbed down and got into her car, Everet now drove them at speed to the house.

"Do not overtake the transporter," Julie said as they closed in on it.

"Sorry Ma'am, I was not intending to, but I thought it would give us cover," Everet said.

"I'll make a soldier out of you yet," Julie said, smiling at her.

Tucked in behind the transporter, Everet could not see what was going on, but Julie pulled the hand brake on hard as the transporter crashed through the front and she turned the wheel to the left, making a hand brake turn to a halt. They jumped out as the bullets began to fly.

Julie pulled her rifle into position as she landed on the gravel drive and fired, Damian was also out and firing at the guards from the grounds as the men in the transporter emptied out, firing. Julie turned over and lifted the radio up.

"Eagle three, attack," she said, rather, shouted.

She rolled back and took out two more guards, the area clear she entered the house with Everet, who had not unusually, taken a moment or two to adjust and accept the situation.

She saw Julie swing the rifle up and fire, a guard tumbled down the stairs to their left, Everet seemed now to wake up, as Julie would have put it and she fired, this time hitting her target.

Julie smiled; she would be alright now, for all the action going on, it was not a long battle. Julie looked at her watch, in less than half an hour they had taken the house and it was now in police hands.

"Well. Ma'am, didn't we do well," Damian said, imitating a TV star.

"Indeed, we did, Damian; we did very well, two injured, one with a gunshot wound, the other slipped and fell, injuring his arm, which just leaves us with the safe room. You did bring the equipment I asked for, didn't you? Julie asked, turning to the driver of the transporter, their friend from the army.

"I am insulted, when have I ever forgotten something, you asked for?" she asked, feigning being insulted.

"I humbly apologise, you are perhaps the only person not to let me down," Julie said, "Now can we get on with it, before you do let me down?" Julie asked her.

"Here we are, I thought a few sticks of C four might do the trick, rather than spend a day with an oxyacetylene torch on the door," she said and began to drill into the concrete.

She drilled a small hole and fed a camera in, with a means to communicate.

"Hello in there, now you have two options, come out, or wait until we blast you out. We will start with a small charge, you see, I was special ops and I have slit many an enemy throat, so, it will not even bother me that, when we get to the big blast, it may very well kill you. For your own safety, I suggest that you get behind a firm piece of furniture to protect you, from the blast and flying debris and lie down on the floor," Julie told them, seeing six of them in there, males and females.

"Ma'am, the house is clear," the officer in charge of the squad said.

"Tell your men to relax then and get the coroner to collect the bodies and an ambulance for the injured. You may as well get your vehicle here to collect you, once the incident has been cleared; that way Sergeant Evelyn Parker can take her wagon back," Julie ordered him.

A shot rang out and Julie was up and out of the room onto the landing. To her left was a lone gunman looking down onto the scene below him, as the officers began to relax.

Lying on the floor of the entrance hall was a police officer, blood coming from his chest. Julie didn't hesitate, she flew at him hard, she hit him taking his gun hand in her hand and twisting it behind him.

He let fly with his other fist into her face, he was not going down without a fight, Julie had surprised him and that had given her the upper hand. But she had not won yet, he was going to fight her, there was a snap as she broke his arm and then after she took another fist in the face, she managed to topple him over the rail onto the floor below where he was pounced on by several officers.

Julie's senses again spiked, the hairs on her neck rose, she knew the house was not clear and turned to see a man raising his gun to shoot her. She now jumped at the nearest door, bursting into the room shoulder first. To avoid the bullet, he fired a fraction of a second too late, missing her as she crashed through the door, landing on the floor.

This was not a time to lie about; she was up and looking around for her advantage. She chose behind the door as he burst in, shooting wildly into wardrobes and cupboards.

Julie slammed the door into him and then gripped the edge of the door and swung her legs around it into his face, as she followed them, landing in front of him. Her fists ready, she landed a swift punch to his belly and one to his chin with her elbow, broke his jaw before she turned him, gripped his head and twisted it and broke his neck. She was panting as she stood over him. It was over in a few seconds, not enough time for Damian, who now stood facing her, to arrive.

"Damian, I want this house cleared fully, you take charge, do not listen to that bunch of amateurs, you make sure I do not want any more surprises," Julie said.

Julie realised it was a variation on a terrorist trick, to plant a bomb, wait until the emergency services arrived and then set off a bigger one. He had the place protected, knowing he would lose, but then called in a second wave when the attackers relaxed, taking back the place, so that he could escape, but he had not counted on Julie's sixth sense or determination. He was going down.

While all this was going on her friend Evelyn had drilled down into the concrete, packed it with explosives and sealed the opening off. This would not open the place up, but it would weaken the wall, the next explosion would create the opening, they needed.

From the spy camera, they could see the people inside getting ready, placing their guns ready to defend themselves. They were not going down without a fight.

Julie was in front of the room with Damian, Everet and two officers; Evelyn was on one of the sides, with four officers. The spy hole was in the front where Julie was, the next hole was in the side and now packed and ready to be set off.

"I will tell you once again to surrender, after this, I will blast my way in, Evelyn, I will count down from five, on zero, hit the button," Julie ordered her.

"You can't do that, it is against the law to murder suspects," he shouted.

"Then all you have to do is surrender, fail to and I come in, what to do? I do not care, bodies, or suspects, either will suit me, your choice." Julie told him.

"You wouldn't dare," he said.

"Five, four, three, two, one, fire," Julie said, and there was the blast as Evelyn pressed the button. "Do not dare me! You will lose, the next one is the big one, surrender or die," Julie said with force.

"You may get through the concrete, but not the steel liner," he said confidently.

"Well, Evelyn, what about a steel liner, can we breach that?" Julie asked her.

"It will take time, but without the concrete either side, it will just be the time it takes to cut through the steel. I suggest some knock-out gas to stop them firing through a small opening at us. I drill a hole and we pump the gas in and then cut our way in with safety.

"Ma'am, there is nothing we can do now, apart from wait, please, get your wound attended to. You're running on adrenaline." Everet said to her.

"If I do that, then I end up in hospital and do not finish what I started, but you can dress it again," Julie said, being obstinate.

"And if I refuse?" Everet asked.

"Then I stay here dripping blood all over the place," Julie said.

"Until you pass out from loss of blood, then you do not finish what you started, anyway," Everet said.

"Stop being logical, I will not pass out, I am too strong for that, Evelyn will be here in less than an hour and I will survive that long," Julie said, being determined and obstinate.

"Do you want me to blast, or wait for you to say?" Evelyn asked her.

"In there, you have until we are ready to surrender. I will not offer the chance again after this; once my guy is ready, they blast, so come out or stay in, your choice," Julie said, and then to Evelyn, "As soon as you are ready, fire! They have until then to come out."

The blast buckled the quarter inch plate steel liner and scattered debris all around the room, destroying furniture with flying debris even after packing the area with mattresses from several bedrooms and solid furniture to direct the blast inward.

Julie looked at the dust that filled the room in a cloud of dense dust; Evelyn smiled at the havoc it caused to the wall.

"Boy, that was a big blast; I even cracked the steel liner, it buckled so much we are lucky the house is still standing," Evelyn said.

The door opened and they came out, their hands in the air. Julie had counted how many were inside and knew they had not all come out; two were still inside, the others looked like ghosts, covered from head to toe in dust. The officers made them lie down and handcuffed them and took them away. This was done mainly by gestures, as Julie had told the officers; the suspects would be deaf after that blast.

Julie stood up, gun in hand, looking at the door, waiting and, as the last two appeared in the haze of the dust, she was ready for them. A gun showed and she fired, not waiting, then there was a shot, useless because the shooter could not see through the dust to take aim, but Julie saw the muzzle fire and shot

311

back to a cry of pain. She couldn't aim, but knew where the shot had come from and fired at that point.

The man she had been after now appeared, holding his belly. He had shot from the hip and being left-handed, as she knew, she just aimed slightly to the left, his right, a chest or belly shot enough to take him down.

"Drop the gun, or I will drop you," Julie said.

He smiled and raised the gun; she fired, hitting him between the eyes.

"Suicide by police," Julie said.

That was when she collapsed and Everet ran to her, putting her hand on the wound over a dressing and yelled for the ambulance men.

They arrived and began to make sure she would survive the journey to the hospital.

Everet went with her in the ambulance, leaving the others to ensure the house was now clear and to clean up. Damian smiled at her as they passed him carrying Julie on the stretcher.

"She is too effing awkward to die, you do know that don't you?" he asked Everet, laughing.

"I suppose I do; can I tell her that the house is clear?" Everet asked him.

"You can. I went into the attic and shot two up there. By the way, nice shooting, make sure she knows you hit his heart, with your shot. Sometimes it is a bullet whizzing past your ear that triggers self-defence, sometimes it is to defend a friend that is the trigger," he said, smiling at Everet.

Chapter 20 - The Aftermath

"Young lady, who the hell do you think you are, Superwoman? I pumped four pints of blood into you after the operation to try and find some skin to stitch. You had ripped every single stitch and I was faced with holes and torn skin. Don't look at me like that. I am your doctor, not a senior officer, your doctor and I can put you to sleep if you do not obey me. One week's complete bed rest. I may if you are good, allow you a visitor," he said smiling at her, yet she knew he meant it.

"I promise to be good, Doctor; we have been here before, haven't we?" Julie asked him.

"Don't remind me, bed rest and that means no squat thrusts by the bed, you stay in it, no press ups, pull ups, or running on the spot, you just lie there for one week," he said laying down the law.

"This is national health, isn't it? So, I can sign myself out, unlike the army where you could order me to stay in bed?" Julie asked him.

"That is the case, but then again, I can place you under arrest for murder and handcuff you to the bed. The charge will not stick, but for the next week, while it is investigated, I can make sure you do as told. The Super has suspended you, as is the law after a death at police hands, which means Ma'am, I can arrest you," Everet said, smiling at her.

"Bring me up to speed and by the way, a nice shot, had I not been ready for him, you would have

313

saved my life, thank you," Julie said, adding a smile.

"It is nice to see you, but I mean it, this time I am in control and you do as the Doctor says. Damian told me that the house was clear, as we were taking you out. We have broken up a major drugs syndicate and taken forty tons off the streets from both warehouses and smaller ones they told us about, when being questioned. It is a massive haul. You will probably be pleased to know that the Super is on the war path, asking why her Chief Inspector had to go and clean up Blyth and she is not happy with you. I would take a low profile for a bit, if I were you, then again knowing you, that will not be happening.

"Our action also led to the gang in London being arrested and charged with Collins' murder. To put it simply, we have a clean slate. I might take a few days off," Everet said.

"Not while I am out of action, you are in charge, unless of course I am declared fit for work, a few days and I will be fine, then I will have Wilkins and you can take a few days off, but until then you have the reins, so time off is out of the question," Julie said, laughing at her as she pulled a face.

Julie was back at work three days later, but restricted to desk duty and Everet got her time off, before the weekend so that they could go and watch the concert given by the band.

Things were back to normal, petty thieves and speeding tickets.

Julie with attitude was declared not fit for the police, she refused to let go of a criminal with a gun when told to.

"I do not know if Little Hampton can cope with two of you," Damian said as he dropped Julie with attitude off at Julie's cottage.

"I had thought about calling my cottage, 'Bitch Residence,' but now I suppose it will have to be 'Bitches Residence,' seeing as there will be two of us," Julie said laughing and cuddling Julie with Attitude.

THE END